S

A Noir Thriller

by

Matthew Legare

Copyright

Author's Note

The Chinese language has two systems of Romanization – pinyin and Wade-Giles. Although pinyin has become the dominant method in mainland China, it was not invented until the 1950s, after the events of *Shanghai Twilight*. Therefore, Chinese terms and places are Romanized using Wade-Giles e.g. Nanking instead of Nanjing, Kuomintang instead of Guomindang, and *lung* (dragon) instead of *long*. It also helps to lend a more vintage feel.

There are many dialects in China, the most important to this novel are Cantonese and Shanghainese. Since Tom Lai is of Cantonese descent, he often uses Cantonese terms e.g. *cheongsam* instead of the *qipao*.

Many Chinese and Japanese terms that have not entered the English lexicon have been italicized, followed by a brief translation e.g. *changshan* long shirt.

In China, surnames come before given names e.g. Lai Huang-fu instead of Huang-fu Lai. In keeping with literary tradition, I have kept this custom for the Chinese characters. Chinese given names also tend to have two parts e.g. Huang-fu, but some have only one e.g. Ping.

Japanese surnames also come before given names e.g. Fukuzaki Jiro, however, to make this story more palatable to Western readers and keeping with the literary custom of my other works, Japanese given names will come before their surnames e.g. Jiro Fukuzaki.

Acknowledgments

I am grateful to my parents, my sister, my brother-in-law, and my friends for the support, my readership, Caroline T. Johnson for her fantastic cover design, especially my other half, Jenny.

Mailing List

Join my mailing list! You'll receive updates, deals, and *Conspiracy in Tokyo*, free prequel novella to the Reiko Watanabe/Inspector Aizawa series! Just visit https://matthewlegare.com/mailing-list/

Thanks!

January 1932

CHAPTER ONE

An ethereal feeling hung in the Shanghai night, and Tom Lai wondered if he was dreaming. As the Bentley passed over the Garden Bridge, Tom stared out the window at his adopted city. Bright neon lights punctured the darkness like blinking flares. They also illuminated the Whangpoo River, alive with Chinese junks, foreign merchant vessels, and two Japanese Navy ships, lying anchored like enormous sea monsters. War could soon devour the city, but Shanghai shimmered in an electric glow – bright, gay, and decadent.

The Bentley soon cruised into Shanghai's glamorous promenade, nestled on the waterfront. Crammed full of clubs, banks, bars, and brothels, the Bund was like a Chinese Times Square, crackling with energy. The people out and about tonight were dressed to the nines – men in three-piece suits, frock coats, and top hats walked alongside women in elegant gowns and long gloves. Most were foreign but a few were native Chinese.

If anyone was concerned, they didn't show it. Tensions between China and Japan had reached fever pitch in the past few months. The newspapers predicted war, but there was little anxiety in this crowd. After all, the Bund was secure inside the International Settlement, where foreigners ruled over a piece of China's territory. They would be spared while the rest of Shanghai burned. There was an eerie unrealness to it all.

The chauffeur turned the Bentley west onto Foochow Road and became ensnarled in traffic. Tom reexamined his overcoat, blue serge suit, and silk gray tie. His usual duds, but thankfully, they were just ritzy enough for tonight. It wasn't every day that a nightclub owner had dinner with an official from the ruling Nationalist Party, the Kuomintang. And at the American Club, no less!

It was about time he received some recognition. After all, his own Club Twilight was one of the most popular spots in Shanghai, even if it was located in the working class Chapei district. It earned him enough money to send a steady stream of donations to the Nationalist Government in Nanking, the only hope for a strong, modern China. Maybe this meeting was to announce that they wanted to dedicate a statue to him? He'd settle for a street in his name.

Tom glanced at his Rolex wristwatch and sighed. Almost half past six.

"What's the hold-up?" Tom asked his chauffeur in Shanghainese.

"There's a demonstration about a blocks up, sir. It's backing up the whole street."

Tom peered through the front window. A snakelike throng lurched down Kiangse Road, grinding all traffic to a standstill. Minutes ticked by, but the river of people passed on and on with no end in sight. Tom grumbled, remembering an old wives' tale. If everyone in China walked past you in a line, it would never end because new Chinese would be born and grow up. He'd have to go the rest of the way on foot or risk being late.

"I'll get out here," Tom said. "Wait outside of the American Club when you manage to get out of this traffic."

The chauffeur gave an obedient nod as Tom exited. Outside, the air was cool and moist, tempering his mood. A thin fog crept through Foochow Road which reminded Tom of his native San Francisco. Just across the street was the six-story brick building which hosted the American Club, the social hub of all Yankee expats in Shanghai. The Stars and Stripes flapped back and forth in the breeze, so close it was almost taunting. Hopefully, he could pass through the crowd without too much trouble. But as Tom approached Kiangse Road, the parade took on a more ominous focus.

People carried placards and banners that read "BOYCOTT JAPANESE GOODS" and "JAPAN GET OUT OF MANCHURIA!" A blown-up photograph of the

Japanese Mikado – Emperor Hirohito himself – was stamped with the word "BANDIT" across it. An illustrated poster showed a Chinese soldier impaling a Japanese devil on his bayonet. Such patriotic demonstrations were a common sight these days, ever since Japan invaded the northeastern region of Manchuria back in September.

From the throng arose an angry chant, "Don't buy from the Japanese devils! Boycott all Japanese goods! Don't buy from the Japanese devils!"

But instead of simple patriotism, Tom could see a lit fuse that threatened to blow Shanghai into dust. Hitting Japan in its wallet was tantamount to declaring war. Not that the Land of the Rising didn't deserve it. But for all the love he had for his adopted country, Tom didn't know which side would win in the coming conflict. Regardless of the victor, he would survive. He always survived. His thoughts turned to Ho Mei-chen, his Beautiful Pearl, waiting for him back at the club. Whatever happened, she would survive too. He'd see to that.

The procession continued uninterrupted, which made it impossible to cross the street. Tom looked at his Rolex again and noticed a couple near him. They were two middle-aged Orientals – a man in a Western suit, coat, and fedora, and a woman in a green kimono. Looking back and forth, the couple conversed in worried Japanese. They must have gotten lost looking for Little Tokyo, Japan's enclave within the International Settlement.

Tom approached them and pointed northward, past the Soochow Creek. The Japanese couple smiled and bowed their thanks, drawing attention from the passing crowd. Three rough-looking men detached from the procession and surrounded the Japanese couple.

"Japanese devils! Get out of Manchuria!" one of the toughs snapped in Shanghainese.

"Get out of Shanghai while you're at it!" another roared, pushing the man forward.

The woman babbled out a stream of frightened Japanese, giving submissive bows and gripping her husband's arm.

"Dwarf bandits," the third man growled. "You come to our cities and don't even speak our language! Just wait until our soldiers throw all of you Japanese devils into the Whangpoo River!"

The ring of men closed tighter and tighter until Tom stepped forward.

"That's enough," Tom said in Shanghainese. "These two didn't invade Manchuria."

"What are you? Some sort of Japanese sympathizer?"

"Better walk away now," a thug growled, a switchblade flicking out from his clenched fist, "or we'll carve you up too."

Tightness gripped Tom's chest and his eyes darted about for assistance. The nearest cop was a few blocks away, helping with crowd control. Even the people in the procession focused their attention straight ahead. Maybe he could reason with these thugs.

"Use your head, friend," Tom said. "Can't you see the headlines in Tokyo now? 'Chinese thugs murder two of the Emperor's subjects!' All the Japanese need is another excuse to attack Shanghai."

Just last week, five Japanese Buddhist monks had been beaten by an angry, patriotic mob. One later died from his wounds. There had been no apology thus far, raising tensions between the Chinese Republic and the Japanese Empire to a boiling point.

The knife-wielder grumbled and spat on the sidewalk. "Let them attack. Those dwarf bandits are no match for the great 19th Route Army!"

Such patriotism was admirable, but foolish. Shanghai's garrison force was stronger than most Chinese units, but even the vaunted 19th Route Army would have a hell of a fight on its hands. The tough drew closer, his knife seemingly growing longer with every step. All too late, Tom regretted not bringing his Browning automatic, tucked harmlessly away back at Club Twilight.

With an angry roar of "Jap lover!" the thug lunged forward, swishing the blade back and forth. Tom sidestepped and let him cut open air. A few other passersby and protesters took notice. One man, carrying a sign reading "STOP THE CIVIL WAR AND FIGHT JAPAN," froze in his tracks and gawked.

Tom grabbed the sign and ripped the paper off the wooden pole, creating a makeshift weapon. The protester looked ready to complain but rejoined the procession. Tom soon saw why. The knife wielder had repositioned himself for another attack and charged again. With a heavy swing, Tom brought the wooden pole down and swatted the blade out of the man's hand, sending it swirling into the air.

Glancing around, Tom realized what a hollow victory it was. The two other thugs drew their own knives, even longer and sharper. The procession finally passed in its entirety; however, the chants of "Boycott Japanese Goods" lingered in the frosty night air. But soon, all Tom could hear was his own heart, thumping rapidly. It looked like he might miss that dinner after all.

CHAPTER TWO

The thugs moved closer, brandishing their knives like butchers. Tom gripped the wooden pole and waited for an attack. Taking advantage of the commotion, the Japanese couple beat a quick retreat. The woman ran so fast it looked like her kimono would tear itself apart. Not that he could blame them. That's what he got for sticking his neck out. The few passersby on Kiangse Road paid them no attention other than a sideways glance. If you wanted to live long in Shanghai, you minded your own business.

One hoodlum slashed forward and Tom thrust out the wooden pole as a shield. The man backed up and repositioned his blade, ready to strike again. A few feet away, the first tough had found his weapon and was back for a rematch. Three against one and no way out. Tom gritted his teeth and prepared for the worst.

A shrill whistle cut through the air, drowning out the fading anti-Japanese slogans. In the near distance was a dark-uniformed police officer. Blowing his whistle like a bleating billy goat, the cop waved a nightstick and charged forward.

The three toughs froze in fear before scattering in different directions like scurrying rats. Tom straightened up, presenting himself to the police officer with a curt nod.

"Thank you, officer," Tom said in Shanghainese, hoping he understood the dialect. In this city, every block seemed to speak a different language.

The cop nodded and said, "What happened here?"

"Those thugs were going to kill a Japanese couple so I intervened."

"Where are you from?" the cop asked, examining Tom with suspicious eyes.

"My accent, huh?" Tom gave a wide smile. "American, born and bred."

The suspicion morphed into contempt. "It's not wise to be so friendly with the Japanese devils these days. My duty obliges me to protect them, but as someone with Chinese blood in your veins, you shame your ancestors."

Tom braced himself. "My loyalties are with China."

After a dismissive scoff, the police officer said, "Your kind have no homeland to be loyal to. You are neither Chinese nor American, yet you pretend to be both." Sliding the nightstick back into his belt loop, the cop added, "Go back where you came from. China doesn't need any more foreign devils."

With that, the police officer turned on his heel and traipsed back down Kiangse Road, a good patrolman returning to his beat. Taking a steadying breath of chilly air, Tom suppressed an inner rage that had been kindling for years. Here he was, halfway around the world from San Francisco, and still treated like a foreigner. For a moment, he heard Mei-chen's soft voice in his head, calming him further. He would see her soon enough. For now, there was no time for anger. His good deed had cost him precious minutes, making him even more tardy. Tom turned around and crossed the street, toward the fluttering Stars and Stripes outside of the American Club.

*****

After walking up elegant marble stairs, Herbert Hoover's dour, lumpy face greeted Tom as he entered the lobby. Even in an official portrait, the thirty-first president of the United States looked like a man twice his age. As a nightclub owner, Tom sympathized. Running a business was hard enough and running a nation – especially during the worst economic depression in history – would age anyone.

"May I help you?" an irritated voice asked.

Tom took his eyes off of President Hoover's picture and focused on a fat-faced white man in a tuxedo, standing behind a podium. The manager of the American Club was a familiar sight but evidently, he didn't remember Tom. Perhaps he thought that Chinamen looked alike?

"Yes, I'm Thomas Lai. I have a reservation for tonight."

"Oh, you speak English," the manager said with a chuckle.

"I would hope so since I'm an American."

A frown creased the manager's flabby face as he scanned the registry book. "Ah yes, you're Charles Whitfield's friend, right? The Chinaman he sponsored?"

"Yes."

The American Club's membership was made up of well-connected white men in the foreign service, finance, and industry. A Chinese-American nightclub owner didn't meet their criteria. However, thanks to a sponsorship by an esteemed Boston Brahmin like Charles Whitfield – along with a hefty donation – Tom Lai had become something of an unofficial member to the American Club. Left off the membership roster, but able to pass in and out with ease.

"Ah, that's right, I see your reservation now. Your guests have already arrived, Mr. Lai."

Handing his fedora over to a Chinese attendant, Tom walked to the nearby elevator and took it to the fifth floor. There were all sorts of gentlemanly entertainment throughout the American Club's six stories– a bar, a billiards room, a library, a mahjong hall, a rooftop garden, along with personal rooms for members and guests. But Tom was only concerned with the fifth floor tonight, the spacious dining hall.

Polished Maplewood floors gleamed from the many chandeliers shimmering overhead. Red velour curtains around the windows were parted to let in the neon glow from the nearby Bund. Most magnificent of all was an enormous oil painting of George Washington in his Continental Army uniform, which made the lobby's portrait of Herbert Hoover look even dumpier by comparison.

The patrons – mostly white men – and staff – mostly Chinese waiters – were half-obscured by a veil of cigar smoke that wafted throughout the dining hall. Several hostile stares greeted Tom through the bluish haze as he walked past, as if he were a heathen violating this sacred temple.

Tom stopped at a table occupied by the only two Chinese patrons in the dining hall and gave a slight bow. The occupants stood and offered Tom firm handshakes and welcoming smiles.

Uniformed in a blue-gray tunic, breeches, and black jackboots, Tung Hsi-shan struck an imposing figure. A graduate of the Whampoa Academy – the West Point of China – Tung was the epitome of a modern officer in the Nationalist Army, the military arm of the Kuomintang. Here was a soldier who fought, not for warlords or plunder, but for the Chinese Republic. Metallic rank insignia on his collar – a gold stripe against a red background and three gold triangles – denoted his rank of infantry captain.

With a large, shaven head and a lean, muscular frame, Captain Tung's presence was both intimidating and comforting, like a trained wolf. Despite their many differences, Tom had managed to befriend the Captain, further ingratiating himself with the Nationalist Government. It was Captain Tung who had set up this mysterious meeting in the first place.

Tom had never met the other man before but his identity was no secret. Thin and bespectacled, Chow Chun-wah looked the part of a government bureaucrat. A pressed gray suit hung off his gaunt body, ornamented with a White Sun insignia on the lapel, the emblem of the ruling Nationalist Party, the Kuomintang. Tom glanced down at his lapel to make sure his own Kuomintang badge was fastened tight.

"May I present Mr. Chow Chun-wah from the Ministry of Finance," Tung said and then gestured to Tom. "Mr. Thomas Lai, the owner of Club Twilight."

Chow gave another good-natured smile and Tom reciprocated, Party member to Party member. With the introductions completed, the men took their seats. Tom pulled out his gold cigarette case and offered a round of

Lucky Strikes, a clear sign of respect to the older men. After lighting up, they took a few moments to enjoy the tobacco before Tom began.

"I apologize for being late," Tom spoke in Cantonese, the language of southern China. The region was not only where the Kuomintang had been born, but also where the Lai family traced their roots. "There was a lot of commotion outside."

Chow's face lit up and he replied back in Cantonese, "You mean the anti-Japanese demonstration? Ah, such a fine display of patriotism!"

"Whatever it is, it caused traffic to back up," Tom said, blowing a curl of smoke.

"Our citizens are outraged at Japan's naked aggression and banditry in Manchuria. They demand action," Captain Tung said, slamming his fist down on the table.

"Well, it looks like they might get it right here," Tom said, "if Mayor Wu rejects their demands to stop these boycotts. It's hurting them in the pocketbook, and in this depression, Japan needs all the money it can get."

Chow scoffed. "The Chinese people won't stand for another national humiliation! Mayor Wu Tieh-cheng will stand firm against Japan's attempt to bully China once again."

Tom wasn't convinced and let it show on his face.

"Remember that Japanese monk who was beaten to death last week?" he asked. "Just a few minutes ago, a Japanese couple was almost poked full of holes by some of those protesters." Tom didn't volunteer who saved them. "All Japan needed was a fake attack on their railroad to invade all of Manchuria. Now, they have plenty of reasons to attack Shanghai under the pretext of 'protecting their citizens.'"

Chow gave a knowing smile between drags on his cigarette. "That is why I traveled all the way from Nanking. Indeed, the next confrontation with the Japanese will be here in Shanghai. And you, Mr. Lai, will pay for it."

CHAPTER THREE

Tom peered through the veil of cigarette smoke and scanned Chow's face for any sign of humor. Unfortunately, there was a disturbing seriousness in the bureaucrat's face. Perhaps a joke would diffuse the situation.

"Sure, I've been keeping a sock full of cash under my mattress for just such an occasion," he said with a wry smile.

Chow chuckled and shook his head. "Perhaps I misspoke. Not you alone. But Generalissimo Chiang expects all Party members to donate generously to the defense of the nation. He needs your help again."

"Anything for Gimo," Tom said, using the affectionate nickname for Generalissimo Chiang Kai-shek.

So that's all this meeting was. Just another collection drive for the Nationalist Government. Still, if anyone deserved the money, it was Chiang Kai-shek. Hadn't the Generalissimo mopped up those feuding warlords with the Nationalist Army and turned China into a unified nation? But the country was still plagued by poverty, banditry, Communism, and foreign aggression. The survival of the Chinese Republic was a dream that Tom Lai would help make a reality, no matter what.

Behind his glasses, Chow's eyes brightened. "I'm glad you feel that way Mr. Lai. Captain Tung tells me that Club Twilight is one of the most popular spots in Shanghai."

"You flatter my unworthy little nightclub," Tom said, blowing out a puff of smoke with a grin.

"Tell me, Mr. Lai," Chow said, flicking the ash off of his cigarette. "Why did you open up your club in Chapei and not in the International Settlement?"

"Well, I want to say it was motivated out of a desire to give back to the Chinese community…but the truth is that real estate's cheaper over there," Tom said with a grin.

The three of them shared a laugh.

"Spoken like a true Chinese," Chow said. "We love to save money." He sighed and continued, "Unfortunately, we cannot afford to be so frugal when China faces its greatest peril. That is why I'm in Shanghai, selling bonds and securing loans from the local businesses and bankers."

"Mr. Lai is a loyal Party member who has come to our aid before," Captain Tung cut in. "He helped finance the last Bandit Extermination Campaign."

A colorful term for civil war. There had been many "Bandit Extermination Campaigns" directed against the Communists who had set up their own Soviet Republic in the southern province of Kiangsi. All of which had resulted in defeat for the better-equipped Nationalist Army.

"As a businessman, Communism offends me," Tom said, after another puff. "But Gimo seems more determined to crush that nest of bed bugs rather than to deal with the ravenous wolf that's right outside his front door."

Chow gave the Captain an offended glance.

"The Generalissimo believes in the policy of 'internal pacification first, external resistance second'," Tung offered after a sheepish cough.

Chow frowned and ashed his cigarette. "You doubt Chiang Kai-shek's strategy, Mr. Lai?"

"It's the American in me," Tom said, holding up a placating hand. "We're accustomed to criticizing our leaders. I just feel that the Japanese are a greater threat. Besides, nothing breaks my heart more than Chinese killing other Chinese, even if they are Reds."

Captain Tung nodded. "The Communists can be finished off in time but only if the Japanese devils are dealt with first."

Chow puffed away on his cigarette. "I actually agree with you and the Captain, Mr. Lai. It is unfortunate that the Generalissimo does not see the danger coming from that island of dwarf bandits. When the fighting begins, Shanghai cannot rely on any help from Nanking."

"Oh? Is Shanghai no longer part of China?" Tom asked, softening the insult with a coy grin.

Chow chuckled. "Well, I'm sure you know that although China is unified on paper, the central government – that is the Kuomintang – really only controls about a third of the country. The rest is ruled by warlords who have pledged loyalty to Generalissimo Chiang and the Kuomintang. It is difficult to have national unity with so many alliances."

Tom shrugged. "Still, China is the most unified it's been since the Manchus were overthrown."

"A fair point, Mr. Lai. However, I'm sure you're aware of the internal politics that are tearing the Kuomintang apart?"

"From what I hear, Chiang resigned as Chairman of the Nationalist Government because of that mess in Manchuria. Now it's a power struggle in Nanking."

"You heard correctly, Mr. Lai," Chow said. "The Kuomintang's left-wing faction, under Wang Ching-wei, are jockeying for power now. There are rumors of a coalition government between Chiang and Wang, but because of this disunited leadership, Nanking can't afford to send any more troops to reinforce the garrison here."

"We do not need reinforcements from Nanking!" Tung roared, banging his fist on the table. "The officers and men of the 19th Route Army are ready! My company has been tasked with guarding the North Railway Station, which I will turn into a fortress! Our commander, General Tsai Ting-kai, is one of the most brilliant officers in the entire Nationalist Army. With him leading us, we cannot lose!"

"I'm sure even Hirohito heard you over in Tokyo, Captain," Tom said, taking one last drag on his cigarette. "Let's have a toast." Flagging down a waiter, Tom switched over to English and ordered, "Three whiskeys, please. Scotch."

A few minutes later, the men received their liquor and raised their glasses.

"To the Chinese Republic! To Generalissimo Chiang Kai-shek! And to victory!" Tom toasted.

"*Kanpei*," Tung and Chow responded before they all downed their whiskeys.

The alcohol soothed Tom's nerves but unease lingered in the air along with the smoke. Suspicious, shifty glares from the surrounding tables made him feel even more like a Chinaman. Part of Tom wanted to relocate to a friendlier bar, but he couldn't lose face in front of his fellow Kuomintang members. After all, the survival of Club Twilight and his future with Mei-chen depended on keeping favor with the Nationalist Party.

"Will two hundred thousand American be enough?" Tom asked, pulling out his checkbook.

Chow gave a faint hissing noise, expressing disapproval. "Unfortunately, that won't be enough. I told Finance Minister Soong that we could count on at least half a million."

Tom blinked in confusion. "That's how much I gave last time."

"Yes, but things have changed," Chow said as he began cleaning his glasses with a pocket cloth. "A year ago, we only had to contend with the Communists. The loss of Manchuria has robbed us of millions of our countrymen, valuable natural resources, and countless factories. Added to that, the world economic depression makes securing loans from foreign nations almost impossible. All patriotic Chinese – especially members of the Kuomintang – must dig deep into their pockets." Placing the glasses back on, Chow added, "You *are* Chinese, aren't you, Mr. Lai?"

At times like this, Tom wasn't sure of what he was. American by birth, Chinese by ancestry, both yet neither. The police officer's insults resurfaced in his mind, along with countless slights, taunts, and cruelty he'd endured back in the States. He'd given so much to both countries and for what? Part of him wanted to write a check out for one million, two million, three million dollars, just to prove his loyalty to China out of spite. But San Francisco entered his mind and quelled his fury.

He would be back there soon enough, where he and Mei-chen would own a nice Victorian mansion together. They'd travel back and forth between Shanghai and Frisco, opening up businesses in both cities and for that, he'd need to save his money.

"I'm sorry, Mr. Chow, but business has been slow over the winter. As you said, the depression has hurt everybody."

"I see," Chow said, irritation flickering behind his glasses like a dimming light bulb. Within moments, it was gone. "May I ask your Chinese name?"

"Huang-fu," Tom said.

Chow pursed his lips and nodded. "*Wealthy future?*"

"My father was a businessman, like me. He wanted us all to be rich."

"And Tom came from…?"

"Thomas Jefferson, of course. He was the most famous American my parents could think of."

Chow gave a gracious smile. "Well, Lai Huang-fu, on behalf of the Chinese Republic and Chiang Kai-shek, I thank you."

"I wish I could give more," Tom replied with some truth. He glanced over to Tung, who couldn't hide his disappointment. The same look that his father had given him so many times. "But with men like Captain Tung leading the fight, victory is assured."

The Captain nodded. "I wish I could have you fighting beside me, Lai Huang-fu." He turned to Chow. "Do you know he served in France?"

Genuine surprise lit up behind Chow's glasses. "You were in the World War? I didn't know America allowed Chinese to fight in their army."

"Of course! There were even Chinese fighting at Gettysburg," Tom said. Tung gave an impressed nod but Chow stared in confusion. "During the American Civil War," he clarified.

"I'm impressed, Mr. Lai," Chow said. "Did you order white men into battle?"

"Never made it past private, I'm afraid. But the US Army did award me the Citation Star." Tom didn't volunteer any further. In Chinese culture, accomplishments should be hinted at but not boasted. Besides, revisiting the war always left him with a hollow, washed-out feeling.

"If you change your mind and wish to fight, there's always a place for you in my company," Captain Tung said.

The hint was clear enough. If Tom couldn't pay the half million, the least he could do was fight for the country that had allowed him to prosper so much. A valid point, Tom conceded. But he'd already done enough soldiering in the mud and muck of the Argonne Forest to last a lifetime. Instead, he settled on a third option.

"Tonight's bill will go on my tab," Tom said. Fighting over the bill was customary for any Chinese dinner, with each man insisting he would pay for the other. Rather than endure that staged drama, Tom would settle the matter here and now.

"Very well, Mr. Lai," Chow said smiling. "What do you recommend here?"

"I'm thinking of an old American delicacy. Have either of you gentlemen had chop suey before?"

CHAPTER FOUR

Club Twilight glowed like an oasis in a wasteland. As he stepped out of his Bentley, Tom felt like a proud parent. Blinking neon signs proclaiming its name in both English and with Chinese characters hung above the entrance. Their cascading glow seemed to warm the crisp night air.

Until two years ago, the structure had been one of the many somber warehouses that dotted the city. Through hard work and connections, Tom had transformed it into one of the most popular nightclubs in Shanghai, despite being located in the industrial Chapei district.

A stream of clientele moved in and out of Club Twilight like flowing rivers. Tom joined their ranks and entered the lobby, where a Chinese boy – one of Shanghai's many orphans – took his hat and coat. Off to the right, another boy sold tickets for taxi dancers, where a line had formed.

Tom turned and almost collided with what looked like a wall wearing a tuxedo. With his massive build, bald head, bulbous nose, and thick mustache, Yan Ping resembled Genghis Khan stuffed into a dinner jacket. Fitting since he had been a veteran soldier in the warlord Sun Chuan-fang's army. That is, until Chiang Kai-shek and the Nationalists had defeated them in battle and occupied Shanghai.

No hostility remained inside Yan though, since Tom paid him good money to be head of Club Twilight's security.

"Welcome Mr. Lai," he said with a little bow.

"Thanks for opening up the club, Yan. It's busy, I see."

"Oh yes, very busy tonight. Whenever there's trouble outside, people try and forget about it inside."

"Yan my friend, you're wiser than Confucius," Tom said with a smile. He made his way into the main hall and looked for Mei-chen. Large American and Chinese flags hung crisscrossed on the walls – the Stars and Stripes locked firm with the White Sun of the Kuomintang.

Fifty or so tables surrounded a large dance floor, completely packed with guests. A few of his taxi dancers stood off to the side, mostly Chinese and Russian girls, willing to dance with any man so long as they paid. Just like taxicabs, these girls had their fares.

The Twilight Band was a motley assortment, drawn from Peking, Canton, Hong Kong, and Shanghai. Despite the lack of standard dialect, they all understood the language of jazz and played as if they were at Harlem's Cotton Club. The long bar was crowded with guests, drowning their worries in liquor.

About half of the clientele were native Chinese, decked out in Western clothes and traditional *changshan* long shirts. The others were foreign, hailing from America, Britain, Italy, France, Germany, Siam, the Philippines, Malaya, Persia, and maybe even Timbuktu. Club Twilight didn't have opium or gambling, but it could boast the prettiest taxi dancers and the best jazz band in all Shanghai. Despite its lack of vice, the club had become a haven for foreign diplomats and Chinese *taipans* looking for foreign connections.

In the sea of dancers, Ho Mei-chen was easy to spot in a red *cheongsam* gown and her signature flared black leather gauntlets. She swayed and twirled with a tall white man in a light gray double-breasted suit. Charles Whitfield was instantly recognizable, and – even though he was dancing with his girl – Tom couldn't suppress a smile.

Blonde, blue-eyed, and strapping, Whitfield looked like a cross between Lucky Lindy and Tarzan. In contrast to his football player physique, he was actually a government bureaucrat, specifically a foreign service officer attached to the US Consulate. He was also one of the few white men who treated Tom as an equal, probably because he was the son of Christian missionaries.

Through the dancing throng, they soon spotted Tom and waved. Whitfield took Mei-chen by the arm and led her off the dance floor. Tom joined them at a nearby table.

"Good to see you, old boy," Whitfield said as they shook hands. "I hope you don't mind me dancing with your lady."

"Not at all, so long as you paid her," Tom said with a wry grin in Shanghainese.

The Consulate man threw back his blonde head and laughed. Fluent in many regional dialects, Whitfield had served all over China, from Peking, followed by Nanking, then Canton, and finally Shanghai. Although a missionary's son, service in the World War seemed to have killed whatever Christian zeal had resided inside Chares Whitfield. Either that or it was Shanghai itself that had corrupted a once nice church boy from Boston into this secular, worldly diplomat.

"Can we speak in English please?" Mei-chen asked, without any vestige of a Chinese accent. "I want to practice."

"Of course," Tom said, switching languages. "I see those Bob Haring records I bought are paying off."

Tom sat down and smiled at Mei-chen, holding her in a silent embrace. Waved black hair surrounded her elegant face down to her chin, accentuating her dark brown eyes. Her slender body filled out the snug-fitting *cheongsam* so tightly, she might as well have been sewn into it. She flashed a smile back but there were no overt displays of affection. Despite the open secret of their relationship, during work hours, Ho Mei-chen was just another one of the many taxi dancers at Club Twilight. Until they were properly married, at least.

"How did your dinner go?" she asked.

"Yes, do tell us all about it," Whitfield said, leaning closer. "Did the Nationalist Party offer anything good this time?"

Tom groaned and rubbed his temple. "It wasn't a business deal. More of a shakedown than anything."

"Again?" Mei-chen practically sneered.

"Confound it, Tom, after all the money you've given them I'm surprised they haven't appointed you the mayor of Shanghai yet," Whitfield said, shaking his head.

"I know, I know, but if Gimo needs the money then I'm happy to give. The Nanking Government is strapped for cash these days."

"That's because the Kuomintang is riddled with thieves," Mei-chen hissed.

The barbed insult stung because it was so true. Although it was the best hope for a modern, progressive China, the Nationalist Party had attracted hordes of unscrupulous riff-raff since assuming power four years earlier. Crooks and grifters flocked to its ranks, using patriotism as a way of lining their pockets. But such was politics in any country.

A white man in a dark blue sailor's uniform approached and offered a little bow. "Scuse me, gentlemen, but is this Miss Ho Mei-chen?"

"The one and only," she said in English.

"Me mates told stories of how you was the prettiest bird in all of Shanghai. I was wondering if I might dance with you," he said, extending a ticket.

The man's cockney accent told that Mei-chen's reputation had traveled far and wide. She glanced back to Tom, who gave an approving nod. She extended her gloved hand and the sailor accepted. They strode out to the dance floor as the band struck up "Chinatown, My Chinatown."

"A fine crowd here tonight," Whitfield said with a sigh. "I imagine this is how Rome looked just before the Visigoths sacked it."

"When do you think it will start?"

"Soon, at least that's the consensus at the Consulate. Tokyo is howling mad about that Nipponese monk being killed by a Chinese mob. But what's really hurting them is the boycott of their goods. In this depression, the Japs need all the cash they can get."

"Can't the American Government mediate peace?"

Whitfield gave him a stern look, like a parent scolding a child. "You've been away from the States too long, Tom. The depression is all President Hoover cares about these days. Apart from saying we won't recognize any government the Japs set up in Manchuria, that's all we'll do. Besides, most Americans can't even tell the *difference* between Japan and China, so there'll be no outcry from John Q. Public."

"What about the League of Nations? Hell, resolving conflicts is why it was set up in the first place!"

Whitfield gave a bitter laugh. "The League is nothing more than a bad joke. Japanese bombers could level Shanghai and all they'll do in Geneva is issue a stern denouncement."

Tom wanted to sink into his chair. "Thanks, Chuck. I appreciate your honesty."

"Well, maybe you'll appreciate some more. You need to get out of Chapei. This is the first place the Japs will attack. Hell, get out of Shanghai altogether."

Now it was Tom's turn to laugh. "All the boats are booked up."

"Then take Mei-chen and high-tail it into the International Settlement or the French Concession. The Japs can't attack there without having to deal with Britain and France."

"I won't abandon my club, Chuck."

"It's just a business, Tom."

"No, it's more than that. I built Club Twilight out of a dilapidated warehouse and greased palms until it turned a profit. This is my ticket to a better life, not just in Shanghai but also in America."

Whitfield raised his blonde eyebrows. "You're going back?"

"Eventually...with her." Tom jerked a thumb over to Mei-chen, foxtrotting with the British sailor. "But until then, I need this club and hell, so does China. It's because of Club Twilight that I can be so generous with my donations to Gimo."

Whitfield snapped his fingers. "Exactly my point, old boy! The Japs know how much you've supported Chiang Kai-shek. Being an American means you're safe in peacetime but during war...well, accidents happen."

Tom snorted. "The 19th Route Army won't just roll over and play dead."

"Aw hell old boy, you know the Japs will lick them."

Of course, Tom had his doubts but such insults from a *gweilo* foreigner couldn't go unchallenged, even if Whitfield was a friend.

"That's to be determined. The Japanese only have their Naval Marines stationed in Shanghai. No Army troops since they're all up north tromping around in Manchuria. The 19th Route Army has General Tsai leading it – probably the best soldier in China except for Gimo – *and* it outnumbers the Japs five to one."

Whitfield pursed his lips. "Do you believe that?"

Tom shrugged. "I have to. Regardless of who wins, I'm not leaving Club Twilight." Tom said, before adding, "My— our future depends on it."

"At least send the poor kid to a hotel in the International Settlement," Whitfield pleaded. "The Cathay or the Astor House—"

"Lots of reporters from out of town have booked up all the hotels there. They're waiting for the fireworks to start so they can have a front row seat."

Whitfield was about to protest again, but closed his mouth as Yan Ping approached their table with rapid steps.

"Mr. Lai, there are several men just arrived and wish to speak with you. I showed them to the back room."

Tom frowned and asked, "Who?"

Worry clouded Yan's face. "The Green Gang," he said, leaning closer. "They said not to keep them waiting."

Only Shanghai's notorious crime syndicate could terrify a battle-hardened soldier like Yan Ping. Not only were they the lords of the city's underworld, but also respectable allies of the Kuomintang. One couldn't refuse their invitation without insulting both parties. Fear tightened Tom's throat and quickened his heartbeat, but he masked it. Face was important in China, especially Shanghai.

"If you'll excuse me," Tom said, standing up. Whitfield gave an understanding nod, sympathy shining in his blue eyes. As he followed Yan past the dance floor, he gave Mei-chen a longing look, just in case it was their last.

CHAPTER FIVE

Three men awaited Tom in the storage room, sitting around a small table. He dismissed Yan with a casual nod. After all, it might insult the Green Gang to keep a bodyguard around and cause a loss of face. Better to stand your ground with a respectful yet stoic manner. After a moment, Yan walked out but not before looking back with a weary expression. Tom refocused his attention on the men.

Two of them wore traditional *changshan* long shirts, flat caps, and the same thick, brutish faces that gangsters of every country possessed. Their leader, however, looked distinctly American in a black pinstripe suit, fedora, and overcoat. Feng Lung-wei resembled a member of the Chicago Mob more than Shanghai's Green Gang. Flanked by two big ears, his large head was decorated with hooded eyes, a wide nose, and thin lips. Barely twenty years old, this fresh-faced brat was the terror of Shanghai, running amok throughout the city like a mad dog with impunity. Being a nephew of Tu Yueh-sheng, the Grandmaster of the Green Gang, had its perks.

"Hello Tommy, what's the bumpus?" Feng asked in English, flashing a grin. He'd learned enough of the language by watching gangster pictures like *Little Caesar* and *The Public Enemy*, and by reading lurid pulp magazines like *Black Mask* and *True Detective Mysteries*.

"Hello, Feng Lung-wei," Tom said, taking a seat across from him. "That's 'rumpus,' by the way."

Feng ignored the correction and said, "Nice joint you have back here. Lots of unused space." He gestured around to the stacked crates of liquor, food, and other supplies. "Plenty of room for an opium den or a gambling house."

Tom shook his head. "Not in my club."

"A Chinese who doesn't chase the dragon or gamble?" Feng shook his head. "You really are a Yankee at heart, Tommy."

"I love the fan-tan as much as anyone, but it's your uncle's domain. That was the deal we made when I opened this place up."

Tom flipped open his gold cigarette case and offered some Lucky Strikes. Feng held up a declining hand.

"Speaking of my uncle, he wants to see you."

Tom lit himself a cigarette, using the pause to prepare a response. Feng's uncle, Tu Yueh-sheng, lived in the French Concession, just south of the International Settlement. The last thing Tom wanted to do was make another trip on such a busy night. Still, it wasn't wise to reject an invitation from the Grandmaster of the Green Gang.

"My club just opened for business. Tell you what, how about you and your men go out to the bar and have a few drinks on me. Give me an hour or two just to make sure everything is running smoothly. Then we'll go to Frenchtown and see Uncle Tu."

The offer was met with cold stares. Tom took a drag on his cigarette and considered his situation. Club Twilight only existed with the Green Gang's tacit approval. A small cut of the club's profits satiated Tu Yueh-sheng, along with a promise to never engage in opium, gambling, or prostitution. Tom knew enough not to encroach on the Green Gang's prized businesses, or even enter into a partnership with them. The bottom of the Soochow Creek was full of men who couldn't fulfill their promises to Grandmaster Tu.

"Perhaps, you don't understand, Tommy," Feng said, his thin lips twisting into a sneer. "It wasn't an offer but an order. When the Green Gang commands, you obey. Savvy?"

Respect for one's elders was commonplace of Chinese culture, but not for Feng. His condescending tone to someone twelve years his senior showed just how much contempt this gangster brat had for Tom. His given name of Lung-wei – Great Dragon – was supposed to showcase his intelligence and strength, since dragons were symbols of wisdom and power in China. But Feng Lung-wei was a dragon of the European variety – breathing fire, terrorizing peasants, and taking fair maidens hostage. To him, few were worthy of a dragon's respect.

Ignoring the insult, Tom flicked the ash from his cigarette and said, "Of course, of course. However, I just came from the International Settlement and would like to stick around for a little bit, just to make sure my guests are satisfied. Between nine and midnight are our busiest hours, you know. Have a few drinks, dance with some of my girls, and then we'll—"

Feng snapped a command with his fingers. The two other gangsters stood up, knocking their chairs over with a loud clatter. Smith & Wesson revolvers slid out of their voluminous sleeves and aimed straight at Tom. He'd seen many of those during the war, but never looking down the barrel of one.

"You can either come with us now or we'll kill you and every single person in your little club." A cruel smile curled onto the young gangster's face.

Tom swallowed hard and stubbed out his cigarette.

"Lead the way."

*****

Feng Lung-wei's Mercedes cruised down Avenue Joffre, the main thoroughfare of the French Concession. Whereas the International Settlement was run by the British – together with the Americans, Italians, and Japanese – France had carved out its own enclave just to the south. Although French in name, it was actually governed by the Green Gang. Police, officials, and just about anyone who mattered were on their take. While Frenchtown was its headquarters, the Green Gang's tentacles spread far and wide all throughout Shanghai.

Sitting in the back seat, Tom puffed away at a Lucky Strike, hoping to mask his concern. Had he done something to offend Tu Yueh-sheng? He'd paid his dues on time and never encroached onto the Green Gang's turf. The gangster lord had even dubbed Tom his "American nephew," which was endearing of him. But the triads – the secret societies of Old China and today's crime syndicates – were notorious for their double dealings, shifting alliances, and betrayals.

Feng Lung-wei sat beside him and chatted away, as if they were out for a night on the town.

"Ever been to the Great World, Tommy?"

Of course Tom had been to the Great World, Shanghai's premier arcade and amusement center. This impudent brat was just toying with him now. He took a drag and nodded.

"Great place, isn't it, Tommy? That's how you met your little twitch, right? Isn't that what they call women in America?"

"Twist," Tom said, expelling a cloud of smoke.

"Oh yes...Mei-chen sure is a great little twist. Isn't she Tommy?"

"She sure is."

Mercifully, the Mercedes slid to a halt and parked outside a storefront. Feng's henchmen hopped out and held the door for Tom, still offering him some level of courtesy. Tom exited the vehicle, tossed his cigarette to the ground, and glanced around.

A lively sea of people flowed to and fro on Avenue Joffre. French couples walked in and out of a dim sum restaurant while Chinese ladies in *cheongsams* and pea coats admired store mannequins outfitted with the latest Paris fashions. An Annamese policeman in French uniform and kepi directed traffic. Tom almost wanted to call for help but suppressed the urge. After all, the Green Gang and the Police were one and the same in Frenchtown.

Instead, he followed Feng Lung-wei into a storefront labeled "*Antiquités d'Orient*," followed by the two hulking gangsters. Inside, the walls were covered in auspicious red wallpaper and dim lighting was provided by low hanging paper lanterns. A moon-faced girl in a *cheongsam* stood behind a glass counter, filled with artifacts from China's ancient past – Ming vases, ceramic foo dogs, and gold statues of the Buddha.

"Not a bad racket we have here, Tommy," Feng said with a proud smile. "All counterfeit but most tourists who come through here can't tell the difference."

Tom peered into the glass case before turning to Feng. "Is the Green Gang branching out into other ventures?"

"It's just a front. Even in Frenchtown we have to be discrete. But that doesn't mean we can't make a little money off of it."

Feng nodded to the store girl, who trotted over to a portion of the red-papered wall and slid open a panel. A large doorframe opened, allowing entry into a hidden back area. A sweet smell wafted up into Tom's nostrils, almost intoxicating him. Opium.

He followed Feng and found himself inside a small room, completely dark except for a few burning lamps. Pallets filled out almost every inch of the cramped area. A few white men and women lay in stupefied bliss next to their opium pipes, but most were Chinese coolies, spending their meager earnings on this demonic drug. Many people – both native Shanghainese and foreign Shanghailanders – lost themselves in this city, swallowed up in a swirling cloud of opium smoke.

Across the room was another door but Feng walked past it and instead, opened another secret panel. Tom and the gangsters followed him down a flight of stairs which led into a murky basement. The door slid shut behind them with a startling whoosh, like a guillotine slamming down. Crates and barrels blocked almost the entire area, but Feng pressed on, squeezing in between the walls of boxes.

A bright electric light bulb illuminated part of the basement and labored breathing cut through the silence. A thick-set Chinese came into view, wearing the same *changshan* long shirt and flat cap as Feng's other two gorillas. The gangster loomed over an Oriental man handcuffed to a chair. The captive took in deep gasps of air, spluttering out bloody phlegm. His blue suit had been torn to rags, which still looked better than his face, now just a maze of cuts and bruises.

"This is why we brought you here, Tommy," Feng said with a taunting grin.

Tom examined the prisoner but there was no recognition. "Who is he?"

"Ever since coming to power, Chiang Kai-shek has tasked the Green Gang to be his eyes and ears in Shanghai," Feng said. "We usually hunt underground Communists, but nowadays we're also looking for Japanese spies." He gestured to the battered captive.

"Congratulations," Tom said. "I'm sure the Generalissimo will give you a medal."

Feng Lung-wei and his thugs stared back with cold, reptilian eyes.

"Wait until you hear what he says." Feng slapped the prisoner hard and asked in English, "Mr. Ono, who was your main contact?"

The man's broken, bloody face lifted up and stared straight at Tom.

"He was."

CHAPTER SIX

The accusation tightened Tom's throat and sent his mind racing. His eyes darted around the dimly lit basement before settling back to Ono's blood-smeared face. Through his myriad of open wounds, a familiar figure began to emerge. Tom had seen this Japanese man before, so much so he'd reserved his own table. Ono could be seen dancing with the taxi girls, conversing with Whitfield and other diplomats, and passing his business card out to anyone who would take it.

"Recognize him now, Tommy?" Feng asked, grinning.

"Yes," Tom admitted. "Goro Ono…he works for some import-export company based out of Nagasaki."

The gangster brat wagged a finger. "That was only his cover. He actually works for Japanese Naval Intelligence. What's more, Ono says that he used *your* club as a rendezvous point for receiving top-secret messages." Feng slapped the Japanese again. "Isn't that right?"

Ono nodded and opened up his mouth to speak, revealing rows of cracked teeth. "Yes…I would," he coughed, "…find messages underneath the table…"

Well, that explained why he always sat at the same spot. But in his confession was Tom's salvation.

"So you admit, Mr. Ono, that you never saw me give you the messages. For all you know, someone else could have been your contact?"

The denial sent an irritated chill through the gangsters. Even Ono looked disappointed.

"Doesn't matter," Feng snapped. "He received the messages at *your* club, Tommy. As far as I'm concerned, you're an accomplice. As they say in your country, 'possession is ninety percent of the law.'"

"That's 'nine-tenths of the law.' And as far as *I'm* concerned, you could have tortured him into saying whatever you wanted," Tom said, bracing his frame. "After all the money I've given the Nationalist Government, you really think I would spy for Japan?"

Feng hissed out a contemptuous scoff. "You might look like us but you're really an American underneath that Chinese skin! And Yankees have no loyalty except to money."

"Let me speak to your uncle. I'll explain myself to him."

"Oh, you will Tommy, you will. The Grandmaster demanded to see you in person to explain your treachery. But first," the gangster turned to the handcuffed prisoner, "I have a spy to execute. You're entitled to a martial firing squad, Mr. Ono. How does that sound?"

The bruised and battered Nipponese spy stiffened his frame into an erect posture. Somber acceptance shone in his eyes. He looked less like chopped up roast beef and more like a proud patriot. Every spy knew that a bullet awaited them should they fail. From Mata Hari to Goro Ono, such grim fortitude was almost admirable.

"I will go to my death as a true servant of the Emperor," Ono said, his gory face alighting with patriotic zeal. *"Tenno Heika Banzai! Banzai! Banz—"*

Feng's hand dove into his jacket, pulled out a Smith & Wesson revolver, and pressed it against Ono's forehead. The Japanese fell silent, closing his eyes in preparation. With its gleaming silver barrel and polished handle, the weapon befitted a Texas Ranger more than a Chinese gangster. Chambering a round, the brat's face glowed with sadistic glee.

But his finger loosened around the trigger. The gun dropped to Feng's side and he snapped his fingers.

"Since Tommy is here, let's use *his* gun," Feng suggested with an ominous laugh, tucking the revolver back into his jacket. One of the henchmen lumbered into the darkness and returned with an enormous firearm – a Thompson submachine gun. From its bulbous drum to its sleek wooden foregrip, the weapon emanated dread and menace, like a metallic demon.

Grabbing the Thompson with both hands, Feng walked to the back wall. The other three gangsters stepped back, but Tom stood transfixed in horror. Feng aimed the submachine gun straight at Ono and fired an inferno of bullets and flame. Bursts of lead ripped through Ono's body, sending small eruptions of blood and flesh up into the air. What remained of the Japanese spy's bloodied face was torn apart as the lethal spray pulverized his nose, jaw, and eyeballs into pink and red pulp. The onslaught struck him with such force that it knocked the chair over, smashing the wood into splinters that mixed together with the crimson gore.

The shooting stopped, replaced by Feng's heavy breathing. The deep breaths lapsed into a fit of high-pitched giggles.

"Tommy gun…like you, Tommy! Get it?"

The other gangsters laughed alongside Feng, like cackling hyenas. Tom stared down at the mass of red mush that had once been Goro Ono and saw his future. A wave of nausea almost overtook him but he steadied himself against a nearby crate of opium. Saving face was more important than ever now.

"Very funny," was all he could muster.

*****

Feng Lung-wei led the entourage back up the stairs and into the opium den. The explosive volley of bullets hadn't disturbed the occupants from their drug-induced slumber. Most stared into nothingness but a few glanced over to Tom with empty, languid eyes. He looked away, over to Feng, who looked like an otherworldly ghost in this haze of opium smoke. Fitting, since there were rumors that Feng Lung-wei had been possessed by evil spirits as a boy.

Such superstitions still ran rampant in China but after what he'd just witnessed, Tom reconsidered their validity.

Gruesome brutality was a common sight in the trenches but this was something different altogether. The white-bone demons that killed and devoured the flesh of travelers would have been more merciful.

They walked across the opium den and to the door on the opposite side. Without knocking, Feng opened it and led them into a spacious chamber, lined with frilled pillows. Two women – one redheaded Occidental and one raven-haired Oriental – lay about half-naked. The stupor of opium had turned their pretty faces into semi-catatonic masks. Tom had seen them before – Feng's Russian and Chinese mistresses. He realized that they were standing in Feng Lung-wei's private chambers.

Two white men stood with crossed arms at the far end of the chamber. Although they wore gray three-piece suits like respectable businessmen, their thick beards and scarred faces identified them as former Cossacks. Millions of Russians had fled their homeland after the Bolsheviks seized power, finding employment in Shanghai as prostitutes, mercenaries, and bodyguards.

The Cossacks flanked a throne-like chair at the far end, ornamented with sculptures of golden dragons. Only someone like Feng would own something so garish, but it was Tu Yueh-sheng who currently occupied it. An elegant silk *changshan* hung off of his wiry body and he beckoned Tom closer with a claw-like hand. A long, sharp pinky nail was visible, symbolizing his status like the mandarins of old.

Thick lips sat at the bottom of his long face while slit-like eyes looked Tom up and down. Two large ears hung off of the side of the gangster chieftain's head, which earned him the almost comical nickname 'Big-Eared Tu.' The family resemblance to Feng was strong in that regard. Although Tu was only twelve years older than Tom, there was something ancient and eternal about the Grandmaster of the Green Gang, like China itself.

But as Tom entered, his once benefactor had taken on an even more sinister appearance than he'd thought possible.

Tu Yueh-sheng was like Al Capone and Fu Manchu rolled into one.

"Welcome, Lai Huang-fu," the gangster lord purred. "Any last words?"

CHAPTER SEVEN

"Yes, I do have something to say, oh illustrious one," Tom said.

Ignoring the fear that weakened his knees, he walked toward Tu and presented himself with a supplicating bow. Ever since the establishment of the Republic in 1911, bowing was reserved for only formal occasions. But Tom knew that despite his support of Kuomintang, Tu Yueh-sheng was still a traditional Confucian at heart. He'd have to pull out all the stops if he wanted to ingratiate himself to the Green Gang one last time. Straightening up, the Grandmaster of Shanghai fixed Tom with an almost satisfied look.

"Thank you for meeting me here, Uncle," Tom said in Shanghainese. He used the familiar Chinese term to address an elder male, regardless of any actual family connection. "I realize how insulting these paltry quarters must be for one so high!"

That earned another pleased expression from Tu. He cast a glimpse over to Feng Lung-wei, standing off to the side, who burned with undisguised fury. It was a rarity to see the lord of the Green Gang outside of his sprawling mansion on Route Doumer. Actually commandeering Feng's private room and opium den intoned that Tu had taken a personal interest in Tom's fate.

"I had to hear Ono's confession with my own ears," Tu began, "and I would never allow a Japanese devil to set foot in my mansion. I am disheartened to bring you here, my American nephew. Out of sentimentality, I allowed you to operate in Chapei at a much lower protection fee than other nightclubs in Shanghai."

"As long as I stayed away from opium and gambling, since they are your domain, oh illustrious Grandmaster. And I have done so!"

"That may be true, but a Japanese spy names you as his collaborator! Aiding the dwarf bandits is a far more serious offense. How do you answer these accusations?"

"Uncle, I deny such slander against my good name. I would never aid Japan."

Tu grunted. "Regardless, he used your nightclub as a rendezvous, picking up and dropping off secret documents to his contact. The Jap told me everything just before you arrived. Although he didn't name anyone specific, we believe that he is in league with Commander Jiro Fukuzaki, a Naval intelligence officer stationed here in Shanghai."

"He won't be saying much of anything now," Feng said with a giggle. Tu's narrow eyes widened enough to shoot his nephew a silencing stare.

"I'm disappointed, my American nephew," Tu continued, shaking his head. "I thought you were a true son of China, despite your foreign birth."

Always the foreigner. Tom needed to think fast or risk losing his only potential ally. Ono's massacred body flashed in his mind, leaving him light-headed. He balled his fist and summoned what strength remained. Above all, he couldn't lose face or show weakness in front of this man. When Chiang Kai-shek first took power in 1927, he relied on Tu Yueh-sheng and the Green Gang to orchestrate the slaughter of Communists rivals in Shanghai. Hundreds of men and women were gunned down in a bloodbath that made the Saint Valentine's Day Massacre look like a church picnic.

"Ono could have been lying to protect his true contact," Tom suggested. "After all, the Japanese are very loyal."

"Something you know nothing about, Yankee," Feng hissed.

"Be silent!" Tu roared, causing Feng to blanch slightly. Turning to Tom, he said, "Generalissimo Chiang has given us the important duty of uprooting spies in Shanghai, be they

Red or Japanese. The Green Gang has become the unofficial secret service of the Nationalist Government. That being said, Goro Ono was suspected of espionage for some time now, so I sent Feng to abduct him. Sure enough, he was found departing from Club Twilight."

The gangster lord slid a slender hand into his voluminous sleeve and pulled out a folded sheet of paper.

"In his possession were secret documents, detailing the American Government's views on the recent conflicts in the Far East. It even elaborates on the probable reaction they would have if a full-scale Sino-Japanese War erupted."

"What does it say?" Tom asked after a moment.

"It's in English, but my nephew can read them."

Tu beckoned Feng Lung-wei closer and handed the paper over. All too late did Tom remember that despite his grandiose power, Tu Yueh-sheng was barely literate in any language.

Feng unfolded the paper and read aloud in English, "'In accordance with the doctrine proclaimed by US Secretary of State Stimson, the United States Government will not recognize any territorial changes in China by force and will denounce anything that might impair the existing Open Door policy. However, the United States will remain neutral in any conflict between the Chinese Republic and the Empire of Japan.'"

Tom clapped and said, "Bravo, Feng. Those pulp rags must be paying off. You sounded like a real Yankee Doodle Dandy."

Feng growled and replied back in Shanghainese, "Make jokes all you want, but I've already translated these for my uncle."

Tom ignored the brat and said, "May I read the documents for myself, Uncle?"

Tu nodded and ordered Feng to hand them over. The two pages were typewritten in English on thick, high-quality paper. The type used in a business or government office. The contents revealed even more. Everybody knew that

America would stay out of a Sino-Japanese War, but there was an air of authenticity to the documents that the average man might not have been privy to.

Even more concerning was that the papers went on to detail the exact strength and size of the US Marines stationed in Shanghai, along with the specs for all American Naval gunboats that patrolled the Yangtze River. In the event of a Japanese attack on Shanghai or a new Boxer Rebellion, these forces could be used – the documents argued – to safeguard US business interests until reinforcements arrived from the Philippines.

Although it lacked any stationary from the United States Consulate, the information had to have come from there. Charles Whitfield's face flashed before Tom's eyes. He almost laughed.

Charles Whitfield, a Japanese spy? A preposterous thought! Whitfield was not only his friend but an ally of the Chinese people. How could the son of Christian missionaries be a spy? Still, he was the only officer from the US Consulate who regularly visited Club Twilight. The thought lingered, gnawing away at Tom's brain like termites.

"Want to confess, Tommy? It'll save us all a lot of time," Feng said, jerking him out of his thoughts.

Ignoring the taunt, Tom kept his focus on Tu. "Uncle, you know that I am a loyal Kuomintang member and supporter of Chiang Kai-shek. They are the only hope for a strong, united China. If I were a spy, then why would I donate so much of my wealth to the only government that could stand up to Japanese Imperialism?"

Despite his leathery face remaining placid, a twinkle shone in Tu Yueh-sheng's narrow eyes.

"However, if this treachery did occur in my nightclub then it is my responsibility to unmask the true spy. Please, give me a chance to prove my innocence. That's all I ask!" Tom followed up his request with another bow.

A cruel laughter punctured the air.

"Uncle Tu, do not believe this foreign devil," Feng said. "His loyalty is to his family in America, not to us or China!"

Tu's eyes darted between his nephew and Tom. With this bloodthirsty brat demanding Tom's execution, Tu had little choice or risk losing face in front of his own men. However, the mere fact that he had met with Tom in person signified a deep conflict within the Grandmaster of crime. His affectionate title of 'American nephew' hinted that he preferred Tom to his actual vile relatives.

"Lai Huang-fu, not only have you always been on time with your payments to the Green Gang," Tu said, holding up a languid hand. "But you have also been most generous to the Chinese Republic and our great leader, Generalissimo Chiang. I do not want to believe these horrible accusations, but as mentioned, you must shoulder the responsibility. I will give you forty-eight hours to produce the real spy. If you cannot…"

"Then rat-tat-tat, Tommy!" Feng said, snickering.

Execution by submachine gun would be a merciful death. The Green Gang was infamous for cutting every tendon of their victims, leaving them quivering, helpless piles of flesh. Tom forced a grateful smile.

"Of course, I understand. Thank you, oh illustrious one! Thank you!"

With a wave of his claw-like hand, the matter was concluded. One of the Cossack bodyguards fetched Tu a long pipe and presented it with reverence. Feng Lung-wei gestured for Tom to follow him out of the chambers. As he walked by, the girls followed him with glazed eyes. With one motion, the Chinese whore dragged a finger across her throat.

Seeing the gesture, Feng snorted and whispered, "It won't be that quick, Tommy. I promise you."

CHAPTER EIGHT

The Mercedes jerked to a halt in front of Club Twilight, flooding the vehicle with a neon glow. Red and yellow lights danced on Feng Lung-wei's youthful face, giving him the appearance of an enormous firefly. Sitting beside Tom in the back seat, the gangster gazed outside the window in transfixed awe.

"I'll admit Tommy, your nightclub is the beat's knees…did I say that right?"

"Bee's knees," Tom corrected.

"Ah yes," Feng said. "Despite everything that's happened between us, I have always had the utmost admiration for Club Twilight. I just want you to know that."

"I'm touched."

"Too bad it's a nest of spies," Feng snapped. In the neon lights, the gangster's face now resembled a red-faced *mogwai* demon, snarling in rage. "You may have fooled Uncle Tu but I have never trusted you. No matter how much money you donate and how fluently you speak our language, you're just a Yankee at heart."

That was the last straw. The constant threats and insults kindled an angry fire deep inside Tom. It had been there all his life, igniting in brief yet destructive explosions. If he only had two days left to live, he wouldn't hold his tongue any longer around this two-bit gunman.

"Listen you turtle's egg," Tom said in Shanghainese, using the closest Chinese expression to 'bastard.' "I'll find the real spy and deliver him to Uncle Tu gift-wrapped. Now go crawl back to that garbage can you call an opium den."

That seemed to strike a nerve, twisting Feng's face into an even angrier scowl. "You have forty-eight hours, Tommy," he responded in English. "Tick tock. Oh, and don't bother trying to leave Shanghai. We'll be watching you."

An understatement. The Green Gang controlled the docks so escape by sea wasn't an option. Taking the train would probably mean being spotted by one of their many spies. Not that he planned on running away. Thomas Lai was no Japanese spy and he would prove it or die trying. Without a word, Tom exited the Mercedes and slammed the door behind him.

Tom paused near the entrance underneath the neon lights that spelled out "Club Twilight," soaking up the warmth. He waited for the Mercedes to drive away and merge with the steady flow of rickshaws and automobiles. Free of Feng's lurking presence, Tom pressed onward into the club and gave his hat and coat a nearby lobby boy. He took a deep breath and walked into the main hall, like a king returning to his castle.

The crowds had thinned but a respectable number of men slow-danced with his taxi girls while the band played "Limehouse Blues." Mei-chen was no longer with that British sailor but now danced with what looked like a Chinese soldier. They contrasted each other like night and day; Mei-chen in her fiery red *cheongsam* and black leather gloves, the soldier in the same blue-gray uniform that Captain Tung wore. Although, Tom knew for sure that he wasn't an officer, since he looked no older than sixteen. A boy soldier on leave before the storm broke. Tom sympathized.

Catching sight of Tom, Mei-chen flashed a smile. He reciprocated but waved his hand, indicating that the soldier's dance was on the house. The boy deserved a little pleasure before his journey into hell. Sauntering deeper into the club, Tom stopped by the bar, ordered a J&B Scotch on the rocks, and made his way over to Whitfield's table. Nursing a whiskey of his own, the US Consulate man rose and greeted Tom with a firm handshake.

Tom smiled, but the nagging thought of Charles Whitfield colluding with Japan chilled his blood. But such an idea was ridiculous. The Whitfields had not only opened schools and hospitals throughout China, they were also one of the most vociferous families demanding a repeal to that insidious Chinese Exclusion Law. Still, alliances could always shift.

"I say old boy," Whitfield said as they sat down. "That devilish mandarin Big-Eared Tu must have given you quite a fright! The color's drained from your face. You almost look like a white man!"

Tom forced a laugh and realized he hadn't had a cigarette since leaving the French Concession. Pulling out a Lucky Strike from his case, he lit up and let the soothing tobacco course through his lungs.

"In all seriousness, I was mighty worried for you, and so was the kid," Whitfield said, gesturing to Mei-chen out on the dance floor. "What was all that rumpus about?"

Tom swirled the ice in his glass. If his friend was indeed a spy, the last thing Tom wanted to give the impression that he was on to him. Best to play dumb.

"It wasn't anything really," Tom said, taking a sip of his Scotch. The fear and anger from earlier began to dissipate as the alcohol slid down his throat. "The Green Gang is upping my monthly protection payments. I guess the depression has finally hit China."

An air of skepticism swept over Whitfield, but it soon passed.

"This damnable depression isn't going anywhere soon. Have I told you about my uncle?"

"The banker in Boston?"

"Yes, that's the one. There was a run on his bank last month. Just about cleaned him out." Whitfield shook his head. "Feels like the whole world is going crazy, Tom."

A desperate uncle might be enough reason to spy, but Tom didn't want to jump to conclusions just now. Instead, he took a drag on his cigarette and said, "I need to ask a favor, Chuck."

Whitfield leaned in. "Anything, old boy."

Although an outright accusation might backfire, suitable bait might encourage Whitfield to reveal himself, if he was indeed the spy.

"The Green Gang is concerned with a certain Nipponese gentleman." Tom sipped his J&B before saying, "Jiro Fukuzaki. Ever hear of him?"

Whitfield's blue eyes alighted with recognition. "Yeah, he's an Imperial Navy officer. I've had a few drinks with him at a pub he owns in Little Tokyo."

"Does this pub have a name?" Tom asked in between cigarette drags.

"The Golden Unicorn…say old boy, what are you planning?"

Tom gave a placating smile. "Nothing. Tu Yueh-sheng and I thought you would know who he is. After all, you know a lot of the Mikado's men, don't you?"

"Well, it's my business to know. After all, along with the British, the Italians, and us, the Japanese run the International Settlement." Whitfield paused, before giving a concerned look through the veil of cigarette smoke. "Say, what are you trying to imply?"

"Nothing," Tom said, raising a placating hand. "I just promised Big-Eared Tu that I'd ask you what you know about Fukuzaki."

Whitfield shook his head. "Dreadful that you have to deal with scum like that. His lot oppress China even worse than the old Manchus ever did, enslaving his own people to opium and brothels."

Tom took another sip. Although he wasn't a Puritan, Charles Whitfield looked down on the Green Gang with the bitter disdain that only a Christian gentleman from New England could. It was a wonder how he could befriend someone in such ill repute as Thomas Lai. However, tonight's little horror show left Tom more cynical than usual. Perhaps their friendship had always been an illusion created by a manipulative spy.

"Tu Yueh-sheng is a necessary evil. After all, a society can't go from feudalism and warlordism to a modern republic without some growing pains. Hell, Al Capone ran Chicago up until a few months ago."

Whitfield didn't respond and sipped his drink. Tom glanced back over at the dance floor, still crowded with couples. But Mei-chen had vanished and Tom suspected where she'd run off to. He drained his Scotch and stubbed out the cigarette.

"I think I'm going to turn in for the night. Rubbing elbows with gangsters always leaves me bushed."

Whitfield nodded before adding, "I don't know what you're planning Tom but I'd stay away from Little Tokyo. There has been a rapid buildup of Jap Marines there. You don't want to be caught in the crossfire when the shooting starts."

Again, sympathy shone in those blue eyes. Tom wanted to believe it was genuine but a dark voice told him to remain vigilant. They shook hands and Tom walked over to Yan Ping, surveying the crowd like a watchful hawk.

"Close up shop for me, Yan," he said in Shanghainese.

"Of course, boss."

Tom looked at the man's thick, mustached face. Yan Ping wasn't the type to ever learn Cantonese, let alone English, so he couldn't have written those documents. This was a simple and loyal man. Tom needed all the help he could get if he was going to venture into the beast's lair of Little Tokyo. That meant his regular chauffeur wouldn't be enough.

"Yan, I'll need your assistance tomorrow morning. Bring my Bentley around at 9 o'clock."

"Of course, boss," he said, his gaze never wavering. Tom nodded and walked off. Enough intrigue for tonight. Mei-chen, his Beautiful Pearl, was waiting.

CHAPTER NINE

As the Twilight Band struck up "China Boy," Tom made his way upstairs. He had carved out a private apartment from the derelict warehouse space on the second story. Feng Lung-wei was right. There was enough unused space for a gambling hall, a private cinema, and even an opium den. But thinking about those empty, glazed eyes from earlier sent a chill down Tom's spine. Pushing the image out of his mind, he opened the apartment door and tried to focus on his Beautiful Pearl.

Ho Mei-chen was sitting on their bed, as vivacious as ever in her red *cheongsam* and black gauntlets. She looked like a living embodiment of those Shanghai poster girls who advertised everything from cigarettes to soap to *loquat* syrup. Her sheer beauty quickened his pulse and knotted his stomach, no matter how many times he laid eyes upon this gorgeous creature. Despite the last few hellish hours, seeing his Beautiful Pearl always banished his troubles far, far away.

"Welcome back darling," she cooed in English, standing up. "I saved the last dance for you."

Mei-chen walked over to a nearby phonograph and put on a record. The jazzy strains of "Sing-Song Girl of Old Shanghai" poured out and filled the apartment. Tom took her gloved hand and they began swaying back and forth on their own private dance floor. Her head lay on his shoulder but Mei-chen's feet were animated, leading both around the apartment. All too soon, the song ended and an irritating clicking noise filled the air. Mei-chen walked over to the phonograph and lifted the needle, bending down in an alluring pose. Tom shifted his eyes and occupied himself with the rest of the apartment.

This was home, despite the sparse furnishings. A phonograph, small nightstand, and a vanity table for Mei-chen, cluttered with cosmetics and makeup. A desk held Tom's important paperwork and a money toad statuette which brought good fortune and wealth to Club Twilight. A few frames decorated the wall – his Citation Star along with photographs of Tom and his family in Chinatown, Tom and Mei-chen along the Bund, and most prized of all, Tom standing beside Generalissimo Chiang Kai-shek himself.

He refocused his attention to Mei-chen and said, "When we're married, you won't have to taxi dance anymore."

"But I like dancing," she said with a pout. "Besides, I bring in a good haul."

"Yes, and thanks to you we're close to our goal. But when you're my wife, the only dancing you'll have to do is for fun," Tom said as he lit a Lucky Strike.

That seemed to please her. She gave a happy smile and sat back on the bed, lighting a cigarette of her own. "What did that vicious little brat Feng want?"

Tom blew out a long curl of smoke as the night's horrors flooded back. A woman, let alone his fiancée, shouldn't be burdened with such troubles. Although he yearned for her support and comfort, it was his duty as a man to solve this problem and keep her in blissful ignorance. For now, at least.

"Tu Yueh-sheng is raising his protection fees," Tom offered.

Mei-chen frowned and took a drag. Her black gloves held the white cigarette like an ivory cane in a sea of tar.

"Greedy bastard," she hissed. "After all you've paid him already. He wants to run you out of business, darling."

"He isn't so bad," Tom said with some truth. After all, it was Tu's mercy that granted him this brief reprieve.

Mei-chen almost spat out the smoke. "Why defend that gangster? The Green Gang has turned Shanghai into the Whore of the Orient! Kidnappings, murder, prostitution, and opium…that's Tu Yueh-sheng's racket. I'll be glad when we get to America and leave his kind on the other side of the Pacific."

Tom shrugged and took another drag. He didn't want to argue but such naiveté couldn't go unchallenged.

"America has its share of problems too, dear. Perhaps you haven't heard of Al Capone or the Tong Wars? Not to mention a depression that's left twenty percent of the population out of work. I don't think they'll be happy to see another Chinaman and his blushing bride either. They passed a law to keep us out, you know."

"The Exclusion Act," Mei-chen said, puffing away. "I'm aware of such prejudices against our kind. But there is a reason why our people, despite the obstacles, still try and enter *Meikuo*."

Meikuo was what the Chinese called America; the Beautiful Country, full of hope and opportunity.

"Look, America is a fine country but so is China. We can't forget our heritage."

"I'll gladly forget this wretched land," she snapped, stubbing the cigarette out. Her venom was surprising.

"You might, but I intend to still do business here even after we settle in Frisco. Shanghai has been mighty good to me and I am going to pay her, and Gimo, back in spades."

With a little sigh, Mei-chen fell back onto the bed. "When will we go to America, darling?"

"Soon, I just have to make a little more money to set us up big in Frisco."

"Why not tomorrow? They say the war will break out anytime now."

Tom scoffed and took a final drag before crushing the smoke out. "Do you want to live in a Victorian mansion on Nob Hill or a roach-infested tenement in Chinatown?"

A little whine was her initial response, but she insisted, "It doesn't matter. So long as we can start a new life together, darling."

Such loyalty was charming but Tom knew he had to prepare himself. If millions of white men were out of work in America, then where would he be? Chinatown was a self-sufficient economy, but he'd been away for so long that perhaps he'd be an unwelcome stranger there. He doubted he could even get a job folding clothes in his father's laundry shop now. After all, he was the ungrateful son who flouted his familial duties by joining up to fight in France. Then – adding insult to injury – he ran off to Shanghai instead of getting married and making grandchildren.

Unmarried at thirty-two was a sin in itself, but maybe his family would be satisfied when he showed them Mei-chen. His older brother would be jealous, naturally, but hopefully his parents would be pleased. After all, Ho Mei-chen was the youngest daughter of a wealthy landlord from the Fukien province. That is, until warlords killed her parents and sister, causing her to flee to Shanghai.

She found work as a taxi dancer in the Great World, that multi-story amusement center that boasted everything from magicians and sing-song girls to Peking Opera and vaudeville acts. After a few charming words, he'd convinced her to come work for him at the newly opened Club Twilight, just across the Soochow Creek.

No need to tell his family that last part. All they needed to know was that Mei-chen would make a suitable *tai tai* and one worthy of bearing many sons. In Chinese culture, one never married for love. Honor, family status, and politics, but never love. He and Mei-chen would be an exception.

"Let's go see a picture tomorrow," she suggested. "Perhaps *Hell's Angels*? Or maybe *Frankenstein* again?"

Tom chuckled and sat on the bed beside her. Only then did he notice the latest issue of *Photoplay* on the nightstand. Greta Garbo cast a seductive sideways glance at the reader while Clark Gable leaned in to kiss her cheek.

"My little actress. Do you want to be a Hollywood star?"

She posed, placing her gloved fingers on her chin. "Aren't I pretty enough?"

"Pretty, yes…but your skin is the wrong color. The best role you could land would be the bride of Fu Manchu."

Mei-chen opened her mouth in mock surprise. "Tell that to Anna May Wong!"

"Didn't she play the daughter of Fu Manchu?" That seemed to shut her up. "Besides, Hollywood isn't in San Francisco."

"Well then, maybe we can see a Chinese picture then. I heard *A Spray of Plum Blossoms* is good. 'Lily Yuen's finest performance' the magazines all say."

"Unfortunately, I have business tomorrow…"

"Fine then, maybe I'll just go shopping." Mei-chen tugged off her leather gloves and tossed them onto the copy of *Photoplay*. "Darling, tell me about your childhood and San Francisco…"

"Again?"

Mei-chen nodded and tucked her head underneath his chin. "I want to hear it a hundred times over. We're going to be living there after all."

Tom stroked her black hair. "Well, one of my earliest memories is the 1906 earthquake. Somehow, my family made it out but the rest of Chinatown wasn't so lucky. When San Francisco was rebuilt, my old man scraped together enough dough to open his own laundry shop."

"But you didn't like laundry, did you?" Mei-chen said, closing her eyes.

"No, I didn't. My big brother was set to inherit the business, so I busied myself with my uncle's affairs."

"Yes, the Tong man, right?"

"The Suey Sing Tong to be correct. He ran fan-tans and mahjong joints in Chinatown. As a ten-year-old, I helped empty spittoons and take out trash. Eventually, he let me take bets and pay out winners. It was more useful training than ironing socks and shirts."

"Didn't your father mind?"

Tom laughed, picturing the old man's disapproving scowl. Not only had the Tong taught him to neglect his duties to the Lai family, but they'd filled his head with such concepts of patriotism and a strong China. As far as Papa Lai was concerned, a country – whether it was America or China – was only as good as the money you could make in it.

"Of course he did, but he wouldn't dare cross the Tong. They'd practically adopted me and taught me the history of China, from the first emperor to the Ching Dynasty. I still remember all the old timers getting their queues chopped off when the Manchus were overthrown."

"A happy day in my family too. My father ordered all of his farmers to unbind their daughters' feet. My father was a progressive man, very supportive of the Republic. He never subjected me to such barbaric customs." Mei-chen slipped out of her high heels and showed off a pair of slender feet.

"My old man would have hated him. I still remember those little stubs my mother walked around on," Tom said, shaking his head. "Anyway, shortly after my eighteenth birthday, America entered the World War."

"Such a terrible tragedy," Mei-chen said with a sigh.

An understatement. Although Tom Lai joined the United States Army with eager enthusiasm, his countrymen relegated him to being the company's laundry boy. He spent almost the entire war washing uniforms and ignoring jeers of "Heathen Chinee" and "Private Chink." That all changed in late 1918, during the final push against the Germans. Manpower was low and Tom was sent to the front lines as a quick replacement. It was there – in the Argonne Forest – that Tom felt comfortable telling Mei-chen what happened next.

"It was a rainy November morning and our platoon leader ordered us to take out a German machine gun nest. We charged just before sunrise. The lieutenant was killed instantly, as were ten more of my comrades. The next few hours were spent taking cover in no man's land until me and another soldier got close enough to take out the Heinie nest with a few grenades." Tom cleared his throat and added, "The war ended a week later."

"So heroic…"

Tom shrugged and said, "General Pershing thought so too. He even pinned a medal on me." He gestured to the

Citation Star on the wall. "Nothing too flashy, since they don't give the Medal of Honor to Chinamen."

"Well, I think you deserve it."

"Thanks. But when I went home, my father was so ashamed. Said I ran off to 'fight a white man's war.'" He sighed. "But it taught me there were more important things than making money."

"Like what?"

"Don't get me wrong, money is important but there are things worth fighting for. I wanted the land of my ancestors to become a strong and modern nation just like America. So when I heard about this dashing generalissimo named Chiang Kai-shek defeating the warlords one by one, I wanted to help in any way I could. So, I played the stock market for a while, made a tidy sum, and gave hefty donations to the Kuomintang."

"I'm sure Gimo was grateful."

"He was indeed. Invited me to China to meet with him back in '27," Tom said, looking at the framed photograph on the wall. Tom, in his finest three-piece suit, standing next to the Generalissimo, wearing a simple military tunic and Sam Browne belt. Pride welled up inside him but he tried to hide it.

"A fortune teller warned my mom about 'impending disaster' so I got my money out just before the stock market crash in '29. In November, I hopped on a steamer bound for Shanghai to start a new life."

"Where you met me. Why Shanghai?"

Tom shrugged. "I'd visited here when I met Gimo and loved it. It made San Francisco look like a city of milksops."

"Milksops? You Americans talk so strangely," Mei-chen said, lifting her head up. Her half-closed eyes looked even more seductive than normal and she leaned in for a kiss. They locked lips, releasing a surge of pleasure inside him. Tom pulled her back onto the bed where they embraced further.

For a brief moment, the night replayed itself. Chow and Captain Tung asking for loans. Feng's bloody execution of Ono. The Grandmaster of Shanghai giving him forty-eight hours to live. They entered his mind for only a moment and then disappeared like fleeting nightmares. Tomorrow, he would go into Little Tokyo, find this Commander Fukuzaki, and determine if Whitfield truly was the spy. But for now, all that mattered was him and his Beautiful Pearl.

CHAPTER TEN

The next morning, Tom awoke and crawled out of bed, leaving Mei-chen still sleeping. He glanced at his Rolex – 9AM. Yan Ping would be pulling up with the Bentley any minute now, but Tom needed to look presentable if he was venturing into Little Tokyo. He shaved and changed into a nondescript dark blue serge suit and fedora. Most importantly, he fastened the shoulder holster under the jacket and pulled out a Browning automatic from his desk. Since coming under the protection of the Green Gang, he rarely used it, but now the gun looked like a long-lost friend.

He fastened the pistol into his shoulder holster, tucked two extra clips into his waistband, and slid into an overcoat. He parted the blind and gazed out at Shanghai, a sprawling giant in the misty dawn. In the distance, towers of industry and finance were waking up from the night's slumber. On the streets below, laborers and workers of all stripes shuffled through Chapei to man the district's factories, warehouses, and cotton mills.

For the past two years, Tom had carved out a private kingdom within Shanghai but now, this city was looking more like his tomb. He shook his head, trying to rid himself of such pessimism. Thomas Lai had survived the 1906 earthquake, the Tong Wars, and the Battle of the Argonne Forest. He'd survive this. But time was running out.

Peering out the window, Tom saw the Bentley – with Yan Ping at the wheel – coast down the street and park in front of Club Twilight. It was time to go.

He turned around and found Mei-chen stirring awake. After a few blinks and a deep yawn, she asked, "Where are you going, darling?"

"Off to run a few errands," Tom said, surprised the lie came so effortlessly. There was no need to worry her just yet. "Go see a picture today. Do some shopping. I won't be back until we open tonight."

Mei-chen looked disappointed but smiled anyway. "Alright darling...just be careful."

"I will," Tom said, starting for the door, but soon hesitated. He turned around, bent over, and kissed her for luck. Her breath was hot and sticky, but feeling her lips against his filled him with visceral pleasure.

"Come back soon, darling," she said, sinking back onto the bed.

"I will," Tom said, opening the door. He cast a final look back at her. "I promise."

*****

The Bentley inched down Soochow Road, halted by an unusual amount of traffic. A sea of automobiles and rickshaws clogged the roads this morning while the sidewalks were thick with pedestrians, wandering in between the cars. Half were probably the usual commuters but the rest, Tom guessed, were refugees who hoped to find safety inside the International Settlement.

A mixture of weariness, horror, and rage was painted on each of their sallow faces. Shanghai was already overcrowded with poor souls fleeing Communism, bandits, and floods. The entire city was fast becoming an enormous cauldron, ready to boil.

Red-turbaned Sikh policemen directed traffic and manned checkpoints, sending all but a few refugees with the right credentials away. In the coming war, the International Settlement offered the best odds of survival. Not that he planned on abandoning Chapei. After all, a man had to protect his house against burglars.

"Damn these refugees," Yan Ping snorted in the driver's seat, blaring the horn at a few pedestrians, walking in and out of the road. "As if Shanghai wasn't crowded enough."

Tom sighed and looked out the window. Settled in the Soochow Creek, the gunboat *Akata* lay anchored near the Japanese Consulate. Its thick guns jutted out of the sides, ready to lay waste to Shanghai. The US Consulate stood next door, the Stars and Stripes fluttering alongside the Rising Sun. Was Charles Whitfield in there, busy writing secrets for the Mikado?

Yan honked again and few pedestrians parted, allowing the Bentley to pass. They pulled off of Soochow Road and went east, deeper into the Hongkew district. Home to over twenty thousand Japanese, the area had become known as Little Tokyo, full of geisha houses, sukiyaki restaurants, sumo halls, and Shinto shrines. But as the motor cruised up Woochang Road, shuttered businesses lined the street. A few shops still remained but Little Tokyo was beginning to resemble a ghost town. The anti-Japanese boycott was even more effective than Tom had thought.

The Golden Unicorn looked open for business and Yan parked across the street. They exited and Tom surveyed the surroundings. Only a few pedestrians were out today, all of which fixed Tom and Yan with quick, suspicious glares. Tom felt like a hornet that entered the wrong hive. Glancing around for a nearby policeman, his heart sank when two Imperial Japanese Marines turned the corner.

With bayoneted rifles slung over their shoulders, the Marines strutted by like they had already conquered the city. However, in their blue jackets, sailor caps, and white gaiters, they looked more like the kid from the Cracker Jack box than the elite of the Japanese Navy. Still, their presence filled Tom with a gnawing dread. Well, this was why he'd brought Yan Ping along…and the automatic, snug in its holster.

Tom took a deep breath of the chilly morning air and entered the Golden Unicorn. Most bars in Little Tokyo were Japanese style *izakayas* with *tatami* mats and red lanterns hanging out front. However, the Golden Unicorn's interior was more of a London pub complete with a long bar counter, stools, and wooden paneling. No doubt the previous owners were British before the Japanese had made their own enclave in Hongkew.

Adjusting his eyes to the dim lighting, Tom looked around for any sign of Commander Jiro Fukuzaki, but there was nobody except the bartender.

"Excuse me, do you speak Shanghainese?" Tom asked.

The bartender, a middle-aged Japanese, responded with a blank stare.

"English?" Still nothing. Best to try the straightforward approach. Summoning all of his paltry Japanese, Tom asked, "*Fukuzaki Chusa wa kokodesu ka?*"

The bartender's eyes widened and he began speaking in rapid Japanese. Most was it was indecipherable, but he caught the last part – "Yoshida-san!"

The door to the backroom opened and out stepped a lanky man in a trench coat, sporting a toothbrush mustache.

"Yoshida, I presume?" Tom asked.

The man nodded, then said in Shanghainese, "Chinese and dogs are not allowed in this bar. What do you want?"

The man's Shanghainese was accented, but otherwise flawless. Tom glanced over to Yan, looming behind his boss like a dutiful bodyguard.

"I'm looking to speak with Commander Fukuzaki," Tom said. "Do you know where he is?"

"He doesn't want to speak to a *chankoro*," Yoshida said, using the Japanese equivalent for *chink*. He pointed to the front door. "Now leave."

Tom looked back to the bartender for any assistance, but he kept his eyes planted on the floor.

"Wait a moment! I know you," Yoshida said. "You're a member of the Kuomintang, aren't you?"

Tom swallowed. Normally, such links were a surefire protection but here in Little Tokyo, connection to the Nationalist Party could be a death sentence. Yoshida barked something in Japanese, and three men burst out from the backroom. Their cruel, sneering faces were unmistakable –

the three Chinese thugs who tried to attack that Japanese couple last night.

Like before, each of them brandished switchblades, ready for a rematch. All too late did Tom realize that Yoshida was a *ronin*. Named after the masterless samurai of old, these latter day *ronin* were civilians in pay of Japanese Intelligence, either to spy or stir up chaos. From the look in their glazed eyes and vacant expressions on their brutish faces, Yoshida's three henchmen were most likely mere coolies looking for their next opium fix.

"Why don't we bring you to Commander Fukuzaki," Yoshida said, flicking open his own switchblade, "one piece at a time?"

CHAPTER ELEVEN

Tom backed up toward the front door but was soon outflanked by the three Chinese coolies. There was no escape this time. Before he could think, one of the thugs lunged forward. The knife seemed to reach out with cold metallic hands, but suddenly stopped. Yan Ping intercepted the brute with a devastating right cross, sending him crumpling onto the floor like a sack of dirty laundry.

Blades drawn, Yoshida and another coolie focused their attention on Yan, forming a human wall between them. The third hoodlum kept his knife trained on Tom, blocking his escape. Luckily though, nothing obstructed Yan's access to the front door.

"Go get help," Tom called out. "Quick!"

Yan flashed a reluctant look, a loyal guard dog to the end.

"Now!" Tom added for emphasis. The order had its effect, spinning Yan around and sending him out the door. Yoshida and his coolies didn't bother pursuing but instead, kept their focus on Tom. He'd have to shoot his way out. His hand reached for the Browning automatic but stopped when another one of the thugs slashed at him.

Tom sidestepped out of the blade's path and grabbed a nearby bar stool. As the coolie struggled to reorient himself, Tom lifted the stool and brought it down like a mallet. A loud crack filled the pub as the thug collapsed onto the floor. The stool broke apart in Tom's hands like melting snow. Two down, two to go.

Yoshida stood off to the side, letting the last coolie henchman lead the attack. The brute charged forward, whipping the knife back and forth, releasing a whoosh in the air. Tom backed up, avoiding the blade's lethal bite, but soon slammed against the back wall. Speed was what was needed now. Tom's hand dove into his coat and whipped out the Browning automatic.

With the muzzle leveled dead center at his chest, the coolie froze like a statue. Tom swallowed hard, the knife inches away from his throat. After a few tense moments, the thug backed off and retreated toward his master. Keeping the pistol trained on them both, Tom's eyes darted about, assessing the situation.

Yoshida and his Chinese henchman burned with impotent anger and tossed their now-useless weapons aside. The two other coolies lay unconscious on the floor, while the bartender cowered in the corner. Part of Tom wanted to apologize to the poor bastard for all the damage he'd done but he didn't dare take his eyes off of Yoshida. Only when the backroom door creaked open did Tom glance to the side.

A middle-aged man entered, attired in a dark blue uniform and peaked cap, stamped with an anchor insignia and gold embroidery. Rank tabs on his collar with a silver cherry blossom design proclaimed he was an officer in the Imperial Japanese Navy. Even more imposing was the officer's face, stern and commanding. Thick eyebrows hung over fierce brown eyes that were settled in a sea of taut skin.

"*Fukuzaki Chusa desu ka?*" Tom asked, still keeping the gun on Yoshida and his cohort.

"*Hai,*" Commander Fukuzaki said with a nod. His narrowed eyes reviewed Tom up and down, back and forth. Switching over to Shanghainese, he said, "May I help you Mr…?"

"Lai. I need to speak with you."

Fukuzaki pursed his lips and examined the two unconscious bodies on the floor. He gestured to the Browning. "Perhaps you can put that away?"

"I tried asking politely before but Mr. Yoshida and his friends weren't very hospitable."

"I see…" Anger swept over Commander Fukuzaki's tight face as he strode over to Yoshida. Raising his white-gloved hand, the Navy officer slapped his subordinate across the cheek. But it was the torrent of verbal abuse that seemed to really wound Yoshida. Commander Fukuzaki unleashed a torrent of angry Japanese for almost a minute until the *ronin* lowered himself in supplication. After apologizing to his superior, Yoshida trotted over to Tom and offered another apologetic bow.

"*Gomen nasai…*" the *ronin* said, unable to hide the anger in his voice.

"Much obliged," Tom said, holstering the gun.

Commander Fukuzaki walked over and bowed himself, although nowhere near as low as Yoshida.

"My sincerest apologies, Mr. Lai," the Commander said in flawless Shanghainese.

"It's not the first time I had trouble with this riff-raff," Tom said, pointing to the coolie henchman on the other side of the pub. "Last time we met, they were attending an anti-Japanese protest."

Fukuzaki glanced over to the Chinese tough – who hung his head in shame – then returned his attention to Tom. "Is that so?"

"I stopped them from killing a Japanese couple. Imagine my surprise to find them working for the head of Japanese Naval Intelligence in Shanghai."

Fukuzaki made an irritated hissing noise through his teeth but said nothing.

"Hell, just last week five Japanese monks were roughed up by thugs like them," Tom jerked a thumb to the two unconscious coolies, sprawled out on the floor. "Maybe they were in your pay as well?"

Commander Fukuzaki drew himself up. "I do not have time to respond to such slander."

Tom waved his hand. "That's fine because I'm not here to discuss that."

"Then what are you here for?"

"Ono-san."

Commander Fukuzaki's taut face remained expressionless.

"Who is that?"

"Your spy."

Yoshida leaned closer and began conversing with the Commander in rapid Japanese. Fukuzaki said nothing but gave an occasional, understanding nod.

"Ah yes, Mr. Lai…now I remember your name. You're the gentleman who runs Club Twilight. I understand that you have connections with the Green Gang?"

Tom considered how best to proceed. A lowly businessman didn't carry much weight but an associate of Shanghai's criminal syndicate lent him suitable authority. But if he revealed Ono's gory death, his bargaining power might vanish.

"Yes," Tom said, squaring his shoulders. "I bring a message from Tu Yueh-sheng."

"Is that so?"

"He says Ono will be executed tonight if you do not reveal the name of the spy in my establishment."

Commander Fukuzaki and Yoshida traded dark looks with each other before resuming their conversation in Japanese. After a few exchanges, Fukuzaki gestured Tom to follow him into the back room.

"Please Mr. Lai, let's talk about this like gentlemen."

Tom smiled. "I thought you'd never ask."

CHAPTER TWELVE

Aside from a few kegs and liquor crates, the back room was more of a small office, complete with a desk and file cabinet. Along with a portrait of the Mikado, a framed painting of a ferocious naval battle hung on the wall. Amid the smoke and carnage, a bright Union Flag fluttered on the ships' masts.

"The Battle of Trafalgar?" Tom asked, gesturing to the painting.

A smile broadened Fukuzaki's tight face as he sat behind the desk. Tom took a seat across from him.

"Very good, Mr. Lai. Are you familiar with British military history?"

Tom shrugged. "Just the highlights. Wellington defeating Napoleon at Waterloo, their victory in the Opium War...and Cornwallis surrendering to Washington at Yorktown."

"Oh yes, you are American, aren't you Mr. Lai?" Fukuzaki said, switching over to English. His command of the language was flawless, without any difficulty pronouncing l's and r's that many Japanese experienced.

Tom nodded, affirming his heritage.

"Forgive me, I'm something of an Anglophile. Japan and Britain are kindred spirits, you know. Two great island empires with powerful navies. I served as an Assistant Naval Attaché in London and fell in love with the city. When this pub was going out of business, I stepped in and purchased it."

"I like the Brits too but they haven't exactly been good Samaritans in Asia. After all, they started a war to protect the opium trade here."

Commander Fukuzaki shook his head. "Such a dishonorable act was not befitting their glorious empire. However, that conflict showed Japan that she needed a powerful Army and Navy to become strong. China did not modernize and look at what she became."

Tom couldn't argue with that. Up until just a few years ago, China had suffered defeat after defeat from foreign powers, along with floods, famines, and endless civil wars. The entire nation was like an enormous drug addict that had finally kicked its habit.

"From what I understand, the Japanese Army is the one winning all of the victories up in Manchuria."

Fukuzaki's taut face itched with irritation. "We will show the world how well the Imperial Navy can fight."

Tom's clenched his hands into fists. "And when will that be?"

"That all depends on Mayor Wu. Our demands are reasonable," the Commander said, holding up three fingers. "One, an apology for the murder of our Buddhist monk. Two, compensation for the other victims of the attack. And three, a suspension of the anti-Japanese boycott."

"Reasonable my foot!"

"Your...foot?"

"I mean, poppycock. Look, you don't want Mayor Wu to accept your demands. Otherwise, you wouldn't employ riff-raff like those coolies out there to manufacture 'regrettable incidents.'"

Fukuzaki sat in silence, his face placid. However, a tempest of anger raged in his narrow, hooded eyes. Upsetting the Commander might sabotage his plans to unmask the true spy, but the humiliations and threats from the last night burned deep inside Tom. He'd tell this Nipponese "gentleman" exactly how he, and the rest of China, felt about him.

"If you boys are jealous of the Army's success, then keep it between yourselves. In the States, they settle their differences with the Army-Navy game. Why don't you boys try that? It'd be a lot simpler than invading countries to see who the Mikado likes better."

Fukuzaki raised an eyebrow. "The who?"

"I mean, the Emperor. You've seen that Gilbert and Sullivan play, right?"

"Oh yes," the Commander said with a chuckle. "An enjoyable opera, but very inaccurate. I would prefer to keep His Imperial Majesty out of our conversation."

"That's fine, I'm more interested in Ono-san anyway."

Despite the slights against his monarch, Commander Fukuzaki nodded thankfully, the very model of a polite Nipponese gentleman. After all, face was everything in Shanghai.

"If you would Mr. Lai, please tell me what Tu Yueh-sheng said."

Everything rested upon the next few moments. If Fukuzaki was willing to trade, then he might just be able to satiate the Green Gang's thirst for blood. But if the Commander felt that Ono was disposable...no, he couldn't think about that now. Instead, Tom summoned all of the skills he'd learned over the years in poker and mahjong for one last bluff.

"He says give us the name of Ono's contact at Club Twilight or he'll be executed. Tonight."

Commander Fukuzaki said nothing for a few moments but his hooded eyes looked Tom up and down.

"If there is a spy operating out of your club, and I'm not admitting there is, why would I compromise their identity just to save an alleged spy who has failed?"

"You would turn your back on a fellow Japanese to save a *gaijin*?"

A smirk crept over Fukuzaki's lips. "And how do you know it's a *gaijin* you're looking for?"

It was a simple question but signified trouble ahead. Yes, how did Tom know they were looking for a *gaijin*, a white foreigner? He thought back to the letter Tu had given him.

"We have evidence that Ono's contact is an English speaker, maybe even someone who works at the US Consulate."

Fukuzaki gave a wry grin. "Is that so?"

"Yes, only somebody who has connections with the American Government could obtain the information that we found on Ono."

"And what was that?"

Tom was about to speak but caught himself.

"Tut tut, Commander," he said, wagging a finger. "Maybe we can throw those documents in as part of the deal. But for now, if you want Ono and what he knows, then you're going to have to name his contact in Club Twilight."

Fukuzaki again retreated into silence and tented his white-gloved hands. Moments passed without a word spoken, but the Commander fixed Tom with such a penetrating stare that he involuntarily averted his eyes to the Trafalgar painting. The stillness was suffocating but he had to maintain his bluff. But a deep thirst for tobacco burned his throat.

"Mind if I have a cigarette?"

"Go ahead," Fukuzaki said. His grin broadened into a triumphant smile, like a poker player laying down four aces. Tom pulled out his Luckies and lit up. Inhaling set him at ease but a sense of dread lingered. Commander Fukuzaki had met his bluff.

"Let me be perfectly honest, Mr. Lai. I do not believe Ono-san is valuable to me any longer, even if he were still alive, which I am beginning to doubt."

Annoyance shook Tom's frame but he steadied himself with a long drag. "So, what should I tell Tu Yueh-sheng? He's not going to like this."

Fukuzaki's triumphant smile grew even larger as he slid open the desk drawer. Before Tom could reach for his Browning, the Commander aimed an automatic pistol straight at his head.

"*You* won't tell him anything, Mr. Lai."

CHAPTER THIRTEEN

All too late, Tom cursed himself for being so trusting. So much for Commander Fukuzaki being a gentleman. The Browning automatic pressed against his side, tauntingly out of reach. Tempting as it was, Tom leaned back in his chair and took another drag off his Lucky Strike. There was no way out now. That is, until Yan Ping arrived back with some help. For now, all Tom could do was stall for time.

"So what now, Commander?"

"Unfortunately, I will have to keep you 'on ice' as you Americans say."

Tom arched his eyebrows and blew out a trail of smoke. "So, you're not going to shoot me?"

"Not unless you force me to, Mr. Lai. I just need you out of the way until tensions subside in this city."

"Well, that's mighty gentlemanly of you."

Commander Fukuzaki smirked. "Besides, I want to find out exactly what you know. I suspect that you haven't been very forthcoming with me."

Tom took another puff. "Well, one has to retain some mystery in Shanghai."

Fukuzaki motioned with the gun to stand up. Tom tossed the cigarette on the ground, stomped it out, but commotion outside kept him seated. The door swung open and in marched Charles Whitfield, clad in a gray overcoat and homburg, his white face splotched with pink from the cold and anger. Yan Ping and Yoshida followed, and the *ronin* berated them both with a barrage of angry Japanese. Tom didn't understand a word of it except repeated instances of '*chankoro.*'

Yan gripped Yoshida's collar and slammed a thick fist across the *ronin's* face. Stumbling backward, Yoshida crumpled to the floor at Fukuzaki's feet. After a moment of awkward silence, Tom and Yan shared a pleased look.

Fukuzaki turned his attention to Whitfield with a gracious smile. "Ah, Mr. Whitfield! To what do I owe the pleasure of your visit?"

"The pleasure?" Whitfield pointed to Fukuzaki's pistol. "Since when does a Japanese Navy officer have the right to brandish firearms at American citizens?"

"But Mr. Whitfield, this quarrel is between myself and Mr. Lai."

Tom glanced between the two of them. Whitfield certainly looked angry enough, but he couldn't shake the feeling that there was a theatricality to it all. Still, Whitfield appeared to be his only salvation.

"Lousy service in this place, Chuck," Tom said. "I ask for a brown ale and get a gun in my face."

"Commander," Whitfield said, "if you continue to threaten an American citizen, I will have no other choice but to file a complaint with my government. Japan doesn't need any more enemies in Shanghai, does she?"

The veiled threat of war seemed to concern Fukuzaki. After a few moments of considering the possibility of a conflict with America, the Commander frowned and placed the gun back inside the desk drawer.

"My apologies...I was rash," Fukuzaki said, bowing to Tom and then to Whitfield. "Please forgive my regrettable actions."

Ever the diplomat, Whitfield shot Tom a stern look, suggesting that he reciprocate. Tom shrugged and stood up.

"Commander, I'm sorry too. Let's bury the hatchet."

Fukuzaki gave a confused look. "Bury the what?"

"Means to forgive and forget," Tom said.

Fukuzaki nodded then turned to Whitfield. "And I hope this hasn't colored our friendship, Mr. Whitfield."

The US Consulate man sighed, any remaining tension vanishing from his pink face. "Not at all, Commander. I understand everyone is on edge in this city. The last thing we need is another *incident*. Isn't that right, Mr. Lai?"

Fukuzaki and Whitfield confirmed the truce with a warm handshake and bright smiles. Was this all for his benefit? Just to lull him into a false sense of trust? Regardless, all that mattered was getting out of the Golden Unicorn without a belly full of lead.

"Of course," Tom said. "No hard feelings."

After a friendly nod goodbye, Whitfield turned and left, followed by Yan Ping.

"I'll find your spy, Commander. With or without your help," Tom whispered.

Fukuzaki snorted. "I doubt that, Mr. Lai. Give my regards to the Green Gang and to Ono-san…if you haven't killed him already."

Tom said nothing as he stepped over the prostrate Yoshida and left the office.

*****

Tom made his way out of the Golden Unicorn and found Yan Ping and Whitfield waiting near the Bentley. Chuck muttered a stream of curses with frosted breath, whereas Yan looked like a worried child whose parents were fighting.

"Want a ride back to the Consulate?" Tom offered in English.

"Confound it, Tom! What the hell were you thinking?"

"Not here," Tom dropped his voice to a whisper. "Hold your tongue lashing until we're out of Little Tokyo."

A few passersby in kimonos and business suits fixed the trio with long stares, like lions sizing up gazelles. Maybe Fukuzaki had a few more *ronin* out today. Whitfield fell silent and nodded. Yan opened the door for them both and hopped into the driver's seat. The Bentley sprang to life and zoomed down the street. Only after the Golden Unicorn shrank from view did Whitfield resume his tidal wave of anger.

"I specifically told you not to go into Little Tokyo!"

"I know, Chuck…"

"Do you realize how much of a mess you could have caused? What if a Japanese military officer had shot an American citizen? For Chrissakes Tom, you could have started an international incident!"

"International incident?" Tom spat out with a laugh. "Commander Fukuzaki already beat me to it!"

"What do you mean?"

"I mean that last night I saved two Japanese from being carved up like Thanksgiving turkeys by those three Chinese thugs. Come today, I learn that the same three scoundrels are in the employ of one Commander Jiro Fukuzaki."

"I see…"

"Perhaps his thugs were the same ones who assaulted those Nipponese monks last week."

"You're suggesting Fukuzaki was behind it?"

"Or someone like him. The Japs are manufacturing incidents, Chuck. Just like they did in Manchuria. That's all this is. Just one big contest between the Mikado's Army and Navy to see whose samurai sword is bigger."

Whitfield sighed and stared out the window. "That may be true. There is considerable rivalry within their armed forces. But this anti-Japanese boycott is authentic and it's killing Japan's economy."

The words sounded almost accusatory. "What are the Chinese supposed to do, Chuck? Politely ask the Mikado to stop invading their country?"

Whitfield turned around and snapped, "Goddamn it, Tom! Of course not! But this boycott is only agitating the Japs! For Chrissakes, am I the only person in this goddamn city who doesn't want to see it bombed flat?"

"Can a missionary's son take the Lord's name in vain?"

"You smug SOB. You're lucky Yan Ping came to my office. Otherwise, you'd be chained up in a Japanese dungeon right about now."

"*Shi shi*," Tom said, thanking his bodyguard. It made sense that Yan would seek help from the only other American he knew.

"Sure thing, boss," Yan said as the Bentley hugged a corner.

"Look Chuck, it's not that I'm ungrateful, but…" Tom said, grasping at what to say next. Any decent man would thank a friend for pulling his fat out of the fryer but suspicions ran across Tom's brain like spiders. Was Whitfield's rescue a mere act? Last night's horrors instilled him with such paranoia, he wondered how actual spies managed to keep their wits together.

"But what?"

"I was running an errand for the Green Gang," Tom said with some truth.

Whitfield raised a skeptical eyebrow as the Bentley slowed to a stop. At the intersection, a line of Japanese Marines paraded by, Arisaka rifles slung over their shoulders. A show of brute force before the shooting started. A brass band followed, banging out a military march. Tom recognized it as "The Brave Sailor," a rousing ditty from when China and Japan first went to war back in 1894.

The Manchu Dynasty thought it would easily defeat the dwarf bandits, but Nippon's modernized military was victorious after only nine months of fighting. As a result, the island of Taiwan was absorbed into the Japanese Empire, which became the leading power in the Orient. But things were different now. The Nationalist Army had received its baptism of fire against the warlords and the Communists. They'd fight the Japanese tooth and nail to defend Shanghai. At least, Tom hoped so.

He looked at his wristwatch. Almost noon. Time was running out. Beating around the bush was getting him nowhere. He'd confront Whitfield directly. But for that, Tom needed a drink to steady his nerves.

"Look, let's talk in your office. Alone."

Whitfield, sensing the looming conversation would be a troubling one, just nodded. A stifling silence filled the car, punctured only by the droning martial song outside.

CHAPTER FOURTEEN

Yan Ping parked the Bentley on North Yangtze Road, which hugged the Whangpoo River, cutting off Hongkew from the rest of the International Settlement. To the south, a flotilla of sampans, junks, and Japanese gunboats floated in the water while to the north, diplomatic buildings lined the street like a miniature League of Nations. Whitfield and Tom exited the car and gestured for Yan Ping to stay put.

The American Consulate was a slim three-story structure, sandwiched in between the consulates of Germany and Japan, all of which buzzed with last minute preparations. Barbed wire and machine gun nests were mounted outside of the Nipponese Consulate, manned by grim-faced Marines in steel helmets, ready for whatever the 19th Route Army could throw at them. The German Consulate was less impressive. Neutered by the Versailles Treaty, a few sandbags and two sentries in *feldgrau* was all it could muster for protection.

The American Consulate was a happy medium. A pair of green-uniformed US Marines with Springfield rifles guarded the front gate while a platoon drilled with bayonets in the main courtyard. Three officers in peaked caps surveyed the Whangpoo with binoculars on the rooftop. Even from the ground, Tom could see their dour expressions, perhaps realizing how hopeless their situation was if the Japanese decided to attack them too.

As Tom and Whitfield approached the gate, a barrel-chested Marine sergeant greeted them.

"Good morning Mr. Whitfield," he said through the bars. "Who's the chink?"

"Hullo suh," Tom said in his best drawl. "I'm jus' a po'boy from Texas who lost mah passport."

It took the Sergeant a few moments. "Oh, you're that Chinaman from Frisco. The one with the nightclub?"

"The one and only. Stop by for a drink on the house."

The Sergeant frowned but Tom was half-serious. A few medals on his uniform indicated that he'd served in France, probably as one of the devil dogs at Belleau Wood. If vets didn't look out for each other, who would? But most Americans in Shanghai rarely ventured outside of the International Settlement's safety. To many white Shanghailanders, the Chinese section of the city was as uncharted as central Africa.

The gate opened, allowing Tom and Whitfield to enter the courtyard. Thanking the Sergeant with a swift nod, he turned his attention to the platoon of Marines, stabbing the air with their bayonets. On the rooftop above, the officers were now looking west toward the Chapei district.

"Seeing all of these uniforms reminds me of the war," Tom remarked.

"Me too," Whitfield said, shaking his head. "Everyone is on high alert. It's 1914 all over again."

The statement was less than reassuring. "You can't be serious," Tom said. A blank expression was Whitfield's response. "Chuck, you said it yourself. Americans don't give a damn about China or Japan any more than they care about the South Pole."

"That may be true but what if bombs and artillery start landing in the International Settlement or Frenchtown? Nations have gone to war over less."

Tom grimaced and cast another look to the drilling Marines. Poor yokels from Kentucky and Oklahoma who'd probably joined up to see the world. Well, here they were in the exotic Orient, right before it blew up. He turned away as they entered the Consulate.

The lobby was a carnival. Shrill telephone rings mingled with frantic shouts in English and half a dozen Chinese dialects. Secretaries darted down the halls, carrying files and paperwork for Yank businessmen and tourists, eager to get out before the shooting started. A few Chinese sat amongst them, all loudly claiming family in America but surprisingly unaware of the Exclusion Law. It was the type of panic one saw during a bank run or on a sinking ship, and yet, strangely controlled. Nobody pushed or shoved or even cursed as if – deep down – they knew Uncle Sam wouldn't abandon them.

They slipped past the throng and walked down a narrow hallway, before taking refuge in Whitfield's office. Closing the door behind them, Whitfield expelled a relieved sigh and looked ready to collapse. Tom took in the room but found it more or less the same since he'd last visited. A desk centered the room and was flanked by a liquor cart, stuffed with everything from Beefeater Gin to Jack Daniel's Whiskey. Officially, Prohibition was still in effect for all Americans but this was Shanghai after all. In a land of limitless whores, gambling, and opium, hooch was the safest thing you could indulge in.

A small shelf held a dozen or so books, but only a few stood out – *The Great Gatsby, All Quiet On the Western Front,* and – like any good China missionary – Pearl Buck's *The Good Earth.* Curiously, no copy of the Holy Bible, not even for show.

Along with a portrait of President Hoover, other pictures were also mounted on the wall. Whitfield graduating from Harvard and a young Charles with his missionary parents, standing in front of the Temple of Heaven.

"When was this photo taken, Chuck?" Tom asked.

"Oh that? On my fifth birthday, in June 1900. Just before the Boxers converged on Peking and threatened to kill all foreign missionaries in the city."

"You were in China during the Boxer Rebellion?"

Whitfield gave a solemn nod. "My family and I hunkered down in the Legation Quarter, praying every day for a miracle. When the armies of America, Britain, France, Japan, and all the others drove the Boxers away, my father said it was divine intervention."

"Was it, Chuck?"

Whitfield stared into nothing for a moment, before replying. "I don't know, but many other missionaries and their converts weren't so lucky."

For over thirty years, the Whitfields had been saving souls in China, but now Chuck looked like a man ready to cut his losses. Perhaps the Boxer Rebellion had embittered Charles Whitfield against God and China, leaving him more cynical than Tom had realized. Such cynicism could lead a man into a nefarious life of espionage for profit. But right now, as he rubbed his temple, Whitfield looked more exasperated than cynical or nefarious.

"Rough day?" Tom asked.

"It's been a madhouse here since five in the morning." Whitfield walked over to the liquor cart and poured them both a brandy, then handed a glass to Tom. "Now, what's so damn important that you had to tell me here?"

Tom took a swig, letting the liquid rest on his tongue. He'd need all the Dutch courage he could get. It wasn't every day you accused your friend of spying for the Mikado. But after the debacle with Commander Fukuzaki, this was his last chance to unmask Whitfield. Although he knew it might be his death sentence, part of Tom still hoped he had been wrong all along.

"I need your help, Chuck. Or rather...the Green Gang does."

"So that's what last night's little visit was really about." Whitfield sighed and threw back his brandy. "Well, let's hear it. What does that old rascal Big-Eared Tu want?"

"We're trying to catch a spy." Tom took another sip, scanning Whitfield for any hint of nervousness. "We've uncovered someone using Club Twilight as a drop off location for secret documents."

"What was in them?"

Tom took a deep breath and recalled every detail from last night. "'In accordance with the doctrine proclaimed by US Secretary of State Stimson, the United States Government will not recognize any territorial changes in

China by force and will denounce anything that might impair the existing Open Door policy.'"

He paused and scrutinized Whitfield again. But only a deep confusion clouded the Consulate officer's face. Licking his lips, he offered, "It...it...sounds like a report I wrote..."

When the bait was good, a hunter took his shot.

"Know anything about the American Yangtze patrol ships? The *USS Luzon, Mindanao, Oahu, Panay, Guam,* and *Tutuila*? Apparently, this spy had the exact coordinates, captains, crews, and armaments for every one of them."

A white sheet slid over the Consulate man's face as he fixed Tom with a wide-eyed stare. He'd seen that same vacant expression in shell-shocked soldiers. It was the look of a man who realized his time was up. The mask had finally come off of Charles Whitfield.

CHAPTER FIFTEEEN

"So it's true," Tom said, setting the brandy glass aside.

Whitfield didn't respond except for a hard swallow, his Adam's apple rising and falling slowly. How did this son of missionaries and self-proclaimed friend of China fall so low? Had it all just been one long con? Enough time spent in Shanghai would make anyone cynical, so maybe this upstanding Christian gentleman had lost his faith.

"How could you work for them?"

After a few false starts, Whitfield found his voice. "What do you mean 'work for them?' Old boy, are you accusing me of spying for the Japs?"

Tom fixed him with an accusatory stare. "If the shoe fits."

Whitfield's initial surprise devolved into revulsion. Angry pink splotches grew across his cheeks. "How dare you! I love China! Why would I aid her greatest enemy?"

"Men and women fall out of love all the time. Maybe you found a new mistress."

Whitfield pinkened further and poured himself another brandy. He threw the whole glass back and fumed with his back turned. His entire frame tensed like a park statue. "I don't know how you can say that."

"A Japanese was found leaving my club the other night with those documents on him. Commander Fukuzaki practically admitted to me that this Nipponese gentleman, Ono, was one of his men. He was basically just a courier, transporting messages and using Club Twilight as a post office."

"Tom, there are hundreds of people who go to your club every night. Many of whom are diplomats."

A fair point. Besides, Ono never claimed to have seen who this contact was. A smart choice. Keeping his spies in the dark was the best way for only Commander Fukuzaki to have any scope of the entire ring. Genuine ignorance prevented anyone from naming names. That didn't let Whitfield off the hook though.

"Fair enough, but you're the only regular from the *American* Consulate. For most of the staff here, anything outside of the International Settlement is bandit country."

Whitfield's shoulders sagged. "Balderdash, the whole rotten lot of it. Why on earth would I ruin my career and sell out China, Tom?" He turned, pink and bleary-eyed. Was he about to cry? Such actions were risky for a man like Whitfield but Tom knew that few people spied for any real political reasons.

"You mentioned your uncle, the banker in Boston, has been having a rough time in this depression."

The insinuation hit Whitfield hard. Any signs of melancholy evaporated, followed by self-righteous indignation. His voice dropped to a whispered growl. "How dare you!"

All the clues lined up like dominos and the clarity of it all was sickening. Missionary work wasn't profitable but having a rich uncle could cover the loss.

"Do I really need to say it out loud, Chuck?"

"Yes Tom," he hissed. "So you can hear how ludicrous it all sounds."

"That you took money from Commander Fukuzaki to help your uncle's bank? No, that doesn't sound ludicrous at all."

"I don't believe this…"

"Explain how I just recited your report, Chuck."

"I don't know!" Whitfield roared, hurling the brandy glass across the office. It collided with the wall and rained down shards onto the floor. "Maybe one of the Chinese porters broke into my office!"

Tom narrowed his eyes. "So when the heat is on, you look for a Chinese scapegoat?"

"For Chrissakes Tom, that's not what I meant. All I'm saying is that it could be anyone."

"Anyone but you, despite all evidence to the contrary? Your reports were found on the Fukuzaki's man, Chuck. Besides, the documents were in English. The most lingo the porters here speak is 'no tickee no laundry.'"

Whitfield rubbed his temple and expelled a bitter laugh. "Balderdash! After everything my family and I have done for China—"

"You're not Chinese, Chuck."

The statement was harsher than intended but it made its point. No matter how many good deeds the Whitfields had and would do, they would forever be *gweilos* – foreign devils, white ghosts, outsiders.

"I grew up in this country, Tom," Whitfield snapped back as if it was his trump card. "I didn't set foot in Boston until I was twelve. While you were playing fan-tan and mahjong with the Suey Sing Tong, my family and I were serving rice to hungry peasants."

Tom almost flinched at such an affront to his heritage but kept his cool with a deep breath. There was no need to get emotional but he couldn't ignore that.

"Things change, Chuck. What's that Bible quote? 'When I was a child, I spake as a child. When I grew up, I put away such childish things'. I put away my games and went to war."

Whitfield scoffed. "I was in the trenches too, Tom."

"Indeed you were and America was grateful, whereas Uncle Sam looked at me like a dog would a tick. You see, Chuck, I've never truly had a country, only half of one. I love China and America but I'm the bastard son of each."

There was another long silence that could have stretched into infinity if they'd let it. Tom glanced at his Rolex. Ten minutes to one. He needed to tell the Green Gang he'd found the spy. Or at least the best he could come up with on such short notice.

"Goodbye, Chuck. Thanks for the brandy."

He turned and walked toward the threshold.

"Wait." Tom turned and stared back at Whitfield. Sorrow and regret were practically written across his face. "I love China, Tom and would never do anything to hurt her." Such sincerity shone in those bleary blue eyes that Whitfield looked ready to swear his innocence on the Holy Bible. If only he had one. Maybe a copy of *The Good Earth* would suffice.

The image dried Tom's throat, leaving him speechless. He gave a curt nod instead.

"Another thing, Tom." An ominous look swept over Whitfield like a thunder cloud. "He who lies down with trash will become dirty."

A subtle reference to the Green Gang.

"Chuck, I've been dirty for years."

Tom turned and walked out the door.

CHAPTER SIXTEEN

Tom walked past the US Consulate's gate and back over to North Yangtze Road. As he approached the Bentley, Yan Ping hopped out and popped open the backseat door.

"Where to, boss?"

A simple question but Tom didn't have an answer. Right now, he wanted to be nowhere. A drive around Shanghai might clear his clouded head.

"Everything alright, boss?"

Worry must have been carved into his face. "I'm fine...let's just take a drive for now."

Yan Ping nodded and they hopped into the Bentley. The motor roared and sped south, over the Garden Bridge. He needed to get as far as possible away from Little Tokyo, from Commander Fukuzaki, and especially from Charles Whitfield.

They passed a steady stream of humanity, mostly refugees from outside Shanghai, but also plenty of city-born coolies, anxious to get further into the International Settlement. Crossing over Garden Bridge and Soochow Creek, the Bentley drove past the Public Garden and into the familiar modernity of the Bund.

Normally, the Customs House with its clock tower and classical architecture of the HSBC Building offered some charming comfort. However, the Bund structures looked like paper mâché now, ready to be knocked over by Japanese warships floating in the Whangpoo River. Memories of the French countryside flashed in Tom's mind, blown to bits by artillery. Would that be Shanghai's fate? And would he even live long enough to find out?

Of course he would. Tom Lai always found a way out. His odds of survival were high now that he'd identified the real spy. Still, turning Charles Whitfield over to the Green

Gang covered him with enough shame that he needed a bath. Or at least a drink.

"Yan, take me to the Great World."

"Of course, boss."

The Bentley took a right on Nanking Road, plunging deeper into the International Settlement. Paying someone else for booze offended his business sense, but the last place Tom wanted to be right now was Club Twilight. Too many bad memories. The Great World was different. That was where his new life in Shanghai had really begun.

As they approached the intersection of Nanking and Chekiang Road, a Sikh traffic cop held up his hand to stop. The four great department stores of Shanghai – Sincere, Wing On, Sun Sun, and Da Sun – loomed before them like sacred shrines. Chic men and women darted in and out, oblivious to the coming catastrophe. Many of the women were foreign, but some were Chinese, decked out in chic Chanel coats, cloche hats, and gloves. One woman looked particularly familiar as she exited the Sincere Department Store, her black leather gauntlets holding a wrapped box.

"Mei-chen!" Tom called out, rolling his window down. Across the street, Mei-chen turned and waved. The Sikh traffic cop beckoned them forward, and Yan pulled the Bentley up alongside the curb. Mei-chen jumped inside and greeted Tom with a kiss.

"Going my way, pretty lady?"

"Depends on where you're going," she said in English, setting the box between them.

"The Great World."

"Then yes. I always like a drink after shopping."

Tom tapped the box. "For me?"

"Not unless you wear T-strap pumps."

"Thanks but I don't have a thing to wear with them." He leaned forward. "The Great World, Yan."

*****

The Great World was a six story amusement arcade, crammed with every form of entertainment from every corner of the world. Fitting, since it straddled the edge of the International Settlement and Frenchtown. A cacophonous mixture of languages – Oriental and Occidental – reverberated throughout the halls. An equal mixing of curious visitors wandered about. White Shanghailanders dipping their toes in one of the seedier areas of the city. Native Shanghainese abounded too, although to them, the Great World was one of the tamer parts of this vice-ridden metropolis.

Sing-song girls outside an indoor tea house beckoned lonely men closer. They showed off their tiny bound feet, a seductive trait to many Chinese men even though the practice had been officially outlawed. Compared to them, Mei-chen looked positively Western in her size 5 pumps. Across the aisle, people clustered around a shooting gallery, taking potshots at model Japanese planes. Pickpockets made their rounds, sizing up any potential marks. With Mei-chen on his arm, Tom Lai was well-known here and that notoriety was protection enough. The pickpockets doffed their hats and continued on to find more obscure prey.

Ascending the stairs to the second floor, they walked down a long hallway, famous for its enclosed bazaars, Chinese acrobats, and one of Tom's favorite bars in Shanghai. Right now, he needed a Scotch on the rocks as if it were water on a hot day.

"What's wrong, darling?" Mei-chen asked.

He must have been wearing his concern like a mask. Was he losing his poker face?

"Nothing dear. It's just business."

"From last night?"

"Yes..." he trailed off before adding, "Nothing to concern yourself with though."

Mei-chen offered a comforting smile, squeezing his arm. They continued down the hall, past vendors hawking herbal medicines, *loquat* syrup, bars of Victoria Soap, toy firecrackers, Pantheon Cigarettes, Buddhist charms, and bottles of Coca-Cola. Unsurprisingly, the booths selling Japanese products were absent. Tom and Mei-chen pushed past the barking vendors until a row of small bamboo cages came into view.

"Tom, look!" Mei-chen squealed. "Crickets!"

Only in China would people buy these irritating little insects, but according to myth, crickets brought good luck and longevity. Bizarre, but his own mother believed these silly superstitions, insisting that these noisy bugs would protect the Lai family.

"The emperors used to keep crickets as pets," Mei-chen said, running her gloved fingers over the bamboo bars. "During the Song Dynasty, aristocrats bred them for fighting."

Tom snickered and scanned the cages. Most were scrawny with spindly little legs. But a large brown cricket on the top shelf gave a loud chirp like a bugle call at morning reveille.

"I'd put my money on that one," Tom said.

Mei-chen leaned forward and inspected. "Yes, he does look lucky, doesn't he?"

Tom agreed but the thought of that screeching insect in the bedroom might kill the mood. However, Mei-chen's imploring eyes were hard to say no to. Tom rubbed his chin and considered it, when three dark shadows draped over him from behind.

Turning around, he locked eyes with Feng Lung-wei, flanked by his two brutish henchmen.

"Hello Tommy," he said, grinning. "Tick tock."

CHAPTER SEVENTEEN

Tom searched the gangsters for any potential threat, but Feng Lung-wei seemed relaxed, almost jovial. Besides, the Great World would be too public for a murder, even for the Green Gang. On instinct though, Mei-chen drew closer and gripped Tom's arm. Feng scrutinized her up and down before extending his hand.

"I don't believe we've been formally introduced," he said, taking her gloved fingers. "Feng Lung-wei. You must be Ho Mei-chen, right?"

She nodded before withdrawing her hand. "Pleased to meet you."

"Darling, would you excuse us?" Tom said in English. "I have…business to discuss with Mr. Feng."

Mei-chen nodded but dread lingered in her brown eyes. Tom and Feng walked down to the other end of the hallway. A crowd had gathered around an acrobat in garish makeup and small band with *guzheng* zithers, *dizi* flutes, and *erhu* strings. Tom recognized the acrobat's outfit as the legendary Monkey King, the magical hero from the novel *Journey to the West*.

"I loved this story as a kid," Feng said, staring at the performance. "Do they have it in America?"

"Yes, my mother would read it to us at night. My brother and I took turns playing the Monkey King and Pigsy."

Feng laughed. "The way he stormed the Dragon King's undersea palace and demanded the best weapon," he gestured to the acrobat's staff, twirling in his spindly fingers. "I admired that. It takes courage to take what is rightfully yours. Not to mention the way he tormented all the deities of heaven *and* hell! Oh, how I craved such power!"

Tom wanted to ask if this gangster brat realized that *Journey to the West* was a story about redemption but dismissed it. Besides, there were more pressing concerns.

"What brings you to the Great World? It's not Green Gang turf."

Feng gave a confused, half-offended look. "Don't you know that this joint was purchased by Huang Chih-jung, just last year?"

"It...it must have slipped my mind."

Pockmarked Huang was a big shot in the Green Gang, not to mention chief of detectives in Frenchtown. The Great World had never been Coney Island, but under new management it was about to reach even lower depths of vice.

"I was just playing a few games of fan-tan myself. People are in a gambling mood these days. Panic does that I guess," Feng said, giving a toothy grin. "And as I was leaving, I said to myself, 'Hey, isn't that Tommy Lai? Why is he strolling around with his little twist instead of spy hunting?' So I figured I'd investigate."

Off to the side, cymbals clanged and *erhus* wailed out a tune as the Monkey King spun round and round, slicing the air with his magical staff. The crowd gave a burst of applause.

"I already found the spy," Tom said, facing Feng. The gangster gave a coy look, followed by a mischievous smile.

"Have you now? Don't keep me waiting, Tommy."

A twinge of regret spasmed in Tom's gut at the thought of turning Whitfield over to this lowlife. Still, Tom Lai was nobody's fall guy.

"Charles Whitfield."

Feng rubbed his chin in thought. "The name is familiar..."

"He works for the United States Consulate and fits the bill for your spy. One, he speaks English and two, he has access to information about American gunboats in China."

The gangster brat shook his head. "Sorry Tommy, I don't like that answer."

Tom's heart sank as the clanging cymbals grew to a crescendo. In the center of the crowd, the Monkey King hoisted himself atop his cane, balancing himself on one foot. Stunned gasps and cries rippled from the onlookers.

"What do you mean?"

Feng gave a dismissive shrug. "Even we have limits. An American diplomat might just be out of reach for the Green Gang." He paused before giving a wolfish smile. "But you're not."

"But I'm not the spy," Tom snapped, his voice mixing with the whine of zithers and *erhus*.

"I'm still not convinced of that. Regardless, if you can produce this Charles Whitfield, with a full confession, then maybe my uncle will believe you."

"Are you suggesting I kidnap a diplomat?"

"I'm not suggesting anything, Tommy. But the Green Gang requires evidence. Right now, we have all the proof we need that *you're* the spy. And that's good enough for me."

"Then I demand to see Grandmaster Tu and explain my case to him."

Feng held up a hand. "Uncle already granted you an audience. You need not waste his time with more excuses."

"But how will I prove that I'm not the spy if you don't even—"

"That's not my concern, Tommy. An American diplomat is too conspicuous to kill. However, nobody would bat an eye if a nightclub owner, a *Chinese* nightclub owner, disappears."

Tom braced himself. "I'm an American too."

"Not like Whitfield," Feng said with a taunting smirk.

The band concluded and the Monkey King flipped off his staff, ending the performance with a bow. The crowd broke out with vociferous applause, Feng included. Tom spun on his heel and stormed back over to Mei-chen. The two henchmen ignored her now, prodding the cricket cages with childlike curiosity.

"Your boss wants to see you," Tom said, jerking his thumb behind him. "Something about wanting to introduce you to the Monkey King."

The two gorillas' faces lit up as they lumbered back over to Feng. Mei-chen rushed to Tom, laying her gloved hands on his chest.

"What's wrong?" she asked in English.

The last thing he wanted to do was worry her in front of the Green Gang. Fixing her with a reassuring smile, he said, "Nothing that lucky cricket can't cure."

Forking over the money, Tom grabbed the cricket and took Mei-chen by the arm. He needed some guidance and he knew where to start. As they waited near the elevator, Tom glanced over to the crowd, now dispersing. Flanked by his two mugs, Feng looked back and gave a quick, ominous gesture to his watch.

Tick tock.

CHAPTER EIGHTEEN

Tom gazed up at the Great Buddha with a mixture of awe and longing. The statue was similar to the ones he'd prayed to in San Francisco's Chinatown, albeit coated in gold. Even the Buddhas were ritzier in Shanghai. A sweet smell of incense wafted up, putting him at ease. The Great World's Buddhist Temple was situated on the fifth floor, just a quick jaunt for anyone needing spiritual guidance. In addition to every vice imaginable, the amusement arcade offered a way for sinners to repent.

It had been years since Tom prayed at a temple, but today he needed all the help he could get. Pressing his palms together, he considered his options. Mei-chen's safety was his top concern but he'd prefer to survive along with her. Out of ideas, Tom bowed his head and asked the gods for protection. For him, for Mei-chen, and for all of Shanghai. They had pulled through during the 1906 quake, during the war, and when he'd first moved to China. Hopefully, they wouldn't abandon him now.

Tom turned to Mei-chen, her hands pressed together in prayer. The worry etched into her face told she was asking for a lot. She bent down and picked up the little cage holding the cricket. The bug was quiet, dozing in the tranquil atmosphere. Turning away from the statue, they walked out arm in arm, back into the land of mortals. Just outside of the Buddhist Temple were rows of peep show machines. Slides showed everything from the latest photos of the Manchurian front to snapshots of undressed women, both Chinese and Western.

A dance hall was on the other side, boasting the prettiest girls in Shanghai. Unlike the tea house on the second floor with its dainty sing-song girls, these taxi dancers were cheap and loose, willing to foxtrot along with the latest jazz music.

Tom and Mei-chen paused to steal a quick glance into the hall. Sultry Chinese women in *cheongsams* danced with men of all nationalities as a jukebox blared "Nighttime in Old Shanghai."

A wistful sigh from Mei-chen was enough prodding for them to move along, the cricket cage swaying in between them. After all, this was where they'd met two years ago. They walked in silence toward the stairs, taking them up to the Great World's rooftop. A high guardrail encased them, save for one small section left open. Those unfortunates who gambled away their savings often used it for impromptu suicides. Nobody was killing themselves today though, giving Mei-chen and Tom some much needed seclusion.

Shanghai spread out below them, dominated by the Bund's distinctive skyline to the east, the facsimile of Paris to the south in Frenchtown, and masses of gray warehouses and tenements to the north in Chapei.

"I love this city," Tom said, leaning over the guard railing.

"You love the makeup Shanghai puts on," Mei-chen said. "Have you seen how hideous she is underneath?"

"San Francisco has an ugly side too."

"Not like Shanghai. No city is like Shanghai."

"That's why I love it" Tom sighed. "Paris of the East, whore of the Orient. She's both."

"Whatever she is, I'll be glad to leave her." A few moments passed by in silence before Mei-chen said, "I never thanked you for rescuing me."

Tom turned to face her. "From what?"

"I'd still be working in that glorified brothel downstairs. A dollar bought three dances. Five dollars bought customers much more."

"Is that why you agreed to come work at my club? I'm sure me being well-connected to the Kuomintang had something to do with it too."

"Well, that and your handsome face."

Tom leaned over and kissed her. They stood, locked in an embrace, alone atop all of Shanghai. A comforting silence engulfed them, washing out all of the horrors from the past twenty-four hours. He didn't know how long they stood there until an obnoxious chirp interrupted them.

Mei-chen held the cricket cage up and smiled. "Maybe he's jealous."

"Next time it happens, he's going to wind up under my shoe."

"Tom, no," she cried, slapping his arm. "It's bad luck."

They shared a laugh until a deep rumbling demanded their attention. They looked over the guardrail, down at the streets below. A procession lurched past the Great World, thicker and angrier than last night. All the usual anti-Japanese banners and signs were there – 'Boycott Jap Goods', 'Japan Get Out of Manchuria', but there were also a few new ones now. 'Retake the Northeast' and 'Liberate Taiwan' stood out in particular.

"This city is doomed," Mei-chen said.

"Don't talk like that," Tom snapped.

"It's true. Shanghai is next. That's why we have to get out of here." Drawing nearer, Mei-chen clutched the cricket cage tightly. "I'm frightened Tom. Time is running out for this city…and for us."

Well, she did have a point. Still, the best thing a man could do is put on a stoic face for his woman.

"There's still time. Mayor Wu could still accept the Japanese demands. Hell, maybe the Mikado will order his boys to stand down."

He pressed her head against his chest. The shouts of "Boycott all Japanese goods" and "Kill the Japanese Devils" thundered from below. Something told him that those protesters probably weren't in the pay of Commander Fukuzaki. That was genuine Chinese patriotism at work. The kind he'd helped Chiang Kai-shek water and nourish for years. Now Tom Lai was reaping the fruit.

"Don't worry. Captain Tung assured me that the 19th Route Army is ready to defend Shanghai. It won't be a walk over like Manchuria."

"That might be, Tom. But what happens if we're all caught in the crossfire?"

He didn't answer that; how could he? There was nothing Thomas Lai could do to stop a war, no matter how many Kuomintang officials he knew or how many palms he greased. All he could do was fight for what was his – Club Twilight, Mei-chen, and his own life. But perhaps Captain Tung could save him as well as Shanghai.

CHAPTER NINETEEN

After dropping Mei-chen and the cricket off at Club Twilight, Yan and Tom drove over to the North Railway Station, located strategically in the Chapei district. People thronged at the gates, held at bay by squads of armed soldiers. Since becoming the headquarters of Captain Tung's company, the North Railway Station still functioned as a railway depot, but just barely. The wealthiest Shanghainese had taken refuge in Frenchtown or the International Settlement, but the middle-classes could only afford to flee to Nanking. The poor – those who had come to Shanghai to escape floods and famine – would have to take their chances in the streets of Chapei.

Weary families – dragging their entire life's belongings in suitcases – made their way toward the gates. Soldiers inspected tickets and then motioned them through with bayoneted rifles. Yan parked the Bentley and Tom jumped out, snaking his way to the front of the crowd. At the gates, a youthful sentry blocked his advance by leveling his rifle straight at Tom's chest.

"Your ticket, sir?"

"Tell Captain Tung Hsi-shan that Lai Huang-fu is here to see him."

The soldier nodded to his even younger comrade, who rang a nearby field telephone. After a brief conversation, he gave a confirming nod.

"Go ahead, sir," the soldier said, lowering his rifle. "He's on the first floor, third door on the left."

Tom nodded his thanks and walked through the gates, trying to shake off the angry stares from the crowd. The courtyard was full of soldiers in blue-gray uniforms, field caps, and tattered cloth shoes. They thrust their bayonets in formation, low-crawled through dirt, and shot at paper targets. Last minute practice before show time.

Inside the railway terminal, families clustered together like frightened mice. Others gathered near the schedule board, checking for any delays. The trains in China were notoriously late, worsened by this mass exodus. A pair of dark eyes stood out in the crowd, belonging to a sly-looking wretch in a long *changshan* shirt and fedora. Although he'd never seen this creature before, Tom could spot a member of the Green Gang a mile away. Feng Lung-wei's promise that they'd be watching the docks and railways was no idle threat. Not that he ever doubted it.

Tom turned and moved past the crowds, trying not to lock eyes with anyone, until he found the third door on the left and knocked.

"Who's there?" a voice barked from behind in Cantonese.

"It's me, Tom…err, Lai Huang-fu," he replied, also in Cantonese.

A few moments of silence followed before a resigned response. "Enter."

Tom walked into an office occupied by Captain Tung and two junior officers, huddled around an enormous map of Shanghai. All wore field caps ornamented with the Kuomintang White Sun cockade, polished black jackboots, white gloves, and high-collared, blue-gray tunics that were starched so stiffly they looked ready to snap in half. As opposed to their motley-looking soldiers outside, Captain Tung and his lieutenants looked more in line to lead a parade than fight in the trenches.

"Ahhh, welcome Lai Huang-fu! Ready to enlist in the 19th Route Army?" Tung said with a grin. The two lieutenants shared a sardonic snicker.

"I'll let you know when – or rather *if* – the war starts. But right now, I need to talk to you about something else."

Captain Tung nodded his dismissal. "You both have your orders. General Tsai has tasked us with defending the North Railway Station no matter the cost."

The lieutenants snapped salutes before tromping out. Tom fished out his cigarette case and lit two Lucky Strikes for them both.

"Let me guess, you want out of Shanghai too?" Tung said, taking a drag. "I *might* be able to get you on a train to Nanking tonight."

Sneaking out of the city was tempting, but foolhardy. That creature lurking in the railway terminal would gun him down before he set foot on the platform. But if anyone could help, it was Captain Tung.

"I appreciate that Captain, but I need something else," Tom said, blowing out a puff of smoke. He gestured Tung toward the door, then eased it open. Through the crack, the Green Gang hood was visible, nestled in between a cluster of anxious families. Tom closed the door and Captain Tung fixed him with a frown.

"Is this about a gambling debt, Lai Huang-fu?"

"No, nothing so humdrum," Tom said, taking another drag. "The Green Gang thinks I'm a Japanese spy."

Tung's brown eyes bulged, then narrowed in thought. Finally, a deep laugh burst out of the officer.

"You? A Japanese spy? What a joke!"

"That's what I said. Unfortunately, the Green Gang thinks I'm as good as guilty. Or rather, Feng Lung-wei thinks so. Big-Eared Tu is a little more neutral."

"Feng Lung-wei? Tu Yueh-sheng's nephew?"

"The very same. He's a real turtle's egg, huh?"

Tung snorted. "An understatement! He's more devil than human. I had the misfortune of seeing his work back in 1927, when we purged the Communists from Shanghai." A strange shell shock appeared in the Captain's squared face. "Most of the Green Gang just shot the Reds they captured. But Feng Lung-wei would stuff firecrackers in their mouths, noses, ears, and then light them."

"Sounds festive. Wait, Feng's barely twenty now. He must have been only fifteen back in 1927."

Tung shook his head. "The Green Gang trains their killers at a young age."

Tom took another puff and pictured himself with a mouthful of firecrackers. What was it Feng had told him, back at the opium den?

'It won't be that quick, Tommy. I promise you.'

"So, you can see my predicament. I need someone to vouch for my loyalty to China."

"It's not that easy, Lai Huang-fu. As loathe as I am to admit it, the Green Gang rules Shanghai, not the Kuomintang."

"I know that, but the Kuomintang rules China. In exchange for his help in killing all the Reds in Shanghai, Chiang Kai-shek appointed Tu Yueh-sheng as president of the Opium Suppression Bureau. The biggest dope pusher in all of China! They both need each other."

After taking a puff on his Lucky, Captain Tung grunted. "True, there is a...*relationship* between Party officials and the Green Gang."

"Relationship? Don't be so coy Captain, they're practically married!"

Tung frowned and took an angry puff of his cigarette. "What right do you have to judge? You come from a wealthy country, not ravaged by civil war. Not since the Manchus has China been united. Generalissimo Chiang and the Kuomintang have saved the nation from those tyrannical, self-serving warlords."

Tom took a final drag and ground out the cigarette beneath his heel. "Captain, remember who you're talking to? I'm no boy scout. Hell, I admire Gimo for everything he's done, and that includes his alliance with the Green Gang. All I'm asking for the Kuomintang to pay me back a little for all my generous donations. I am a Party member, after all."

"I'll try, Tom, but it won't be easy. The Green Gang is like Chiang's pet tiger. It can perform tricks for him sometimes, but it's still a wild beast."

Tom grimaced. "Can you ask that man from the Finance Ministry…oh hell, what was his name?"

"Chow Chun-wah."

"Yes, Chow. Just ask him to make a phone call to Big-Eared Tu and tell him how valuable my regular donations are to the Nationalist Government."

"Perhaps. I must admit, Mr. Chow was rather offended by your most recent donation."

"Offended?"

"Yes, he was expecting more."

Anger surged through Tom, tensing his throat and clenching his fists. After a deep breath, he managed to snarl out in English, "Greedy son of a bitch!" before switching over to Cantonese. "He was expecting more so he could line his pockets. I know these Kuomintang officials take at least ten percent."

Captain Tung said nothing and finished his cigarette.

"Look, I'm desperate here. The Green Gang is looking for a patsy and I'm it. As much money as I give to Gimo, the least he could do is save my life."

Captain Tung nodded. "Alright, Lai Huang-fu. I'll talk to Mr. Chow. That's the best I can do."

The tension throughout Tom's body began to unknot. Perhaps it was the uniform or his chiseled, heroic face, but there was something about Captain Tung that could make anyone feel protected.

"Thank you, *dai go*," he said, using the Cantonese word for elder brother. The term wasn't used blood relatives, but for any kind-hearted older man. Tung Hsi-shan was only a year older than Tom, but now, he seemed more like a father figure.

They shook hands and Tom walked out the door, back to the main terminal. A shrill whistle sliced through the air. Through a pair of open windows, a lumbering train came into view and lurched to a stop at the main outdoor platform.

Mounted loudspeakers squawked out, "Now boarding for the 4:15 to Nanking."

Families grabbed their luggage and children, then swarmed through the doors to the platform outside. They queued up outside the train cars, shoving, pushing, and punching to keep their spot in line. Soldiers paced alongside the throngs, trying to maintain order.

As the main terminal emptied out like a deflating balloon, the sly-looking Green Gang man kept still. Pressed up against the wall, the lanky thug kept his hands hidden in voluminous shirt sleeves. A gun, knife, or hatchet waited inside those sleeves should Tom try and board the Shanghai-Nanking Express.

Locking eyes with the man, Tom braced himself, then strode directly toward him. The gangster tensed, his hands fumbling inside the sleeves.

"That won't be necessary, friend," he said. "Tell Feng Lung-wei and Grandmaster Tu that I'm not going anywhere. Shanghai is my home and Lai Huang-fu is no coward."

The slinking hoodlum bit his lip, and slowly drew his hands out his sleeves. With a supplicating bow, he croaked out, "Of course, Excellency."

Without a word, Tom turned and walked back to the exit, away from the shrill train whistles and desperate cries of panicked passengers.

CHAPTER TWENTY

Yan Ping parked the Bentley and Tom hopped out, where a rush of chilly air met him. Pausing for a moment in front of Club Twilight's glowing neon sign, Tom soaked up its warmth. The club would be open for business soon, so he needed to plan his next move. Hopefully, the Kuomintang's pressure would get Tu and Feng to back off, but if not...

Holy hell, did he need a drink. Yan Ping opened the front door and they walked into the main hall, resplendent with its crisscrossed American and Chinese flags. The staff was busy setting up – bartenders stocked liquor, taxi dancers applied last minute makeup, and waiters laid out silverware. Tom glanced over to Charles Whitfield's table and wondered if he'd ever see the US Consulate man again.

Tom gravitated toward the bar and ordered a J&B on the rocks. Sipping the drink, he weighed his chances of surviving past tomorrow. Probably sixty-forty in favor of being shot, firecrackered, or whatever Feng Lung-wei's diseased little mind could come up with.

Behind him, a squeal of saxophones and trumpets erupted. Tom turned around to observe the Twilight Band rehearsing a pleasing rendition of "Shanghai Honeymoon." He took another sip of Scotch and let the music seep in. If he really was going to die tomorrow, then he'd spend all the time with Mei-chen he could, dancing to jazz until time ran out. Drink in hand, Tom walked upstairs to their private apartment and knocked.

"Come in!" Mei-chen's voice sounded like honey.

Tom entered, closing the door behind him. The caged cricket sat on the floor, beside his Beautiful Pearl who busied herself in front of a vanity mirror with eyeliner. Her reflection flashed him a bright smile. A record played on the phonograph, and Tom recognized the nasally voice of Li

Ming-hui singing "The Drizzle." The charming ditty was China's first foray into modern music, lighthearted and frivolous. The jukebox had played it when he and Mei-chen first danced together at the Great World, filling him with warm memories ever since.

"How are you, darling?" she asked in English.

Tom took a swig of Scotch before answering, "I've been better."

Her pretty face scrunched into a pout. "Why's that?"

Making his way across the room, he hovered over his desk before removing the Browning automatic from his coat. Club Twilight was his domain after all; he was safe here. Appearing too cautious might be a loss of face in front of his staff and guests. After tossing the pistol inside the drawer, Tom plopped himself on the bed and swirled his drink. His eyes moved from the Scotch and over to the table, where Mei-chen's flared leather gauntlets lay next to issues of *Photoplay*. He envied her ignorance. Only after polishing off the drink did he lift his gaze to Mei-chen's warm brown eyes.

"Darling, what's wrong?"

He sat there mute with a lump in his throat. How could he explain everything to her? Tom Lai had never been superstitious, but admitting he might be killed tomorrow was like tempting fate. Even more, Ho Mei-chen had always had a special venom for Shanghai, and now it seemed like this city would actually be the death of him. He hoped she wouldn't say 'I told you so.'

Clearing his throat, Tom said, "Turns out I might only have another day to live."

Horrified surprise stretched out Mei-chen's face. "What are you saying?"

"That meeting with Tu Yueh-sheng wasn't about raising his protection fees." Tom took a deep breath. "Somebody has been using my club to pass along secrets to Japanese spies. The best part is that the Green Gang thinks I'm one of them."

He forced a laugh, hoping to hide his worry. Mei-chen said nothing and stared at the ground. "Why do they think that?"

Tom shrugged. "They tortured a man named Ono into confessing everything he knew. I don't like the Japs much, but I felt sorry for this poor bastard."

He shook his head, trying to rid his mind of Ono's bloodied corpse.

Mei-chen's pretty face twitched. "Wh-what did he say?"

"That he used Club Twilight as a rendezvous spot to pick up documents. Apparently, he never even saw his contact, but that doesn't matter. It's my club so it's my responsibility." Tom expelled a bitter sigh.

"S-so, you don't know who Ono's contact was?"

"Unfortunately, I do..."

"...who...?"

"Chuck."

"Charles Whitfield?" Mei-chen's concern seemed to evaporate, replaced by a strange confusion. "B-but why would he spy for the Japs?"

"Who knows?" Tom said with a shrug. "The depression has hurt everyone, even Boston Brahmins. Maybe his family needs some extra dough."

"I see...how unfortunate..."

"The Drizzle" faded out and silence spread throughout the apartment, broken only by the cricket's bleating chirps and the record scratching. There was no time to sit around and wallow in self-pity. Better to make the most of the time they had left. Tom stood and went over to the phonograph. He put on the same record from last night – "Sing-Song Girl of Old Shanghai" – and extended his hand. Mei-chen donned her leather gloves and took it. She rested her head on his shoulder as they swayed to and fro, animated by the jazzy melody.

As they danced, Tom's thoughts drifted to the past, the present, and the future. Perhaps if he had been more careful about who he let into Club Twilight, then maybe none of this would have happened. Hopefully, Captain Tung and Chow were working hard right now to save his life. And, if he did die tomorrow, what would his parents and big brother say when they found out? An image of the Lai family lighting incense and praying for his soul filled him with a deep, shameful sorrow. And what would become of his Beautiful Pearl? He'd have to write a farewell letter to them all, just in case.

A knock at the door halted their steps.

"What is it?" Tom said, switching back to Shanghainese.

"A visitor," Yan said from behind the other side.

"Tell them I'm busy."

"But boss, it's that Japanese from earlier. Yoshida."

Tom released his grip on Mei-chen's hand and said, "Excuse me." Opening the door, he leaned out and asked Yan in a whisper, "What does he want?"

"He says he has a message for you," Yan said, lowering his voice. "I asked him to wait in the storage room."

Tom nodded and followed Yan down the stairs and into the back hallway. Yan opened the door to the storage room, where Yoshida, wearing a khaki trench coat and fedora, sat at the small table. The *ronin* glanced up as they entered, his dark eyes following their every move.

"Yes? What do you want?" Tom snapped, leaning against a crate full of liquor.

"I need to speak to you about something," Yoshida said. He shifted his gaze over to Yan Ping. "Alone."

Tom's curiosity was piqued, but he'd be damned if he was going be alone – unarmed – with this *ronin*.

"Search him Yan," Tom ordered. "Then leave us."

The beefy bodyguard nodded and walked over to Yoshida, who rose slowly. A glint of metal flashed in the overhead electric lights, reaching out to strike. Yan Ping stumbled backward, blood bursting from his torso. After a few jerking steps, he crashed hard onto the floor. Gore flecked his thick mustache while his eyes searched for some desperate, pitiful way to escape. Finally, they settled on Tom with a sad, apologetic look before glazing over. Loyal to the end.

Yoshida advanced forward, his trench coat wide open and a short sword in his hand. Tom recognized it as a *yoroi-doshi*, a short sword sheathed in wood and weapon of choice for Japanese rabble rousers. Made for piercing samurai armor, it was just small enough to conceal inside a trench coat. Apparently, this *ronin* took his namesake quite literally. Locking the blade in place, Yoshida prepared to deliver a killing blow.

"I just wanted to say '*sayonara.*'"

CHAPTER TWENTY-ONE

The *yoroi-doshi* gleamed in the electric light, allowing Tom to catch a brief glimpse of his reflection in it. Pale and wide-eyed, he looked like a prisoner awaiting execution. Here he was concerned about the Green Gang when he should have been more worried about the Japanese.

Releasing a battle cry, Yoshida charged and swung the blade horizontally – perfect for a beheading. Tom dropped to the ground and rolled, avoiding the lethal slash. Crackling glass filled the storeroom, as a row of liquor bottles shattered in the wake of Yoshida's sword. The *ronin* steadied himself, realigning for another attack. Springing up, Tom turned toward the door and ran.

He burst out into the hallway and found himself dashing into the main hall. Taxi dancers and bartenders gawked at him with dumbfounded expressions.

"Call the Police!" Tom managed to shout in between gasps of air.

Glinting metal drew closer in his peripheral, and Tom dove straight toward the band pit, scattering its members. Tom landed hard on his stomach, knocking the wind out of him. Tubas, trumpets, and saxophones clattered to the floor as the musicians fled in fear. The taxi dancers shrieked in unison, their panic almost palpable. Grasping for any semblance of a weapon, Tom gripped a nearby tenor saxophone and swung around.

Yoshida rushed closer, the *yoroi-doshi* raised high above his head, ready to deliver the coup de grace. Tom heaved the sax up into the sword's path. The blade bit into the instrument, but met firm resistance, allowing Tom to swing both across the band pit.

Disarmed, Yoshida lashed out his fists, allowing Tom to grip one of his arms and pull the *ronin* down to the floor with him. Tom managed to land a punch to Yoshida's face, but the blow wasn't enough to waylay the *ronin*. Within moments, Yoshida quickly recovered and dashed toward the sword laying impotent across the room. Tom heaved himself to his feet and glanced for help.

The taxi dancers pressed themselves against the wall, squealing in terror, while the bartenders took refuge behind the counter. Not that he blamed them. After all, he paid Yan Ping for security, not them. He shook his head free of guilt, at least for the time being. He needed to concentrate on staying alive, then he'd have the rest of his life to mourn poor Yan.

The only thing that could beat a sword was a gun, and unfortunately, his was upstairs. Tom glanced over, seeing Yoshida pry the *yoroi-doshi* from the saxophone. He'd only have one shot at this. Turning, Tom ran out of the main hall, into the narrow corridor of storage rooms, and then up the stairs. Halting in front of his apartment, he almost ripped the doorknob off as he stormed inside.

Mei-chen sat on the bed, busy reading an issue of *Photoplay*. Only when Tom slammed the door behind him did she glance up with wide, surprised eyes.

"Darling, what's wrong?"

Tom didn't respond and ran over to the desk, where his Browning automatic was nestled inside. With twitching, nervous fingers, he tore open the drawer and fumbled for the gun. Behind him, a loud whoosh announced the arrival of Yoshida. Tom grasped the Browning and swung his aim around, but it was too late. With a quick dash, the *ronin* made his way across the apartment and sank an iron grip around Mei-chen's neck while the *yoroi-doshi* sword raised up to her throat. *Photoplay* slipped from Mei-chen's gloved fingers and crumpled on the floor.

"Drop the gun," Yoshida growled, "or I'll cut her throat."

Tom kept the gun pointed, but adrenaline distorted his aim. Situated behind Mei-chen, the crafty Nipponese held all the cards. There was no way Tom could get a clear shot now, even if he weren't shaking like a leaf.

"Let her go first," he managed to rasp out.

Yoshida growled again, animalistic and annoyed. "You are in no position to give orders! Drop your gun or she dies!"

The Browning rattled in Tom's hand, now moist with sweat. Without thinking, he knelt down, placed the pistol on the floor, and rose a defeated man. Yoshida left the safety behind Mei-chen, but still kept the sword locked under her throat.

"It won't be so easy for either of you. This is a matter of honor. I want you to feel the same loss of face I experienced when you humiliated me in front of Commander Fukuzaki." The *ronin* eyed Mei-chen like a cat playing with mice. "I'll hack your little whore to pieces in front of you...first her ears, then her nose, then her..." The blade glided down to Mei-chen's breasts.

Tom swallowed. Just like the samurai of old, he thought, who plucked the noses and ears off defenseless peasants. A silent tension spread out before them, soon punctured by the caged cricket's loud chirps. The annoying bug was soon drowned out by a barrage of angry Japanese. Yoshida remained quiet with widening eyes. Mei-chen talked, berated, and demanded in fluent, accentless Japanese. Tom hadn't a clue what she was saying, but the words *"Fukuzaki Chusa"* were repeated over and over.

The sword retreated from Mei-chen's body and hung limply at Yoshida's side. The *ronin's* stupefied face went pale. He offered a slight but apologetic bow, giving Tom an opening. With one fluid motion, he dropped down, grabbed the Browning, aimed, and fired. Bullets tore bloody holes in Yoshida's torso as he tumbled backward, plopping onto the bed. A death rattle wheezed as the *ronin's* fingers slackened, letting the sword tumble to the floor with a loud clang.

Tom took enormous gasps of air, trying to steel his jangled nerves. The gun shook in his hands as he looked at the corpse. How the hell was he going to explain this to his staff? But a more troubling thought appeared. He looked over to Mei-chen and didn't see his Beautiful Pearl anymore. Here in his own apartment was the Japanese spy.

CHAPTER TWENTY-TWO

Tom aimed the Browning automatic straight at Mei-chen's face. She glared at it, her brown eyes cold and analytical. What was going through that dark mind of hers, full of so many secrets? Maybe she was thinking about what a sucker he'd been. Shame and humiliation burned through him. He glanced over to Yoshida's bloodied body, sprawled out on the bed—their bed. A slight nausea prickled his stomach.

"What are you going to do, darling?" she asked in English. In that blazing red *cheongsam* and black leather gloves, she looked like a beautiful Satan. Tom lowered the gun to her chest.

"Get some answers for starters. Who are you, really? What's your real name?"

Mei-chen heaved a sigh, full of melancholy. "Does it matter?"

No, it probably didn't. On to the next question. "Are you Japanese?"

"No..." she said with another sigh.

"So, you betrayed your country?"

An angry defiance swept over Mei-chen's face. "I never betrayed *my* country."

"I don't know what that means, but you can explain to the Green Gang." Keeping the Browning locked on her, Tom inched over to telephone.

"Please don't do that," she pleaded, clasping her hands together.

"Why not? After all, you were going to let me take the fall. That's all I was to you, huh? An American rube."

Mei-chen didn't answer, but tears welled in her eyes.

"And I swallowed it, hook, line and sinker. What an idiot I've been! Thinking about marriage, living in San Francisco..." he scoffed, trying to hide his own tears.

Although Tom hated to admit it, her betrayal hurt worse than any physical pain he'd endured. He could handle a stab in the back from Whitfield, but had anything between them been real? It had been for him at least. That made the pain even worse.

"You were going to let the Green Gang kill me! You set me up, didn't you?"

"No, that's not true, I swear it!" she cried, balling her hands into fists. "I had no idea the Green Gang discovered my notes. Please Tom, I didn't want to spy for Japan…but…but Commander Fukuzaki forced me to!"

Mei-chen – or whatever her name was – fixed him with a pitiful, morose look. Her eyes were so bleary from tears that they looked like shimmering diamonds. The gun shook in Tom's hand, but he took a deep breath to steady it.

"Commander Fukuzaki? He's your handler, isn't he?"

"Yes, he said he'd kill me if I didn't spy for him." With careful, dainty steps, she inched toward him. "Please Tom, protect me from him. All I want is to go to America and start over…with you."

Tears had smudged her mascara, but she still looked radiant. His brain went numb, his muscles slackened, his will bent. Suddenly, Tom had a newfound sympathy for opium addicts. Oh God, why was he so weak around her?

"Darling, I would never hurt you," she cooed. "I swear it."

Her gloved hands pressed themselves against his chest and for a brief moment, nothing else mattered. She was his Beautiful Pearl once again. Yoshida's corpse, Commander Fukuzaki, the Green Gang, all of Shanghai, vanished. Nothing else existed except them. A swift jerk dragged him back to reality. Mei-chen knocked the pistol out of his hand, sending it tumbling across the apartment. She flashed him a wide-eyed glare, like an animal ready to strike – and pushed him hard. Tom stumbled backward and lost his balance, slamming down against the cricket cage.

After a moment, Tom returned to his senses, a man waking up from a dream. Mei-chen darted out the door, the clacking sound of high heels following her. He heaved himself off the little cricket cage, now twisted and bent. Even worse, the bug was now crushed into a greasy smear. So much for bringing good luck. Tom scooped up the Browning and ran downstairs, back into the main hall. The staff was clustered around the bar, shaken and afraid. Tom's sudden appearance brightened their forlorn faces, a man who'd returned from the grave.

"Boss, boss!" a bartender said, running up to meet him. "Thank heaven you're alive! We just telephoned the Police and—"

"Where's Mei-chen?" Tom snapped.

Only then did the bartender notice the Browning pistol. "She um…she um…"

"Where?" Tom snarled, his voice an angry bark.

"She just ran out. We thought you'd been killed."

"Out of my way," Tom said with a forceful push.

He raced out of the lobby and into the streets of Chapei, clogged with factory workers returning home. Tom searched the passing throng of blue workman coveralls for a red *cheongsam*, but to no avail. He plunged into the human river and let himself be carried along down the street.

Tom rounded the corner and zeroed in on Mei-chen's red dress, like a blazing flame in the blue sea. Oddly enough, she wasn't headed east toward Little Tokyo, but south to the Soochow Creek. She maintained a good lead, but those high heels slowed her down. Tom shoved his way through a number of slow-moving pedestrians and gained on her. Mei-chen turned with widened eyes and froze.

Lashing out a hand, Tom gripped her by the arm and squeezed hard. Yanking Mei-chen toward him, Tom drove the pistol into her side.

"Going somewhere?"

Mei-chen twisted and squirmed in vain. Her only response was a pained grunt.

"You're coming back with me," Tom growled in a low whisper, "and then we'll invite the Green Gang over."

She met his eyes and said, "Go ahead and shoot me. Now!"

Tom's finger stiffened around the trigger, unable to move. She'd called his bluff. Even after complete betrayal, he still couldn't kill his Beautiful Pearl. But that didn't mean he would die for her. Tom Lai was nobody's rube.

"We're going back to Club Twilight," he said, jamming the pistol deeper into her side.

Flashing her eyes from side to side, Mei-chen looked like a cornered alley cat. Although her heels were planted firmly on the sidewalk, one sharp tug dislodged her and pulled her along.

"Help!" she cried in Shanghainese. "Please help! This man is trying to kidnap me!"

The shuffling crowds on the street halted and several people scrutinized them with hostile eyes.

"Let her go!" somebody cried.

"Call the Police!"

The penetrating stares loosened Tom's fingers, allowing Mei-chen to wriggle out of his grip. She retreated and disappeared into the mass of people, her red *cheongsam* swallowed by walls of blue and gray.

"No, you don't understand," Tom said. "She's really—"

"He's got a gun!" another shouted, sending a ripple of terror through the throng.

All too late, Tom holstered the pistol to placate the onlookers, but the terror was spreading. The crowd convulsed and split to and fro in panic. A shrill whistle blew through the chilly air. Tom glanced over his shoulder and saw an enormous police officer hulking toward him. In his dark blue uniform, peaked cap with white band and Kuomintang badge, he looked like a Chinese Frankenstein monster. Truncheon drawn, he parted the mass of people and headed straight for Tom.

"You're under arrest for disturbing the peace with a firearm," Frankenstein snarled in Shanghainese. Tom glanced at his collar rank insignia – this lumbering giant was only a sergeant.

Catching his breath, Tom wheezed out, "A Japanese spy…she's running…please catch her."

"Shut up!"

Sergeant Frankenstein lashed out with his truncheon, striking Tom across the head with a shattering blow. Within moments, he was on his knees and sank into a black abyss.

CHAPTER TWENTY-THREE

The darkness opened up and returned Tom to consciousness. He lay on his back in a dingy bed, while a musty stench hung in the air. Ignoring a throbbing pain at back of his skull, Tom heaved himself to a sitting position and took in the room – a dank jail cell. Iron bars to the right, a ragged, emaciated cellmate to the left. The man stared back with a glazed, stupefied look. An opium addict no doubt, but was he just a vagrant or something more sinister? Thirsting for tobacco, Tom fumbled through his pockets for a Lucky Strike, but found his cigarette case was missing. Where had that damn thing gone to?

But the more pressing question was, how long had he been out? Tom glanced at his wristwatch but saw only bare skin. *Sons of bitches*, he thought to himself. At least the cell contained a slim, barred window where a darkened sky could be seen. It was still night but an exact time was unknown. Taking the Browning pistol was understandable, but his Rolex too? Still, what did he expect from Shanghai cops?

The city really had three police forces. The best was the Shanghai Municipal Police, in charge of the International Settlement. Run by esteemed British gentlemen, they'd fashioned it into an Oriental Scotland Yard – professional and competent, for Shanghai at least. Next was the French Concession's *Garde Municipale*. Although nominally run by the French with their Annamese officers and Russian auxiliaries, Tu Yueh-seng's henchmen had so thoroughly infiltrated the organization that it was now the Green Gang just under an alias.

Lastly was the Police Department for the Chinese section of Shanghai – the Public Security Bureau. Officially controlled by the Nationalist Government, it was made up of former warlord soldiers, brutes, sadists, and Green Gang informants. Since he had been arrested in Chapei, that's who must have taken him. Regardless, he could now supply them with the name of the real spy – Ho Mei-chen.

Rubbing his sore head, a wave of memories flooded Tom's mind – dancing with Mei-chen for the first time, luring her away to Club Twilight, their first time making love, and the moment he realized how hard he'd fallen for her. It all seemed like a serene, magical dream that he'd awakened from. Just then, a nightmare approached. The hulking copper from earlier – Sergeant Frankenstein – loomed on the other side of the bars, glaring at Tom. His uniform seemed to blend in with the darkness, but one item stood out – a ritzy Rolex fastened around his thick wrist.

"Hey, you," Tom said in Shanghainese, hopping off the bed. He pointed at the watch – his watch – and said, "For as much as I pay your superiors in protection money, the least you could do is not steal from me."

The Sergeant cracked a smile full of uneven teeth. "You're lucky that's all you lost. I could have cracked your skull open if I wanted."

Ignoring the stinging pain, Tom grabbed the bars and leaned closer. "I'm an American. I have my rights. Call the US Consulate and…" he trailed off, remembering the bitter words between him and Whitfield. Besides, he wasn't in the International Settlement; he was in the real Shanghai. A Chinese contact made more sense.

"Look Sergeant, call Captain Tung Hsi-shan of the 19th Route Army," Tom said, taking his hands off the bars as a token of subordination. "He can vouch for me."

A gruff laugh burst out of Sergeant Frankenstein. "Fine then, Mr. Yankee. You'd better pray I can reach this Captain Tung of yours. For now, you'd better get some sleep. Lieutenant Kuo will question you tomorrow."

"Won't be hard after your little love tap," he muttered in English. Frankenstein made a sour face and walked away, leaving Tom alone with the doped-up vagrant. No sense in staying awake. He crawled back into bed and shut his eyes, letting sleep embrace him. Before he dozed off, Mei-chen appeared in his mind's eye, beautiful and haunting, forever running just out of reach.

*****

A harsh, jangling sound stirred Tom awake. He groaned and rubbed his head, still sore but no longer throbbing. Sunlight leaked through the narrow window, illuminating the jail cell. It was January 28th, 1932, possibly the last day of his life.

"Rise and shine, Mr. Yankee!" Sergeant Frankenstein bellowed as he opened the barred door.

Tom slid off the bed and walked out the cell. Frankenstein guided him down the long hallway, passing cells overcrowded with the riff raff of Shanghai – beggars, dope addicts, pickpockets, and thieves. Small timers to be sure, since the major league criminals were the ones running the city.

They reached a white door marked "Interrogation" in English and Chinese. Frankenstein opened the door and pushed Tom inside. A slim police officer in similar dark uniform and white collar patches sat at a desk across the room. A wry grin clashed with his hooded eyes and sharp, thin face.

"Lieutenant Kuo, I presume?" Tom said, taking a seat across from him.

"Yes. It's a pleasure to meet you Thomas Lai...or should I say Lai Huang-fu?"

"You can call me Charlie Chan so long as you let me out of here."

Lieutenant Kuo waved his hand, dismissing Sergeant Frankenstein, who closed the door behind him. He reached into his tunic pocket and pulled out Tom's cigarette case.

"Would you care for a smoke?"

"I was wondering where that went," Tom said, plucking a Lucky Strike out.

"Forgive me, but I do love foreign tobacco, so I had a few," Kuo said with an apologetic smile. "I'm sorry for your treatment. The Sergeant didn't know you were *the* Thomas Lai."

Lighting up, Tom took a drag and said, "After all the donations I've made to your superiors, I'm glad *someone* here knows who I am, Lieutenant."

"I've been to Club Twilight several times, but we received a very distressing call last night." Lieutenant Kuo slid two photographs across the table; Yoshida full of bloody holes, and Yan Ping sliced nearly in half. Guilt and shame squeezed Tom's gut, leaving him shaken. He took a deep drag to steady himself.

"The poor bastard on the right is Yan Ping, my bodyguard. He died protecting me from this turtle's egg," Tom tapped on the *ronin's* photo. "His name is, or was, Yoshida, a Japanese agent. Tried to *hara-kiri* me next but luckily I managed to reach my pistol."

Apart from his slight grin, Lieutenant Kuo remained expressionless. "Yes, we have a file on Gen Yoshida. He has been stirring up all sorts of trouble in the International Settlement. Your staff gave statements that this man tried to kill you last night."

Tom blew out a trail of smoke. "Great. So, I'm free to leave now?"

"Not quite. Perhaps you can enlighten me as to why a Japanese agent was in your club in the first place?"

"I made his boss, a Japanese Navy officer by the name of Fukuzaki, lose face. You're aware of how important that is, right Lieutenant?"

Kuo nodded with a widening grin. "Oh yes, I'm very aware. I wonder if Yoshida was there for another reason?"

"What do you mean?"

"Before you were arrested, you mentioned a Japanese spy."

Tom took another puff and rubbed the back of his head. "Before your sergeant knocked me out, I was pursuing..." he trailed off, considering how to explain their relationship. "Ho Mei-chen is who you're after. She's a Japanese spy."

"Oh yes, your staff mentioned her," Lieutenant Kuo said, his grin subsiding. "But we don't have any record of her in our files. Neither do our colleagues in Frenchtown and the International Settlement. Somehow, I doubt she has much of a history."

Tom scoffed and stamped out his cigarette. "There's no doubt Ho Mei-chen is an alias..."

"And apparently, she lived with you for two years, yet you do not know her real name?"

Tom didn't like where this was going. Throwing his hands up, he said, "What do you want me to say? She duped me! I have no idea who she really is! But try the Sincere Department Store, she likes to shop there."

"That is troubling, Mr. Lai. You must understand our concerns. You claim that this woman is a Japanese spy, yet you lived with her. Can you expect me to believe you didn't know about her double life?"

Well, it *did* sound ridiculous when said aloud.

"Look Lieutenant, I was blinded. The Green Gang informed me about a spy working at my club and unfortunately, it was my woman."

Lieutenant Kuo stroked his chin, scrutinizing Tom up and down.

"I'm not sure if you're telling me the truth, Mr. Lai. But I have ways of finding out," Kuo purred, tenting his spindly fingers together.

That didn't sound reassuring. From Death by a Thousand Cuts to being impaled by bamboo, China had a long history with brutality. A common torture used by Chinese cops these days was sliding needles under fingernails, then tearing them out – the old Shanghai manicure. Tom swallowed and braced himself. Face was everything in this city, especially in front of police officers. Lose it and you might as well be dead.

"I'd like to make a phone call before you do, Lieutenant," he said, keeping a steady gaze.

"Oh, I don't think so Mr. Lai. Not until I let the Sergeant interrogate you first."

Interrogation sessions with Sergeant Frankenstein were probably as gentle as a cattle stampede. Still, Tom kept his cool and reached for another cigarette. Before he lit up, the door creaked open and in walked Frankenstein.

"Ah, Sergeant," Lieutenant Kuo said. "We were just talking about you."

Frankenstein regarded his superior with a stiff nod before locking eyes with Tom. "You have a visitor, Mr. Yankee."

CHAPTER TWENTY-FOUR

Tom traded glances with Lieutenant Kuo across the table. Confusion swept over the Lieutenant's sharp, beaked face, but he regained his composure quickly.

"Very well," Kuo said, standing up. "Let's see who your visitor is, Mr. Lai."

Tom rose and followed the Lieutenant out of the interrogation room. Sergeant Frankenstein led them down the hallway and into the main lobby. A few uniformed cops stood guard, impressive in their dark blue uniforms. However, they paled in comparison to Captain Tung, looking gallant in his stiff blue-gray tunic, field cap, and polished jackboots. Kuo and Frankenstein halted and presented Tung with supplicating salutes.

"Good morning," the Captain said with a curt nod. "Thank you for watching him, but I will be taking custody of Mr. Lai."

Lieutenant Kuo stepped forward. "I'm sorry, Captain. However, I still need to question Mr. Lai in relation to the events of last night."

Tung thrust out his chin. "Which are?"

"My apologies, but we are not at liberty to discuss an ongoing investigation."

"That may be, but Lai Huang-fu is a valuable asset to the Republic and specifically to the 19th Route Army," Tung said. "Or would you like to speak to General Tsai personally?"

Lieutenant Kuo kept a placid face, but his head lowered as a slight admission of defeat. No one could resist the demands of the 19th Route Army, not when war loomed so close. Kuo gave a curt nod to Frankenstein, who left the lobby for a few minutes before returning with Tom's Browning automatic.

Tom grinned, tucked the pistol in his waistband, then gestured to the Rolex on the Sergeant's bulky wrist. "I'll be needing that too."

Frankenstein flushed, then sheepishly slid the wristwatch off and pressed it into Tom's palm. He snapped it into place and checked the time – 11:30AM. Tom glanced over to the two cops, heads lowered like disciplined schoolboys. Loss of face was especially hurtful for the arrogant Shanghai Police, and Tom savored their humiliation as if it were a piece of Hershey's chocolate.

Clicking his heels together, Captain Tung said, "Thank you for your cooperation, gentlemen."

"We'll have to finish those questions later, Lieutenant. Drop by Club Twilight for a few drinks," Tom said with a mocking wink. Lieutenant Kuo and Frankenstein stared back with expressionless faces, but a murderous rage blazed in their eyes. Tom followed Captain Tung out the doors and descended down the steps to an Army staff car waiting at the curb below. A Chinese soldier sat ready at the wheel but Tung didn't enter.

Instead, the Captain drew himself up into an even more rigid pose and said, "I'm sure you're aware how busy am I. War is imminent and coming to bail you out of jail only distracts from my duty."

"That's what friends do for each other, Captain. Don't think I'm unappreciative. From now on, you drink for free at Club Twilight!"

Tung snorted. "You're lucky that sergeant actually did telephone me. Otherwise, you'd still be rotting in there. Lieutenant Kuo is a known Green Gang informant."

"Hell, all of Shanghai is an informant for the Green Gang," Tom said with a grin. "In all seriousness, thank you, Captain."

Tung gave an affirming nod, the limits of his sentimentality. "The Police told me that your bodyguard was killed last night. I'm sorry."

"Yeah, I am too."

"At least you killed that Japanese devil, Yoshida. Excellent shooting, Lai Huang-fu. There's still a spot for you in my company if you're interested."

"Thanks, but I have a spy to catch."

"Oh? You found him?"

"Yes…it was…" Tom trailed off as a wave of shame and sadness seemed to strangle him. Swallowing hard, he finally said, "Mei-chen…"

Sympathy shone in Captain Tung's blocky face, the type of concern that only a *dai go*, a big brother, could show.

"Ah, I see," he said. "I'm sorry to hear that, Lai Huang-fu. Still, it is not surprising. Deceit comes naturally to women, especially in this city. As Confucious said, 'Chaos does not come down from Heaven, it is caused by women.'"

"Sounds like a man who's never been in love."

An awkward silence spread between them, so Tom looked out into the street. Only a few coolies in silk shirts and skullcaps roamed about today. Poor wretches who stayed behind while middle-class Shanghainese managed to flee.

"Still think there's going to be a war?" Tom asked.

"Mayor Wu has until today to accept or reject the Japanese demands." Captain Tung cracked his knuckles. "Regardless, we're ready for a fight. The 19th Route Army will pay those devils back for what they did to Manchuria."

"You know a war will destroy Shanghai."

Captain Tung scoffed and fixed Tom with a steely gaze. "If we don't slay this ravenous wolf now, how many more provinces will it devour? Better all of Shanghai be destroyed if it saves China."

"Speaking of China, have you managed to contact that man from the Finance Ministry, Chow? If there's ever been a time I needed a favor, now is it."

"No, I'm sorry. He won't return my calls. Lai Huang-fu, if you're not going to fight, I suggest you leave the city. I say that as a friend."

Tom couldn't hold back a bitter sigh. "I would, but the Green Gang has all exits covered. I'm a dead man if I run, I'm a dead man if I stay. Unless I can find…" He trailed off again. Her name kept getting caught in his throat.

"It will be difficult. There are three million people in Shanghai, but if I were you, I'd start looking in Little Tokyo. That little snake probably slithered off to her handlers for protection."

"No, she wasn't heading toward Hongkew. She was running south, to the Soochow Creek."

What was down there for her? Surely, Mei-chen would find safety in Little Tokyo. Commander Fukuzaki probably had a room ready for her in the Golden Unicorn. Maybe there was a Nipponese safehouse down in the International Settlement, or maybe she was running away from the Japanese. Charles Whitfield had an apartment there, near the American Club. Whitfield had never invited him over, since they usually just met at Club Twilight. Suddenly, those top secret documents appeared in his mind. The details about several US Navy gunboats had been written in English, as if it had been written by a native speaker.

Mei-chen had been studying English in preparation for their new life in San Francisco. Charles Whitfield had access to those documents. Suddenly, all of his concern for that *"poor kid"* took on a new dimension. How could he have not seen it before? Betrayed by his woman *and* by his best friend. He really was a first-rate sucker.

Balling his fists, Tom choked down his rage. He couldn't lose control in front of Tung. Asking the Captain for help was out of the question since he'd helped enough already. Besides, the 19th Route Army had no authority in the International Settlement. Tom needed to get down there as soon as possible before Whitfield smuggled Mei-chen – or whatever her real name was – out of Shanghai forever.

"Captain, I have one more favor to ask," Tom said. Tung raised an eyebrow. "Mind giving me a ride back to Club Twilight?"

CHAPTER TWENTY-FIVE

The staff car halted in front of Club Twilight, filling Tom with a bittersweet sadness. He was home, but now it was tainted with nightmarish memories. Even worse, every happy moment he had shared with Mei-chen now seemed phony and hollow. No, he wouldn't wallow in self-pity. Tom Lai was nobody's rube. Instead, he'd find Mei-chen and Whitfield to get some answers.

Sitting next to him, Captain Tung extended his hand. "I wish you the best of luck, Lai Huang-fu."

"You too, Captain. Thanks again for all your help."

They shook hands, and Tom gave a friendly squeeze for emphasis. Just in case this was their final meeting, he wanted to remember the Captain this way; a stoic warrior, but also a tender-hearted friend. Unlike that two-faced snake, Charles Whitfield. There was an old Chinese saying – '*Good iron doesn't make nails, and good men don't become soldiers.*' Captain Tung Hsi-shan proved such talk was bullshit.

Tom exited the car and a chilly breeze blew against his face. He walked toward Club Twilight, but Captain Tung called him back.

"Remember Lai Huang-fu," he said, through an open window. "There are many women, but only one China."

Tom nodded his understanding. Just like a soldier to put patriotism above all else, especially love. Building a New China was what had lured him to Shanghai in the first place. But now this New China might just be the death of him. Maybe he should have just stayed in San Francisco. He shook such thoughts out of his head, and waved Captain Tung off. The staff car pulled away from the curb and into the streets of Chapei.

Turning around, Tom marched into Club Twilight, the prodigal son returning. However, as he entered the main hall, a thick, evil sensation engulfed him. Most of the staff didn't begin work until later, but a few porters and bartenders stood off to the side, as if they were facing a firing squad. A quick inspection told why.

Feng Lung-wei and his entourage toured the club like evil spirits. With him were the two brutish gorillas from yesterday, along with an auburn-haired white woman. Tom scrutinized her face and remembered her glazed expression back at the opium den – Feng's Russian mistress. Clad in a fur-trimmed coat and feathered hat, the woman clung to that gangster brat as he led her around like a dog on a leash. They inspected the crisscrossed American and Chinese flags, the tables, and fully stocked bar.

Wearing a black overcoat over his shoulders, along with a black pinstripe suit and fedora, Feng Lung-wei swaggered about as if he owned the damn place. Tom walked straight toward them, making his presence known.

"Looking for a job?" he asked in English as Feng and his cohorts turned to face him. "I'm afraid we're not hiring at the moment."

Shock and disbelief swept across the gangsters' faces. Feng's eyes bulged, but after a moment he regained his arrogant composure and greeted Tom with a sly grin.

"Tommy! I'm surprised to see you here."

"Obviously so," Tom muttered.

"Lieutenant Kuo telephoned me this morning and said you'd been arrested. Knowing the Lieutenant, I figured you'd be his guest for a very long time."

Tom flashed a smile. "Sorry to disappoint you, but I have connections in this city as well."

"Well, it appears I underestimated you, Tommy." Feng turned toward the rest of his party and said, "Give us a little privacy?"

The two mugs nodded, but the redhead began complaining in rapid-fire Russian. An angry scowl contorted Feng's face as he slapped his hand across her cheek, leaving behind a bright pink splotch. The Russian girl showed no emotion, no hint of pain. Perhaps all that opium had eaten away at her nerve endings. After a brief, stupefied moment, she gave a supplicating nod and retreated with the two henchmen over to the bar.

"Russian women," Feng snorted with a resigned shrug. "They think just because they're white, they can talk back to our kind. At least Chinese girls know when to shut up."

"Speaking of which, where's your other skirt?"

Shaking his head, Feng said, "Such a tragedy. Opium finally consumed what was left of her brain. Our people are more susceptible to that drug. She was almost catatonic, so my men disposed of her yesterday. That's why I was at the Great World." His grin broadened. "Fan-tan always cheers me up."

Tom wondered how the poor girl had been disposed of. Probably nothing too brutal. A gunshot to the head or drowning in the Whangpoo River. The most vicious Green Gang killings were reserved for men who couldn't pay their debts, rival gangsters, Communists, and spies. Could he really subject Mei-chen to that horror? Well, it was either him or her, and Tom Lai was a survivor.

Feng bent over and scrutinized Tom's hands. "Still have your fingernails? I suppose Lieutenant Kuo didn't have time to give you the Shanghai manicure!"

Tom balled a fist. "Disappointed?"

"More like surprised. Imagine my shock when Kuo rang me up, telling me you'd been arrested last night. Something about assaulting a woman, along with *two* dead bodies at your club? A boy scout like you! I almost didn't believe it!"

"I'm full of surprises."

"Who killed the Jap? You or that little twist of yours?"

"Me."

"Coming here to silence you, now that your cover was blown up, eh?

"That's 'your cover's been blown.'"

"Yes, yes, a blown cover! But you got the drop on him first, eh?"

"No," Tom said through gritted teeth. "You know how the Japanese are about honor. Apparently, my visit to the Golden Unicorn caused Yoshida to lose face with his boss, Commander Fukuzaki. He thought he could regain it by removing my head."

Feng shrugged again. "Regardless, since your time is almost up, I figured I might as well swing by, since this whole joint will soon become property of the Green Gang."

"Sorry to spoil your plans, but I've identified the spy."

"Yes, yes, Charlie Whitman or whatever his name is. I told you before Tommy, we can't just kill an officer working at US Consulate. If he was a private citizen, then perhaps…"

"His name is Charles Whitfield. And he wasn't working alone." Tom glanced over to the Russian woman, looking almost comatose as she just stared at the bar. The two beefy gangsters searched her up and down with prying eyes. Could he really turn his Beautiful Pearl over to this scum?

"Well, don't keep me in suspense, Tommy. Who was this other spy? I'm dying to know."

The name was caught in his throat again, but he forced it out. "Ho Mei-chen."

Genuine surprise widened Feng's eyes and slackened his jaw. Shock gave way to sadistic delight. "Oh, that's rich," he said with a laugh. "Your little twist, a Japanese spy! Oh, Tommy, I almost feel bad for you." He shook his head and pointed to the redheaded Russian. "If one of my dames ever did that to me, I'd cut out her tongue and make her eat it. Where is she now?"

"She took a run-out powder. Look, I still have until tonight to find her. You can't kill an American Consulate officer, but I'll give you Ho Mei-chen gift wrapped."

Feng gave a dismissive snort. "I'm still not convinced you're innocent, Tommy. It sounds like you're just trying to save your own skin by ratting out the others. That's why Yoshida was here. To silence you both."

"Believe whatever you want, I don't care. All that matters is what Grandmaster Tu thinks. I'll drop by Frenchtown this evening with her and—"

"No!" Feng snapped. "My uncle will not allow a Jap spy in his villa. He ordered me to handle this matter personally. You're only alive right now because my uncle is fond of you, otherwise you'd be full of bullets alongside Goro Ono. I will come back here tonight, and you'd better not empty-handed when I do."

"Tonight? Aren't you afraid of a war breaking out? Chapei will become a battleground."

An ominous snicker escaped Feng's lips. "You don't know from nothing, do you Tommy?"

"I'm beginning to feel like those three monkeys," he said with a shrug.

"Well, I have it on good authority that there won't be any war."

"There won't?"

"No. Mayor Wu will accept the Japanese demands. Another national humiliation! First Manchuria, now this?" Feng shook his head bitterly. "I'll have to take my anger out on a Jap spy. Perhaps it will be your little whore, or maybe you, Tommy."

Reaching into his pinstripe suit, Feng jerked out a Smith & Wesson revolver. Leveling it, he fired and blasted a bottle of Bacardi Rum into pieces. Brown liquid burst outward, dousing the Russian woman's red hair with alcohol and glass shards. Other than a pair of widened eyes, she showed no emotion.

Feng Lung-wei holstered the revolver and slid into his long black overcoat. Snapping his fingers brought his henchmen and mistress over to an immediate orbit.

"See? There will be lots of fireworks later tonight! So you'd better not try and skip town."

Tom gave a slow nod. "Like I told your man, I'm not running."

"Good, because you won't get far," Feng snickered again, then glanced at his wristwatch. "Goodness, it's half past noon. You only have a few hours left. Use them well, Tommy."

With an ominous laugh, Feng Lung-wei led his entourage out the doors. After their exit, a black cloud seemed to lift from the entire club. The porters rushed to his side like frightened children.

"Boss, we're so glad to see you!"

"We were so worried!"

Tom gave a paternal smile. He couldn't lose face, especially not in front of his employees. Better to show confidence no matter what.

"Well, you heard what that turtle's egg said! There won't be a war, so Club Twilight will be open as usual. Let's get ready!"

The porters smiled, then rushed to their posts. Tom slid behind the bar counter and poured himself a tall glass of J&B Scotch. He skipped breakfast, so this would have to suffice. Draining it with thirsty gulps, he felt his fighting spirit return. Tom Lai was a survivor and nobody's fool. He wiped his mouth and headed toward the doors. Time was ticking, and he had some spies to catch.

CHAPTER TWENTY-SIX

Secure in the Bentley, Tom headed east on Soochow Road and into Hongkew like a tank plowing through enemy territory. He drove himself, rather than risk his usual chauffeur ending up like poor Yan Ping. Traffic was thick and heavy, the last remnants of the Chinese middle class driving whatever they could into the International Settlement. Up ahead, several full-sized trucks carrying Japanese Marines drove the other way toward Chapei. If war came, the Mikado's men would be in Chinese territory within minutes.

But according to that gangster brat, there wasn't going to be any war. Feng Lung-wei was well-informed, Tom had to admit that. But would Mayor Wu really accept those humiliating demands? Well, China had been swallowing humiliation after humiliation for almost a century now. The Opium War had not only shattered China's arrogance, but also created the International Settlement, transforming Shanghai from a dreary port into this seething metropolis.

Cruising further east, the magnificent Astor House Hotel appeared on the left. Standing six stories with a stone edifice and grand arched windows, the hotel was the premier place for foreign visitors to stay in Shanghai. A stream of white men and women entered and exited the Astor House, greeted by an astute doorman in a garish uniform and epaulettes. Most doormen in Shanghai were Russians, former officers of the White Army who'd been licked in the Civil War by the Bolsheviks. At least the poor bastard still got to wear a uniform.

Even more insulting was the Soviet Consulate that stood on the opposite side of the street. Thankfully though, this hive of intrigue had been abandoned since China and the USSR had severed diplomatic relations after a brief border war in 1929. Tom parked his car across from the Astor House, giving him a clear view of both the German and American consulates down the road. Whitfield would have to leave sometime.

*****

After three hours of waiting, hunger finally caught up with Tom and demanded his attention. After all, he hadn't eaten since last night. Up ahead, several Chinese clustered around a food cart. Tom hopped out of the Bentley and caught a savory whiff. He recognized it immediately – steamed *bao* buns.

Tom ordered one and bit into it, savoring the pork filling inside. The taste reminded him of his mother's cooking, although the meat in her *bao* was always glazed with sweet *hoisin* sauce. What would his family think about the mess he was in now? His mother would probably cry and burn a few incense sticks at the family altar. His big brother would be angry, but ready to fight whoever attacked a member of the Lai clan. And his father? Papa Lai would probably say how ashamed he was that his foolish son chose misguided patriotism – whether for America or China – over his familial duties. After all, a nation was nothing. Family was everything.

For a moment, he wondered if the old man was right. But picturing himself slaving away in the Lai Family Laundry Shop discouraged the thought. Shanghai was his home, for better or worse. He devoured the rest of the pork *bao* bun, then ordered three more. Each tasted better than the last. Across the street, a newsboy hawked papers next to the entrance of the Astor House Hotel.

"Extra, extra! Mayor Wu accepts all Japanese demands! War averted! Extra, extra!"

Tom swallowed the last of his *bao*, then crossed the street. He bought an issue of the *Shanghai Evening Post & Mercury*. Reading a Chinese newspaper required memorization of thousands of complex characters, but thankfully, the *Shanghai Evening Post* was in English. Skimming the headline story confirmed Feng Lung-wei's earlier promise. Mayor Wu Tieh-cheng had indeed accepted the Japanese demands. The Chinese Republic would apologize for the murder of the Japanese monk, compensate the other victims, suppress anti-Japanese organizations, and most importantly, end the boycott on Japanese goods.

Tom folded the newspaper and breathed a heavy sigh. There wasn't going to be a war. Shanghai was saved. Now, he just needed to save himself.

"Thank goodness," an Australian voice said behind him. Tom turned and found a white couple, dressed to the nines, reading a copy of the *Shanghai Evening Post*.

"Looks like the Japs won't attack," the Aussie man said. "Good thing, since it would have been a blood bath."

"I hope they do the world a favor and wipe each other out," his companion, a petite blonde, sneered. "Oh, the yellow races behave so beastly!"

"And that's why we stopped these Oriental termites from infesting our country," the man said, puffing his chest out. "Australia is for white men and by God, it'll stay that way!"

"I get the most unsettling feeling the way that these slant-eyed coolies leer at me," the blonde Aussie whined. "Oh, I can't wait to go home to Melbourne!"

"Be patient dearest," the man said, taking her arm. "As soon as my business with these yellow monkeys is finished, we'll leave this dreadful place." The Australians turned and strolled past Tom and the newsboy, secure with their own racial superiority.

Anger boiled inside Tom, stoked from years of similar snide comments. A sock to the man's jaw and shoving that newspaper in the blonde's mouth would placate his rage. Still, assaulting a white man and woman would be enough to land Tom in jail for at least a year, despite being an American. He didn't have that long.

Instead, he lit a calming cigarette and went back to the Bentley. In between drags, he read through the rest of the *Shanghai Evening Post & Mercury*. Japanese forces were advancing on Harbin in northern Manchuria, expecting the city to fall within days. After Harbin, the entire region would be secure in Japanese hands.

Wang Ching-wei – Chiang Kai-shek's main rival within the Kuomintang – had been sworn in as premier of the Chinese Republic. However, the Generalissimo was expected to still exercise considerable power as commander-in-chief of the Nationalist Army. Economic depression left many out of work all over the world, especially in America. However, President Hoover proclaimed that "rugged individualism" could get the country through these hard times.

An hour passed, then two. Tom went through five more cigarettes, but there was no sign of Whitfield. In light of today's events, everyone at the US Consulate must have worked late. The sun sank over Shanghai, coating the city with a gloomy darkness. Thankfully, across Soochow Creek, the neon lights of the Bund brightened the sky.

Then, at 8:04, a figure in a light gray overcoat, suit, and homburg, exited the gate and approached a waiting sedan. Although dark, Tom could spot Whitfield's wardrobe of gray double-breasted suits anywhere. The sedan pulled out onto Soochow Road. Tom started the Bentley and followed after them.

CHAPTER TWENTY-SEVEN

Tom maintained a safe distance behind as he followed Whitfield across the Garden Bridge. The dread that choked the city had lifted, replaced by a gay frivolity. Bathed in neon lights, the Bund pulsated with activity as rickshaws, automobiles, and cable cars ran up and down the street. Junks and cargo freighters glided along the Whangpoo River, while the Japanese gunboats just floated there, rendered impotent and harmless.

Whitfield's car turned right on Foochow Road, and Tom steered the Bentley around the corner. He braked at the intersection of Szechuen and Foochow, where a red-turbaned Sikh police officer halted traffic. Tom peered into the distance across the street and saw Whitfield's vehicle pull over at the corner of Kiangse and Foochow, diagonally across from the American Club. The US Consulate man exited the car and let himself into a brownstone building.

In his peripheral, Tom saw a procession approach. Led by an officer on horseback and wearing khaki uniforms and peaked caps, a formation of British troops marched past. The young, apple-cheeked Tommies were cheerful enough as they sang out "It's a Long Way to Tipperary." But the officer's ashen face looked like he'd seen hell itself at the Somme and Passchendaele. Lucky for these lads that there wasn't going to be any war. Not now at least. Maybe they'd get their chance for glory next time.

After the remainder of the British soldiers passed, the Sikh policeman waved Tom through. The American Club loomed on his left, a reminder of simpler times. Had it really only been two nights since he had dinner with Captain Tung and that man from the Finance Ministry, Chow? So much had happened since then; it felt like a dream in a past life. No, he couldn't think about that now. Tom parked in a nearby alleyway a block over, then double backed to the brownstone where Whitfield had entered.

That son of a bitch never mentioned just *how* close he lived to the American Club. This was prime real estate, even for a diplomat. Old money must travel far. Tom hopped out of the Bentley and walked up the steps to the entrance, where a uniformed doorman held up a hand.

"Whot do you vant?" he asked with a heavy Russian accent. "Zis building has no Chinees tenants."

Tom searched for a placating excuse. Something told him this doorman wouldn't believe he was American, which might tip off Whitfield. He cleared his throat and forced out his best pidgin accent.

"Me am Mr. Whitfield new servant."

The old Russian's face wrinkled further with a smile. "*Da, da*, his new house boy! But, dressed like that?"

Tom glanced down at his dark blue serge suit and overcoat.

"Mr. Whitfield say, 'dress to impress.'"

"*Da*, that sounds like Meester Whitfield! His apartment is 402," the Russian said, opening the door.

"*Shi shi*," Tom said with an ingratiating bow. As he climbed the stairs, anxiety began shaking his legs. What was his plan? The Browning automatic – snug in his shoulder holster – was all he could think of. Approaching the fourth floor, a tremor of fear ran through his body. It was either them or him. After a deep breath, he knocked on room 402.

After a moment, the door creaked open, revealing Whitfield's startled face.

"Tom, old boy! What the devil are you doing here?"

Tom gave a cocky grin. "Surprised, Chuck? I hope you're not still sore at me. I…er…came by to apologize. Why don't you invite me in for a drink?"

Whitfield's blue eyes darted to the side, then back over at Tom. "Tonight's not ideal. The place is a mess. I hope you understand."

"What's the matter, Chuck? Got company over?"

"No, that's not it. Look, perhaps we can have a drink over at the American Club. What do say to th—"

Tom plunged his hand into his jacket and whipped out the Browning. Jamming it into Whitfield's cheek, he pushed himself inside the apartment and shut the door behind him.

"Tom, old boy! Have you lost your mind?"

"On the contrary, Chuck. My head is quite clear now," Tom said, guiding Whitfield out of the small vestibule and into the apartment's living room. Oriental knick-knacks clashed with upholstered furniture and a glass coffee table. On it lay several papers, documents, even a passport, and a pair of black leather gauntlets. Ho Mei-chen – still in her red *cheongsam* – sat on the couch, looking at Tom with a stern glare.

"Now I see why you never invited me over, Chuck. Afraid I'd uncover your little love nest?"

Whitfield gulped. "Look, I'm sorry you had to find out this way…"

Tom jerked the pistol over to Mei-chen, then back at Whitfield. "How long has this been going on?"

Shame cast Whitfield's blue eyes downward. "About six months now. I'm sorry Tom, I truly am. It just happened." He swallowed again, then drew a long breath. "Take your anger out on me, but please leave the poor kid out of this."

Tom kept the gun level at Whitfield's chest. "Save your apologies, Chuck. I'm almost impressed by your little scheme. You pass secrets along to Mei-chen at my club, then let me take the fall. The Green Gang bumps me off, then you two love birds resume your little espionage escapades?"

Genuine confusion shone in Whitfield's face. "What the devil are you talking about, old boy?"

The reaction caught Tom off guard. He glanced over at Mei-chen, staring back without emotion. Could it really be that Charles Whitfield was another of this spider woman's dupes? Still keeping the gun level, Tom made his way over to the coffee table and scooped up one of the documents. It was an American passport with Mei-chen's photograph.

Only she wasn't Ho Mei-chen anymore, but rather Margaret Wong. He slid the passport into his pocket, then picked up two other documents. A birth certificate for this mysterious Margaret Wong, born in Chinatown, Los Angeles, and a travel visa.

"Forgeries?" Tom said, sliding the documents into his pocket.

Whitfield nodded. "Please try and understand, Tom. The kid just couldn't wait any longer for you to take her to America. And with war on the horizon, she asked me to get her out as soon as possible."

"So you made phony documents? You'd jeopardize your career for her?"

After several moments of silence, Whitfield gave a slow nod.

Tom couldn't hold in a laugh. "So she used you too, huh? You know she's a Jap spy, right? Ho Mei-chen isn't even her real name."

Sudden realization illuminated Whitfield's face. How else could those top secret documents gotten out? Fury streaked the Consulate man's face as he turned toward Mei-chen, busy putting on her black gloves. "Is this true? Are you really a spy?"

She stood up and regarded Whitfield with a cold glare. "Of course not. Tom is the spy. It was his club. I found out about his double life and he tried to kill me."

"You lying two-timing bitch," Tom growled, slapping her with his free hand. The blow forced Mei-chen back down on the couch, leaving a bright pink splotch across her cheek.

"Don't touch her!" Whitfield roared as he rushed Tom, slamming him up against the wall. Air whooshed out of his lungs, loosening his grip on the Browning. The pistol practically flew out of his hand and clattered onto the floor. Tom swung his hands out for some weak spot, but Whitfield's body was solid muscle. Instead, Whitfield landed a hammering punch into Tom's gut, doubling him over.

"Stop it right now," Mei-chen's soft voice commanded.

Grasping his stomach, Tom lifted his head up. The Browning was now in Mei-chen's hands, aimed straight at Whitfield and Tom.

CHAPTER TWENTY-EIGHT

Tom eyed the Browning automatic as it swayed between him and Whitfield. With that pistol, Mei-chen looked like an Oriental gun moll, tough and threatening. But a slight tremor in her gloved hand betrayed the fear she must have felt.

"Mei-chen," Whitfield began, "what the devil is this all about?"

"Isn't it obvious?" Tom cut in. "She used both of us. At my club she could meet important rubes such as yourself, whom she could pry secrets out of. Ho Mei-chen isn't even her real name."

Shock gave way to anger, reddening Whitfield's chiseled face. "Is this true? Was it really you who made copies of my documents?"

Despite her trembling hand, Mei-chen radiated a casual confidence. "You should always keep your briefcase locked, Charles, even when you're at home."

Whitfield fumed, balling his hands into tight fists. "How could you?"

"It was easy. You're a heavy sleeper," she quipped.

"No, how could you betray me—" he glanced over at Tom "—betray us, like this? Are you really Japanese?"

"Absolutely not," she snapped with enough forced to echo off the walls.

"Then how could you betray your country?" Tom demanded.

"I have no country," she said coldly. "It doesn't matter who I really am, because I'm leaving Shanghai forever. Tonight." She bit her lip, and the gun shook again. "Nobody will ever find me in America. I'm sorry to both of you. I truly am. But I won't anyone stop me. Now step aside!"

"You two-faced tramp," Whitfield roared, stepping forward. "I'll be damned if I help a Japanese spy into my country!"

Mei-chen jerked the pistol toward Whitfield's chest, now rattling in her trembling hand. "Stay back! I don't want to hurt you!"

Ignoring her warning, Whitfield gripped the pistol and twisted. After a brief struggle, the gun muzzle flashed and a shot rang out. With awkward, halting steps, Whitfield let go of her and backed up. Against the light gray suit, a hideous red patch grew over his chest. Strained groans rasped out of his throat just before he collapsed face-first through the coffee table. Glass shattered and burst out in twinkling shards.

Tom didn't miss the opening. He lunged forward and snatched the Browning out of Mei-chen's hand, now loosened in shock. She didn't resist, and instead sank to her knees with a dumbfounded expression. Tom returned his attention Whitfield, who had rolled over onto his back. Thick spurts of blood oozed over his lips. Thanks to the broken glass, raw cuts and scratches now crisscrossed his face like tic tac toe. Tom knelt down and cradled him in his arms.

"S-sorry...about all of this, old boy," Whitfield said in between bloody coughs. "I-I never meant to hurt my best friend. Me and Mei-chen...it...it just happened one night..."

What could Tom say to that? A tempest of conflicting emotions swirled inside Tom. Part of him wanted to ring this backstabber's neck, but he also wanted to cry. They'd been best friends ever since they'd met at the US Consulate, in November of '29, although it seemed like a lifetime ago now. Charles Whitfield was one of the few white men to treat Tom with any respect, and here he was dying in his arms. Although it seemed ludicrous, he felt a twinge of guilt about this whole, sordid affair. Choked by emotion, Tom just nodded.

Whitfield's blood-soaked mouth turned up in a ghoulish smile. Eyelids fluttering, he rasped out a final wheeze then went stiff. Tom laid him back down and turned to Mei-chen. Still on her knees, she stared blankly at Whitfield's body. She showed no emotion at first, but tears soon blotted her brown eyes.

"I…I didn't mean to shoot him…" she muttered. "This wasn't supposed to happen."

It was surprising how genuine her words sounded. Perhaps this Oriental Mata Hari wasn't so coldblooded after all. Tom glanced at this Rolex – 8:55. There was no time to waste crying over the dead.

"Get up," he ordered, gesturing with the pistol. "We're going for a ride."

Tom slid the Browning into his coat pocket, but kept it leveled at Mei-chen's back. With his free hand, he guided her down the stairs.

"Keep quiet and let me do the talking," he said. Mei-chen gave a dumb nod.

They walked outside where the Russian doorman greeted them with a bright smile. "Leafing so soon?"

"Oh yessiree, Mr. Whitfield very busy with work. He ask me to take Miss Ho shopping."

"*Da, da*! Haff a goot night!"

They walked out the steps, crossed the street and toward the Bentley, parked in the nearby alley. Tom glanced around from side to side, confirming it was still deserted. A chilly wind blew through them both, and Mei-chen let out an involuntary shiver, rubbing her bare arms to warm up. Tom looked her over. Her short-sleeved red *cheongsam* and leather gloves were scant protection against the cold.

Tom opened the Bentley's trunk, small and compact, but big enough for a person. He gestured for her to go inside with the Browning. A deep fear radiated from her eyes and trembled her lip.

"What…what are you going to do, Tom?"

"Don't ask questions! Just get in," he snapped. There was enough anger in his voice to let her know there wouldn't be any debate.

Mei-chen took a dainty step inside the trunk, then curled up inside. Shivering from the cold, she fixed him with a pitiful, helpless look, the kind that would have melted him a day before. Despite everything that had happened, Tom couldn't repress an urge to protect his Beautiful Pearl. He slid off the overcoat and tossed it inside.

Curling up inside it, Mei-chen gave a thankful nod as Tom slammed the trunk shut.

CHAPTER TWENTY-NINE

As Tom drove the Bentley northward toward the Chapei district, his mind wandered. How the hell did he get here? He'd never considered himself a gangster, despite his long association with organized crime. Yet here he was, fleeing the murder scene of his best friend with his former lover locked in his trunk. At what point did Tom Lai's life go astray?

Probably early on. Some of his happiest memories were with his uncle and the Suey Sing Tong. They'd groomed him early on to be a member, letting him run fan-tan games and listening in on important meetings. Tom's enthusiasm for the Suey Sing was dashed during the Tong Wars, when a rival gangster buried a hatchet deep into his uncle's skull. After that, he promised never to dive too deep into the underworld.

The World War had focused his attention to patriotism, but the seeds of corruption and crime had already been planted. They grew and grew when he moved to Shanghai, ingratiating himself with Tu Yueh-sheng and the Green Gang. He always tried to keep an arm's length while maintaining a cordial relationship with Shanghai's grandmaster of crime, or at least that's what he told himself. Tom Lai was like a man sinking deeper and deeper into the swamp who insisted that he could pull himself out at any time.

The Bentley plowed across the Soochow Creek via the Garden Bridge, passing into Hongkew. Hanging a left, he cruised past Consulate Way on the left and the Astor House on his right. A gaggle of ritzy-looking white foreigners poured out of the hotel, all set to live it up now that crisis had been averted. He continued westward into Little Tokyo, still barren and desolate. Curiously, units of Japanese

Marines remained in position, as if they still thought there was a war afoot.

As he passed into Chapei, Tom realized why the Mikado's warriors hadn't stood down yet. The streets with thronged with thick, furious crowds. They carried signs, placards, and banners that proclaimed slogans like, "MAYOR WU SHAMES CHINA" and "RESIST THE DWARF BANDITS WITH BLOOD AND BULLETS." A group of students, no older than teenagers, waved Chinese flags while setting a Japanese standard alight. The White Sun fluttered while the Rising Sun burned.

As Tom pressed deeper and deeper into Chapei, the mobs only grew larger and angrier. An effigy of the Mikado was pelted with rocks before being ripped apart. Patriotic songs echoed throughout the streets. There was an incessant chanting for Mayor Wu to "Reject the demands and throw the Japanese devils out of Shanghai." Most disturbing was a Japanese couple, identified by their kimonos, surrounded by a ring of enraged students. Like sharks to chum, they attacked, pummeling the couple with unrestrained ferocity. Within seconds they were bloodied and battered, their kimonos shredded rags. Something told Tom that this wasn't the machinations of Commander Fukuzaki and his *ronin*. This was patriotism at its ugliest.

The Chinese police officers struggled to intervene, but they were impotent to temper this fury. It had been bubbling up for decades, even before the invasion of Manchuria, way back to 1894 when Japan had trounced the Manchu Dynasty in Korea and annexed Taiwan. Being defeated by the mighty British Empire was one thing, but by little Japan? China could only endure so much humiliation before she erupted like a volcano.

*****

By the time Tom reached Kungwoo Road in western Chapei, the angry throngs had thinned out. Tom pulled the

Bentley in an alleyway behind Club Twilight and checked his Rolex – 9:30. Feng Lung-wei would arrive soon, eager for someone to kill. He'd hand Mei-chen off to that gangster brat without any of his staff or guests being none the wiser. Tom hopped out of the car, circled back around to the trunk, and opened it.

Shivering underneath his blue overcoat, Mei-chen stared back at him like an innocent lamb. He helped her out before reclaiming his coat.

"Darling, please—" she began before Tom pressed his hand over her mouth. He couldn't risk falling for her sweet talk or calling for help like last time.

"Shut up. We're going upstairs and you won't say a damn thing. Understand?"

Mei-chen nodded and Tom removed his hand. Guiding her through the backdoor, Tom took a sharp right up the stairs, hoping no staff would see them. The blare of jazz and cacophonous voices leaked out from the dance hall, indicating that Club Twilight had a full house tonight. Tom kept the Browning automatic in his coat pocket but pressed firmly into Mei-chen's side as they ascended to the second story. No sign of any porters just yet, but he wasn't taking chances and went straight to his apartment.

Pushing Mei-chen inside, Tom slammed the door shut and locked it. He gestured for her to sit next to the vanity table and searched for something to tie her up with. Rummaging through the closet, he pulled out a few scarves and went to work, pinioning her arms to her sides with cloth. In her red cheongsam, black gloves, and bound with multi-colored scarves, Mei-chen looked like a wrapped-up Christmas present. Tom expelled a relaxed sigh, knowing this tricky snake wasn't going anywhere.

"Darling please, if we could just talk, we could work something out—"

He cut her off by wrapping a silk handkerchief around her mouth, knotting it tightly.

"You've done enough talking," he said. "Why don't you have a time out and think about what you've done?"

Mei-chen protested into the gag, turning her words into gibberish. That ought to keep her from calling out for help, but Tom still didn't want any disturbances. He'd lose face if his staff found a bound and gagged woman in his quarters.

"Don't go anywhere," he said, then stalked out of the apartment and shut the door.

Following the hypnotic melodies drifting from below, Tom walked down the stairs and into the main hall of Club Twilight. The band streamed out that Oriental ditty "Little Yella Cinderella," fitting background music for the legion of taxi dancers out on the dance floor with their clients. Tom swept his gaze across and took in the packed house.

Each individual table was occupied, including Whitfield's usual one. It was hard to believe he was never coming back. An ocean of different races mixed together – brown, black, yellow, and white – all united by frivolous decadence. Men and women dressed to the nines toasted each other at the bar, celebrating that Shanghai wasn't going to blow itself up after all.

The air was thick with the smell of cigarette smoke and perfume, and Tom breathed it all in. Mounted on the wall were the flags of his two countries – the Stars and Stripes with the White Sun – filling him with a proud patriotism. More guests crammed onto the dance floor, frolicking without a care. Tom imagined this must be how Babylon looked just before the fall. But it was all his. This was his club, his city, his world.

Tom approached the bar and ordered a J&B on the rocks. He grabbed the glass and leaned closer.

"I'm going to be up in my room," he said, raising his voice over the music. "I'm not to be disturbed under *any* circumstances." He paused, then added, "That is, until Feng Lung-wei arrives."

Concern shone on the bartender's face, but he responded with an understanding nod. Tom raised his glass to the frolicking mass.

"Cheers, Shanghai," he said, before walking out of the main room and back up the stairs.

CHAPTER THIRTY

Tom shut and locked the door and Mei-chen fixed him with an agitated glare. Through her gag, she bombarded him with muffled complaints, all of which he ignored. That supposedly "lucky" cricket still lay on the ground, smashed into a brown paste. Tom knew how he must have felt.

With his Scotch on the rocks in hand, he sauntered over to the bed, now splotched with brown stains of dried blood. They'd hauled Yoshida's corpse out but didn't bother taking the sheets. What did he expect from Shanghai cops? Evil spirits tended to linger in areas of violent death, and needed monks to exorcise them. But after what he'd been through, evil spirits didn't scare Tom much anymore. He plopped down on the mattress with an exasperated sigh.

Roped up in her chair, Mei-chen inched around to face Tom, then gave another strangled protest.

"If I remove the gag, you have to promise not to scream for help like last night," he said, in between sips of his J&B. "Deal?"

Mei-chen gave eager, impatient nods. Tom reached over and yanked the gag off.

"What are you going to do with me?" she demanded in English.

Tom took another sip of whiskey. "That's for Feng Lung-wei to decide, sweetheart."

Fear widened Mei-chen's eyes and sent her lip trembling. "You would really turn me over to that monster?"

"Better you than me."

"I never knew you could be so coldblooded," she scoffed.

Anger and bitterness raced through Tom, tightening his fingers around the glass.

"You're one to talk," he snapped. "You used me. All the 'darlings' and the 'I love yous' were all just a con, weren't they? All you were ever interested in was my club and who you could meet through it. Me and Chuck were just little bugs caught in your web. How many others did you snare?"

Mei-chen went silent and lowered her eyes to the floor.

"Plenty, I'm sure," Tom said. "Your lies are finally catching up with you. It's your fault that Yan and Chuck are dead." He glanced over to the dried blood patch. "Yoshida too, although I'm more upset about my ruined sheets. I would have been victim number four, since you set me up to take the fall."

Still looking downward, Mei-chen said, "That's not true. I didn't want to involve you."

"Well, you know everything about me. I poured my heart out and you lapped it up, just like a good spy. You know who Thomas Lai is, inside and out. But I don't know anything about Ho Mei-chen other than the lies you fed me about your family being executed by a warlord." Tom sipped his J&B and exhaled. "So, let's start with your real name. What is it?"

Mei-chen lifted her eyes up and met him with a sorrowful gaze. "As I said before...does it really matter?"

"It does to me. I want to know who I spent the last two years of my life with."

With a heavy sigh and resigned nod, she began. "My birth name is unimportant. You see, I'm an orphan, born and raised in Taiwan."

The statement snapped everything else into clarity. Taiwan had been Japanese colony ever since China's crushing defeat in 1895. It all made sense. Her Fukienese accent made sense, since many Taiwanese ancestors originally came from the Fukien province. Furthermore, the Japanese had outlawed foot binding years ago. It wasn't a progressive father who'd saved Mei-chen from that barbaric practice, but rather the Mikado. Most importantly, her declaration back at Whitfield's apartment – '*I have no country*' – made sense now.

Tom took a gulp of Scotch, then asked, "So when did you begin working for the Japanese?"

"I grew up in an orphanage, but was sent to primary school. Most girls stop attending in their teens to become wives, but I showed an aptitude for languages. This attracted the attention of the Colonial Government and officers of the Japanese Navy."

"Let me guess. Was Commander Fukuzaki one of them?"

Mei-chen nodded. "Yes, but he was only a lieutenant back then. I still remember the day we met. It was hot and humid, but he looked magnificent in his white uniform and epaulettes. He told me as a citizen of the Japanese Empire, it was my duty to use my skills to serve the Emperor."

"Sounds like you were the perfect candidate."

"Orphans usually are," she said with a little smile. "I was taken to a special school run by the Navy where I learned so many dialects and languages. After graduation, I was sent to Shanghai where my tongue could be put to good use."

Tom sighed. "There *are* more languages than people in this city."

"My first assignment was at the Great World as a taxi dancer. It was easy to meet foreign businessmen – British, American, French, Italian. Over drinks I could pry secrets out of them. Why they were in Shanghai, the financial dealings of this or that bank, insider knowledge of stocks. That sort of thing. But after a while, Commander Fukuzaki wanted more political intelligence."

"And this is where I come in?"

"Yes…you had just opened up Club Twilight and already ingratiated yourself with the Nationalist Party. I realized the potential, since so many diplomats attended your club. When you visited the Great World that night, I asked you to dance and—"

"I fell for it like a mark at a poker game," Tom said with a bitter sigh. "How many other men were there besides me?"

Shame pushed Mei-chen's gaze downward. "Three, all of whom worked at different consulates. Charles Whitfield was the latest."

An enraged part of Tom wanted to hurl the glass across the room, but another even more cynical side couldn't help but laugh at what a fool he'd been.

"Guess now I know where you really went during your mid-day shopping excursions."

"A girl can do two things in one day."

That earned a chuckle out of Tom and he took another sip of J&B.

"So, did Commander Fukuzaki order you to America?"

A look of anger swept over Mei-chen and she shook her head. "No, absolutely not. I was going to America on my own accord."

"A freelance spy?"

"No, all I wanted was to start over. This life...spying for the Japanese...it's killing me, Tom. I'm not cut out for it. I hate this city and what it's turned me into." Tears moistened her eyes. "I'm so ashamed for everything I've done to you. To Charles."

"You killed him."

"It was an accident!" she said with a little sob. "Don't you think I feel terrible?"

Tom barked a cynical laugh. "Do you now? Weren't you just using him?"

"Commander Fukuzaki wanted information on US gunboats in China and what America would do if a Sino-Japanese War broke out in Shanghai. So, I struck up a relationship with Charles behind your back. It wasn't hard, since he was genuinely fond of me."

"I'm aware of that now."

"Oh, Tom...I really did want to start a new life with you, I truly did. But you were taking so long to move to San Francisco, I just couldn't wait. War was looming."

Tom sighed and swirled the ice in his glass. Perhaps if he hadn't waited, none of this would have happened. After all, he was only saving money to afford that fancy Victorian in Nob Hill. He even shortchanged the Kuomintang on his annual donation, all for this beautiful creature trussed up before him.

"After I passed those documents along," Mei-chen continued, "I asked Charles to forge the right credentials. I was to become Margaret Wong, an American citizen and leave Shanghai behind me forever. He sympathized and risked his career for me."

"And his life."

She grimaced and bit her lip. "I…I didn't mean to. All I wanted was a new life…in *Meikuo*."

"Well, if you had just waited then you would have gotten your ticket to San Francisco," Tom said. "Or haven't you heard? There isn't going to be any war. Mayor Wu accepted the Japanese demands."

A mocking laughter filled the room. "You don't know the Japanese like I do. Manchuria made the Navy jealous. They want war to prove to the Emperor that they're true warriors. Besides, it's not just Commander Fukuzaki provoking these incidents."

"What do you mean?" Tom asked.

"Remember those Japanese monks who were assaulted?"

"How could I forget?" Tom asked with a shrug.

Mei-chen continued, "An Army attaché, Major Tanaka and his mistress, a Manchu princess, paid Chinese thugs to attack them. Shanghai was already a powder box, and they hoped that incident would ignite the conflagration. At least, that's what I've heard."

"Commander Fukuzaki must have been jealous of their plans. Two nights ago, I saved a Japanese couple from three Chinese hoods in the pay of Yoshida," he said, pointing to the blood stain.

Mei-chen gave another laugh. "The Imperial Army and Navy compete over everything, even staging phony attacks."

Tom almost howled at the absurdity of it all. Phony attacks with real victims. He thought back to the fight with

Yoshida in the Golden Unicorn pub, then to Yan Ping's murder, and near decapitation of Mei-chen. Then it dawned on him.

"Yoshida didn't know who you were? That's why he almost killed you."

"With spies, everything is compartmentalized. The less people know, the less they'll reveal under torture. That's why Yoshida tried to kill too, in a misguided attempt to regain his honor. He didn't know you ran the club that supplied Fukuzaki with intelligence. Why should he? Yoshida was an agent provocateur, not a spy."

Tom rubbed his neck involuntarily. "Well, face is *everything* in Shanghai," he said, before polishing off the rest of his Scotch. The burning liquid slid down his throat, leaving him relaxed. Ho Mei-chen – whoever she was – was more of an enigma than he thought. Whether this latest version of her past was the truth or complete fiction was impossible to tell, and perhaps it didn't really matter anymore. She wore different masks for different people – but what was the real face behind them all? Perhaps there wasn't any.

Still, two questions remained and refused to be unanswered.

"Tell me," Tom said. "Did you love Whitfield?"

"No."

The answer came unforced, unrehearsed, and unemotional. Tom dreaded the next question, but he was unable to stop it from leaving his mouth.

"Did you ever love me?"

A brief melancholy shone in her brown eyes, before they settled to the floor. Her response was almost a whisper.

"No."

Well, at least she was honest. Tom reached over to the nightstand and set his empty glass atop an issue of *Photoplay*. Tears began to form, but he squeezed his eyes shut. No, he couldn't let her know how much she'd hurt him. Instead, Tom stood up and walked over to the phonograph, his back turned to her. Drying his eyes, he put on the record "Sing-Song Girl of Old Shanghai" and let the now-haunting melody fill the room.

Tom let his eyes wander everywhere else except to her – his US Army Citation Star, the framed photograph of him with Chiang Kai-shek, the squashed cricket on the ground. Anywhere but those alluring brown eyes that had hypnotized him so many times. He thought back to every dance, every kiss, every laugh, every night they'd shared together – all lies. He fumbled for his cigarette case and lit a Lucky Strike.

"Can I have a puff?" Mei-chen asked, raising her voice over the music.

Tom turned around to face her. Despite her pathetic condition, she wore a small smile. He pulled the cigarette and wedged it between her lips. She took a deep inhale, held it for a moment, then breathed it out through her nose. Tom took a drag and sat back on the bed.

"Don't all spies ask for a cigarette before they're executed?" he asked, looking up at the ceiling. "Just like Mata Hari."

"I hope I die beautifully," she said with a wistful sigh. She looked back over and added, "I never tried to frame you, Tom. I don't know why the Green Gang thinks you're involved in this sordid business, but I'll make sure they know you're innocent."

"Well, it is my club. But thanks anyway."

"Whatever happens…I…I just want to thank you…for everything. You're a decent man, Lai Huang-fu."

Tom couldn't suppress a smile. Perhaps it hadn't *all* been a lie.

A sudden knock at the door sounded like a machine gun.

"Who's there?" Tom demanded.

"Tick tock, Tommy!" Feng Lung-wei's reedy voice came through the other side. "Your time's up!"

CHAPTER THIRTY-ONE

Mei-chen flashed Tom a worried look, but within moments, a grim stoicism appeared on her pretty face. Tom hopped off the bed and opened the door. Feng Lung-wei – flanked by his two hulking henchmen – stared back at him. As always, he wore an overcoat over his black pinstripe suit, matching fedora, and an arrogant grin.

"We would have been here sooner but it's a damn madhouse out in Chapei," Feng said, walking inside the apartment. His two goons followed and slammed the door shut behind them. Focusing on Mei-chen, he said, "Well well, looks like you kept your promise, Tommy. You delivered the spy – gift wrapped!"

Feng's two gorillas shared a laugh.

"I'm surprised, Tommy," Feng continued, slapping Tom on the back. "Didn't think you had it in you. Figured you as too soft."

Such praise made Tom's skin crawl. He cast a forlorn glance over at Mei-chen, who wore a dignified expression even in such humiliation.

"Just take her and go," he managed to say.

Feng didn't respond and instead circled the tied up girl, his eyes crawling all over her. After a moment, he took her by the chin and leaned closer.

"Are you really a Japanese spy?" Feng asked. "Or are you just taking the fall for your little boyfriend?"

"Tom had nothing to do with my activities," Mei-chen fired back. "He is completely blameless."

Tom shot a thankful smile at Mei-chen. She didn't respond and fixed the three gangsters with a defiant glare.

Feng straightened up with a sigh. "That's too bad. You know, I really thought you two were working together with that American diplomat."

"I told you I was innocent," Tom said. "Now get out."

"Oh, not just yet Tommy. We just got here."

A cruel smile curled Feng Lung-wei's lips like a crawling centipede. He walked toward the door and beckoned for Tom to follow.

"Wait here boys," Feng said to his henchmen, now leering at Mei-chen's bound figure. Tom followed the gangster out the door and down the stairs. The main hall was still convulsing with life, now dancing to the tune of "Chinatown, My Chinatown." Feng Lung-wei gazed out into this multiracial sea of humanity with scornful eyes. A protective instinct went through Tom as a mother would feel toward her child.

"Why are you still here?" Tom demanded, raising his voice over the band. "Just take her and get the hell out of my club."

"That's what bothers me, Tommy. I don't think you deserve Club Twilight anymore."

Confusion and irritation loosened his tongue. "What was that? Get out of here before I throw you out!"

The threat did nothing to temper Feng's arrogance. "Let's talk in private. Order these," he gestured to around the room, "*people* to leave."

"Go to hell," Tom snarled.

With a shrug, Feng Lung-wei slid his hand into his jacket and pulled out a revolver, raised it into the air, and fired. A vicious shot rang out through Club Twilight, strangling the band's music into dead silence. Mute horror rippled over the guests, who gawked at Tom and Feng with incredulity.

"Tell these nice people to leave," Feng Lung-wei said, lowering his voice to a dull growl, "or I'll have my men barricade the doors and kill every single one of them."

A malevolent twinkle in Feng's eye confirmed it was no idle threat. After all, sadism came as naturally to this gangster brat as if scratching an itch. Tom swallowed, stepped forward, and summoned his most dignified and authoritative voice.

"I'm sorry, but Club Twilight is closed for tonight. We must ask you all to leave."

There were a few offended gasps and hushed protests, but the guests began filing out in an orderly fashion. There was an understanding as they grabbed their hats and coats – after all, this was Shanghai. Crime and chaos were part of the charm, especially in the rough and tumble Chapei district. There were always more tame nightclubs in the International Settlement. Customers threw back their drinks and headed out, while one of the bartenders trotted up to Tom.

"Boss, is everything okay?"

Maintaining composure was always important, especially in front of subordinates. Tom gave a confident nod and sent the bartender on his way. Within twenty minutes, Club Twilight had been drained of its guests like a deflating balloon. The band and bartenders hesitated, looking back at Tom with worried expressions. Tom dismissed them with a jovial and good-natured wave of his hand.

The doors shut and Tom turned to face Feng Lung-wei. "What the hell is this all about? Are you going to kill Mei-chen right on the dance floor?"

"No, not her," the gangster said with more ominous tone than usual.

Tom realized he was deeper in trouble than he'd thought, like a swimmer carried out to sea by the tide. He reached for the Browning automatic in his shoulder holster but it was too late. Feng Lung-wei had his revolver leveled straight at his forehead.

"Easy now, Tommy. Let's not do anything rash."

Feng reached inside Tom's jacket and pulled out the pistol, then pocketed it in his coat. With the revolver, he gestured Tom over to the bar, where he took a seat on one of the stools. The gangster then looked up toward the stairs and called out, "Come on down, boys!"

Within moments, the two gorillas thundered down the steps and into the main room. One of the mugs had Mei-chen tossed over his shoulder, laughing as she squirmed against her bonds. He plopped her down on a barstool next to Tom.

"Careful you idiot," Feng complained. "We mustn't damage the merchandise. Release her. I want a better look."

The gangster's thick, meaty hands gripped the binding scarves around her body and ripped them asunder like strings. Despite being free, Mei-chen remained rigid on the stool.

"Come here, beautiful," Feng Lung-wei said, beckoning nearer. Mei-chen glanced over to Tom, then slid off the stool and walked closer to the gangsters. Feng inspected every inch of her – her legs, her breasts, her neck, her face – unable to hide his lust. With delicate precision, he began lifting the slit in her *cheongsam* with his revolver barrel. It raised up and up, until Mei-chen ended his fun with a gloved slap to the face.

The two thugs edged closer, but Feng waved them off. Rubbing his cheek, he laughed and gave her a final look over.

"Quite feisty, isn't she Tommy? How did you ever handle her?"

Tom had wondered that himself. Now he knew. She had allowed him to.

"Go ahead and shoot me," Mei-chen said, bracing her frame. "Just make it quick."

Feng burst out a snarling laughter. "Oh it won't be…for either of you."

"I told you! Tom Lai is innocent!"

"Yes, I can see that now." Feng gave resigned shrug. "But it really doesn't matter anymore."

"What the hell are you talking about?" Tom said, leaping up from the barstool.

Feng held up a silencing hand. "I'll explain every as soon as my partner arrives."

Mei-chen and Tom traded confused looks. Partner? What was Feng talking about? For a brief, frightening moment, he pictured Commander Fukuzaki walking through the door.

Was he really the victim of a dark conspiracy coordinated by the Green Gang and Japanese Naval Intelligence? After the past two days, it wouldn't surprise him. Tom looked down at his Rolex. Two minutes passed. Then five. Then twelve.

Finally, the door opened and in walked a nondescript Chinese man in a gray overcoat and hat. His bespectacled face was bland, without distinguishing features but Tom recognized him instantly. The man from the Finance Ministry – Chow Chun-wah.

CHAPTER THIRTY-TWO

Tom stared in stupefied disbelief. What the hell was this little bureaucrat doing here? Unless…Captain Tung had finally managed to reach Chow! Tom's heart fluttered with apprehensive joy and he slid off the barstool to his feet. But Chow passed Tom with a contemptuous glare, before shaking hands with Feng Lung-wei. Tom felt like a drowning man taking a final gulp of air before going under. There was no escape now. But if he were to die tonight, he'd at least know why.

Tom balled his fists. "What are you doing here, Mr. Chow?" he asked in Cantonese.

Feng and Chow turned to examine Tom like a rat in a cage.

"Mr. Feng invited me here to take a look at our new club," the Finance Ministry man replied in English. There was more to this snake than he let on.

"*Your* new club?"

"Yes, Tommy," Feng cut in, spreading his arms wide to take in all of Club Twilight. "This has so much potential! So much space! So many extra rooms! And so many patrons! And yet you squander it all! No opium, no gambling, no whores! Bah!"

"That was the deal I made with Tu Yueh-sheng," Tom fired back.

"Yes, Uncle Tu has always had bad judgment when it comes to you. Luckily, I found a different investor," Feng said, clapping Chow on the shoulder. "He will provide the initial capital for renovations. After all, we'll have to add a gambling hall, an opium den, and—" Feng cast a wolfish glance at Mei-chen "—a brothel. Club Twilight will become Feng Lung-wei's Pleasure Palace! It will be my answer to the Great World!"

Anger, regret, and humiliation all clamped around Tom's throat like a vice. He looked at Mei-chen, staring at him with a longing sympathy. Everyone in Shanghai had made a fool of Tom Lai – his mistress, his best friend, the Japanese, the Kuomintang, and especially that cackling jackal in the pinstripe suit.

"You set me up as a Japanese spy just to steal my club?"

An offended look swept over Feng's face. "Nobody set you up, Tommy. I was telling you the truth. My uncle did task me with finding Jap spies. We tracked Ono down to your club and picked him up. He didn't know exactly who his contact was, but he figured it was you since you owned the joint, spoke English, and had a friend in the American Consulate. Little did Ono know that it was actually your little twist over there." He leered again at Mei-chen.

"You're still going to kill me, even after you know I'm not the spy?"

"I was prepared to kill you as soon as I saw that Ono slithering out of Club Twilight. Unfortunately, Uncle Tu restrained me. He told me we have to wait and see what Mr. Chow says."

That was surprising. "Since when does a bureaucrat from the Finance Ministry give orders to the Grandmaster of the Green Gang?"

Adjusting his glasses with a sly smile, Chow said, "I've had a business relationship with Mr. Tu and Mr. Feng for several months now."

"Let me guess? Kickbacks? Government contracts? Siphoning off taxpayer money to line your pockets?"

Chow and Feng shared an agreeable nod. "Yes, to all three," the bureaucrat replied. "You see, Tu Yueh-sheng informed me about your alleged espionage activities, since he knew I was going to ask for a donation. I told him that you were too valuable a donor to lose, even if you were a spy. Of course, my opinion changed when you gave wrote a check for an amount far less than I had anticipated. I suppose Club Twilight isn't as profitable as it had once been. After our dinner at the American Club, I called Mr. Tu and told him that the Kuomintang has reconsidered your usefulness. Under Mr. Feng's stewardship, I expect this club will yield much higher returns."

"Now, Mr. Chow will get a permanent cut of the profits when we reopen this joint," Feng said. "A much better deal than begging you for scraps."

A sickening humiliation gnawed at Tom's stomach. He looked again at Mei-chen, who stared shamefully at the floor. After all, he had only shortchanged Chow in order to save for their new life in San Francisco – a Victorian in Nob Hill, a maid, a butler, and a new nightclub. His devotion to her had written him a death warrant. It was as if all Shanghai had conspired against him.

"So, this is how you treat fellow Party members?" Tom managed to croak out. "Does Chiang Kai-shek know about what you're doing?"

"The Generalissimo is a busy man," Chow said with a shrug. "Too busy to delve too deeply into this matter. I'm sure he will believe the evidence provided confirming that Lai Huang-fu was actually a Japanese agent."

Tom fought down a bitter bile rising in his throat. Everything he'd done for Chiang, the Kuomintang, and for China – all just a bad joke. Maybe his father had been right all along. Patriotism was for suckers. He focused his attention back on Feng.

"So, Tu Yueh-sheng signed off on your little scheme?"

A dark bitterness clouded Feng Lung-wei's youthful face. "No, my uncle is too soft on you Tommy. That's why he gave you forty-eight hours to prove your innocence. He really didn't want to believe you were a Jap spy."

It was so absurd that Tom almost laughed. In the end, the two most trustworthy people in Shanghai turned out to be the stoic soldier Captain Tung and the crime lord of the underworld, Big-Eared Tu. Tom Lai was the conduit for the high and the low in society.

"The only reason you're still alive is out of respect for Uncle Tu's wishes. In exactly," Feng paused to glance at his wristwatch, "three minutes, you'll be executed as a spy."

"Tom had nothing to do with this! Let him go!" Mei-chen cried out.

Another bout of cackling poured out of Feng and his thugs. "It doesn't matter if he did or didn't. The important thing is, Uncle Tu will *think* that Tom Lai is a treacherous Jap agent. But don't think I've forgotten about you." A hideous smile spread across Feng's lips. "You'll become a permanent attraction here."

Mei-chen's eyes widened as Feng took rapid steps toward her.

"We can't have this beauty go to waste," he said, taking her by the chin. "But some modifications must be made. First, I'll cut out her tongue so she won't go blabbing the truth. Then we'll dope her up with enough opium to turn her brain into soup. From there on, Ho Mei-chen will be a living, breathing toy, just conscious enough to spread her legs for the next customer."

As Feng leered, Mei-chen kept an aloof poise, but a tremble in her lips betrayed her fear. Despite everything that had happened, despite all the trouble she'd caused for him, Tom couldn't suppress a protective instinct for his Beautiful Pearl. If he was going to die, he'd at least go out fighting. He rushed forward toward Feng, but was blocked by the two gorillas forming a human barricade around their master. One henchman hammered his rocklike fist into Tom's gut, sending him keeling over.

"Aww, too bad Tommy," Feng hissed with taunting laughter. He pushed Mei-chen into the arms of a nearby thug, who gripped her like iron. "Now everything you had is mine. Your girl, your club," Feng checked his watch again, "and now your life. It's eleven o'clock and that means your time is up."

Although his insides twisted with pain, Tom managed to prop himself up against the bar counter. Chow and the gangsters laughed again, relishing his misery and humiliation. Tom steeled himself and met Feng Lung-wei's mockery with an air of unbroken defiance.

"Go ahead and take it. Stealing is the only way bums like you get anything in this world."

The cruel laughter faded.

"The truth is I've always been better than you," Tom continued, his posture stiffening with every word. "And you're jealous. I've built one of the most popular nightclubs in Shanghai and all you have is that little rat's nest you call an opium den. That's why you hate me. Because I'm better than you in every way."

Now it was Tom's turn to laugh. A thick silence filled the empty club, like the early portents of an approaching disaster. Feng Lung-wei's youthful face convulsed with bitter hatred, before he finally erupted.

"Shut up! Shut up! Shut up! You don't know the shame of having the great Tu Yueh-sheng prefer a *foreigner* over his own…his own…"

Feng trailed off, realizing his slip. But Tom didn't need to hear the actual word. These weren't the rantings of a slighted nephew, but rather the cries of an unloved, bastard son who needed his daddy's approval. How could he have not realized it sooner? There were plenty of rumors about Tu Yueh-sheng's illegitimate children birthed from his many concubines. The Grandmaster of the Green Gang must have been too ashamed of this vicious whelp to even admit Lung-wei was his own son – albeit a bastard son – which explained the story of him being a mere "nephew." Not that Tom blamed Big-Eared Tu for the cover up. Feng's cruelty was more on par with Jack the Ripper than the ruthless professionals in an organized crime syndicate.

Feng straightened up and continued his rant.

"To hear him doubt your sanity! But I've always tried to make him proud. I killed dozens of Communists for him, but all he gave me was that pathetic little opium den to manage."

Spittle and phlegm shot out of Feng's mouth like a mad dog. His angry, reddened face and big ears combined to make this sadistic brat look like an actual *mogwai* demon from hell. After a long, calming breath, Feng regained some semblance of composure. Continuing a temper tantrum like that meant severe loss of face.

"But now, I've caught two Jap spies! And when I open my new pleasure palace, even the great Tu Yueh-sheng will be impressed! At long last, he will boast how proud he is of me!"

"So that's what this is about? God, you're even more pathetic than I thought," Tom said, shaking his head. He fixed a contemptuous gaze straight on Feng Lung-wei. "Go ahead and shoot me. I don't even want to live in the same city with a worm like you."

A cruel smile plastered itself across Feng's lips. "Oh no, Tommy. I promised you it wouldn't be that quick. For starters, I think I'll cut every tendon in your body and turn you into a human jellyfish. Then I'll leave you in a cellar for a few days before deciding what to do with you next."

Cacophonous laughter filled the club, like devils shrieking with pleasure. Tom and Mei-chen shared a final, sympathetic look, wondering whose fate was worse. Just then, an explosion of gunfire ripped through the air.

"That came from outside!" Chow exclaimed.

Feng ordered one of the gorillas to investigate. Within moments, the thug had walked out the doors and then returned in a panicked hurry.

"Boss, it's the Japanese!" he cried, his thick face contorted with terror. "They're attacking!"

CHAPTER THIRTY-THREE

"What do you mean they're attacking?" Feng Lung-wei snarled.

"I just saw a truckload of Imperial Marines," his henchman blubbered in panic. "They must be all over Chapei!"

Tom couldn't hide his surprise, until he remembered the angry mobs he'd driven past burning Rising Sun flags, hanging effigies of the Mikado, and pummeling Japanese civilians. Perhaps Japan felt war was better than national humiliation.

"You idiot," Feng roared at Chow. "Your information was wrong! You said the Japanese wouldn't attack!"

The bureaucrat couldn't disguise his terror. He wrung his trembling hands and darted his eyes back and forth. "Mayor Wu accepted the demands, didn't he? I don't know why they're attacking! Oh, we have to get out of here! They'll kill us!"

"No!" Feng barked. "We stay and fight." He snapped his fingers at one of the gorillas. "The Thompson is in the Mercedes' trunk."

"But boss, the Japanese devils might shoot me—"

Feng jammed the Smith & Wesson revolver into the gangster's cheek. "Either they will or I will! Now go!"

The henchman nodded and again lumbered out the front door. More sounds leaked through as he left – the crackle of gunshots, thunderous explosions, and horrified screams – all mixing together in a dreadful symphony. But in that moment, an opening presented itself. Feng's attention was on Chow and the terror outside. Now or never. He pushed himself off the bar and raced forward.

The revolver whooshed around and aimed straight at Tom's heart.

Feng Lung-wei wagged a finger. "Uh, uh, uh, Tommy. Don't make me finish you off like this. I have something more fun planned for you."

The front doors opened and in walked the hulking thug, clutching a menacing black object. It was the same Thompson submachine gun that had blown Ono to pulpy bits two nights ago. Tom swallowed hard as he saw his future in its barrel. Well, at least it was better than having every tendon sliced.

Feng and his henchman exchanged firearms, and the Thompson swung around in Tom's direction. The gangster brat gripped its handles and eyed him up and down, accentuating the power he held. However, Chow was less impressed.

"Mr. Feng," he whined. "We can't waste any time. I'm an important man in the Ministry of Finance! They might hold me for ransom or—"

"Shut up!" Feng roared. "Are you a man or a woman? As soon as I finish off Tommy, we're going to kill every single one of those Japanese devils outside."

"Fight? Are you quite mad? We're not soldiers," Chow protested with a quivering voice.

"No, but we're Chinese! And we will defend our city to the death!" Feng cried. His patriotism was stirring, Tom conceded. Perhaps it wasn't for suckers after all. "But first, I have to tie up this knot."

Tom ignored the butchered idiom and backed up until he hit the bar counter, his eyes fixated on the submachine gun's barrel and drum. It was all over now. The only option now was to accept it.

His mind wandered to his parents, and if they would ever know what happened to their second son. He tore his eyes off the Tommy gun and focused on Mei-chen, helplessly squirming in one of the gangster's firm grasp. He closed his eyes and bid farewell – to his family, to Mei-chen, and to Shanghai. But an eerie whistling noise opened his eyes. He'd heard that strange sound before in the trenches of France. It was the same scream of a falling bomb or incoming artillery shell.

Just as realization set in, the world exploded.

*****

The black river carried Tom downstream. Unable to resist, he lay on his back, stupefied and numb like an opium addict. Why fight it anymore? It was better this way. Painless and comforting. In a few moments, he'd be swallowed up by the abyss.

A hand dove into the dark water and gripped his arm. It heaved and pulled against the murky current, dragging Tom out onto the dry shore. He opened his eyes.

Mei-chen was crouching over him, rubbing her gloved hand across his cheek. No, not rubbing. A hard slap brought him further out of his daze. His ears were ringing, but the high-pitched drone was beginning to fade. He sat up, and found that his legs were covered in debris – splintered wood paneling, nothing too heavy. Mei-chen began pushing the rubble off. He groaned and kicked his legs free. Tom then took in the rest of his surroundings and found a wasteland.

Half of Club Twilight was completely destroyed, blasted to bits and powder. Only a gutted, skeletal frame was left behind. Broken glass, chunks of concrete, twisted metal, and ripped plaster covered the ground like an uneven, jagged carpet. He looked up and the roof had been ripped clean off, revealing a moonless night. Strangely, most of the bar had remained intact – bottles of Jack Daniel's, J&B, Bacardi Rum, and Beefeater Gin stood erect and unfazed. Neon lights from the International Settlement illuminated the sky just enough to see the dark outlines of airplanes buzzing above. Had it been a bomb or a shell that had hit them? Didn't really matter now, did it?

The ringing in Tom's ears faded out completely, replaced by his own panicked breathing and his heart thumping against his ribcage. Club Twilight – his business, his home, his kingdom – was gone. He'd given his heart and soul to this place and it had all gone up in smoke in a matter of seconds. He wanted to cry, but no tears came. His nerves, his mind, his soul, went numb. His eyes swept the carnage, trying to find some proof that it was only a dream, a hideous nightmare, but found only more horrors.

A mangled corpse lay sprawled out a few feet away, singed and blackened. A pair of shattered glasses was enough to identify the body as Chow. Beyond him was another corpse, pulverized underneath a heap of debris. Blood oozed out as if he'd been put in an enormous vice and squeezed till his whole body burst. Although grotesque and swollen, Tom still recognized the poor bastard as one of Feng Lung-wei's two henchmen.

But where was that gangster brat himself? To his surprise, the other muscle-bound gorilla – very much alive – was busy helping his boss out of the rubble and to his feet. Feng Lung-wei still clutched the Tommy gun like a mother would her child. Although his pinstripe suit and overcoat were ripped in places, Feng was unscathed, albeit a bit groggy. He wobbled back and forth, steadied only by his henchman's firm hand.

The Tommy gun swooshed in Feng's shaky hands and unleashed a barrage of bullets. But his aim was off and the lethal spray poured into what remained of the bar, shattering the liquor bottles with violent explosive bursts. His mind and will deadened, Tom just sat there next to Mei-chen as the broken glass rained down like crystal showers. The Tommy gun fire arched and stopped as Feng Lung-wei – still woozy – almost keeled over. The beefy thug grabbed him and strained to keep his boss upright.

Mei-chen's gripped Tom by the shoulders, jerking him back and forth.

"Tom, we have to get out of here!" she cried.

After a few moments, Tom's numbness faded rand was replaced by a visceral instinct. She was right, they had to get out of there. Feng Lung-wei would recover soon and finish them off anyway. There was one opportunity for escape – the Bentley out back.

Summoning the entirety of his strength, he rose with Mei-chen and plodded their way through the wreckage, navigating in between the bombed-out hallways and walls that were left standing. Reaching what had once been the back door, they discovered a new shock. The Bentley was still there, but a pile of debris had caved the roof in as if it were a tin can. All four tires had burst under the pressure, just to add insult to injury.

"Son of a bitch," Tom growled, slamming his fist against the twisted hood. Mei-chen tugged at his arm, leading him away from the Bentley and into a back alleyway.

"We have to go, Tom! He'll kill us!"

Shots of rifle fire echoed through the night, confirming that the fighting was still on. But war or no war, they'd have to lose Feng Lung-wei in the streets of Chapei if they hoped to survive the night. Tom took one final look at the ruins of Club Twilight and said his farewell. Bitter tears surfaced but he blotted them out. Then, he turned with Mei-chen and ran for his life.

CHAPTER THIRTY-FOUR

The streets of Chapei were a choked with panicked people running pell-mell. An animalistic terror hung in the night air, so thick it was palpable. The fleeing throngs were made up of every facet of Chinese society – lowly coolies, overeducated students with protest signs, factory workers, women from the cotton mills, refugee peasants who'd fled famine and floods and now ran from bombs and bullets. The seething crowds rushed eastward, toward the International Settlement and safety.

Tom gripped Mei-chen's hand as they ran alongside this sea of humanity. A loud buzzing drone up above demanded his attention. He looked up and – despite the moonless night – saw the outlines of several biplanes buzzing around over Chapei. Bombs released from their undersides, falling to the ground with a hideous whine. Explosions ripped apart buildings, sending plumes of smoke surging up into the dark sky.

Those bastards were bombing the city! Similar raids had happened during the fiendish savagery of the World War, but technology had improved much in the last eighteen years. How much damage could modern airplanes do? In that billowing smoke, Tom could see the future of warfare. Everyone – soldier and civilian – would be a combatant.

Tom swallowed his anger and kept running, never lessening his grip on Mei-chen's hand. How strange to be running with a woman he'd handed over for certain death less than an hour ago. But out here, in this hellish night, nothing made sense any longer. People pushed, clawed, and trampled over each other just to gain a few extra feet. Maybe this is what Pompeii looked like just before it was smothered by volcanic ash.

Up ahead was the intersection of Kungwoo and Washun Road, where another swarm of people merged into with the stampeding horde. They were still deep in Chapei but nearing the International Settlement with every step. Sure, they'd be in Little Tokyo when they crossed over, but the Chinese Army wouldn't dare cross the border lest they provoke all of the Western powers. The injustice of it left Tom with a bitter taste in his mouth. Even after Mayor Wu had accepted the demands, Japan had struck the first blow without warning. He could only hope men like Captain Tung were up to the challenge.

Behind them came a loud revving engine, like the roar of some enraged celestial dragon. Tom whipped his head around and saw a gleaming black Mercedes piling toward them. Gripping Mei-chen's hand, he pressed them both up against a building as the car sped past, plowing through the tail end of the fleeing throng. Pedestrians were catapulted aside and thrust up onto its hood in stunned disbelief. Primal screams merged with the existing chaos of the night, adding to the atmosphere of insanity. The car skidded to a grinding halt at the intersection of Kungwoo and Washun. People slid off the Mercedes, some dead, some howling in pain, but nobody stopped to help. The mad rush eastward didn't stop.

A door opened and out stepped Feng Lung-wei, Tommy gun in hand. He unleashed a volley of bullets, tearing huge gashes into the brick building Tom and Mei-chen were up against. Training leftover from the US Army kicked in, and Tom slammed his body to the ground, pulling Mei-chen down with him. Blazing away with the Thompson, Feng Lung-wei took halting, jerky steps toward them, laughing with sadistic glee. Still, his aim went awry, arching up and down, side effects from earlier. Although probably suffering from a concussion, this gangster brat was as dangerous as ever.

More people surged forward, paying little attention to this giggling madman with a Tommy gun. The firing stopped as Feng peered into the onrushing crowd. Crouching down,

Tom led Mei-chen to a nearby alleyway and braced himself. He'd only get one shot at this. He needed to put every ounce of his strength into this one blow. Balling his fist, Tom let his anger surge within him. Bitter memories surfaced – Feng Lung-wei's sadism, Chow's treachery, Mei-chen's double life, Whitfield's betrayal, and Club Twilight's utter destruction. They flowed through his veins, leaving him quaking with rage. Even more memories bubbled up. His uncle's murder, his father's constant criticisms, and a lifetime of slurs – Chink, Heathen Chinee, Slant Eyes, Yellow Monkey.

Feng Lung-wei turned into the alleyway, probing for a clear shot with the Thompson. Like a spring, Tom launched upward with a devastating uppercut, hurtling the gangster brat backward into the street. He followed up the attack with a hard right cross, and a swift blow to the gut. Feng doubled over, but Tom gave him no reprieve. Gripping Feng's collar, he hammered another punch dead center in his face. The gangster brat stumbled backward, collapsing a few feet away from the Mercedes, still parked at the intersection Kungwoo and Washun.

Although he still held the Tommy gun in an iron grip, Feng spat out a gory cocktail of blood and broken teeth. He looked up at Tom with a groggy, pained expression, and tried to lift the submachine gun, but wheezed and fell over. Taking huge gulps of air, the gangster struggled to maintain consciousness as he writhed about on the ground. Blood droplets flecked his white shirt and pinstripe suit. At this moment, Feng Lung-wei looked more like a wounded animal than a man. One stomp on his throat would finish off this vile creature. But before Tom could land the killing blow, Feng's henchman lurched out of the Mercedes to defend his master.

A frigid breeze rustled the thug's silk *changshan* shirt as he strode forward. Tom braced to defend himself and thrust out a quick jab into the gangster's meaty chin. The punch startled the brute but did little else. Drawing his thick fist backward, the thug landed a shattering punch into Tom's stomach, like a lion swatting a fly. The gangster landed another across his face. Before he knew it, Tom sagged to the pavement. He took in large gulps of the chilly night air to cool his burning lungs and tried to stand. But the thug's punches were too powerful, and he collapsed again.

Panicked masses continued to rush past them like a great surging river. Some glanced over at the strange scene unfolding before them, but still, nobody bothered to intervene. The brutish gangster loomed over Tom, a cruel sneer plastered over his thick lips. He rummaged through one of his voluminous sleeves and withdrew a pistol – Tom's Browning automatic. The thug pressed the muzzle against Tom's forehead for a quick execution.

But before the bullet came, two gloved hands wrapped around the gangster's thick, blocky head. The thug vomited out a guttural scream as he thrashed about, trying to dislodge his attacker. Mei-chen's slender body held tightly behind him, her fingers pressing deeper and deeper into the gorilla's eyes. The opportunity was quick, but Tom didn't hesitate. He launched forward and pounded the thug in the gut, doubling him over and sending the Browning pistol clattering to the floor.

Tom scooped it up and jerked it straight at Feng and his henchman. Mei-chen released her clawing grip and rushed over to Tom's side. The two gangsters stared in helpless horror. Blood drooled out of Feng's mouth but he said nothing, while the henchman held up pleading palms.

"Please…don't shoot venerable sir," the thug bawled out. Tom spat in disgust. Like so many tough guys of the underworld, they turned yellow when the shoe was on the other foot. Tom wanted to toy with them, make them squirm the way he had, but there was no time. Placing a bullet in their bellies so they could bleed out slowly would be fitting retribution. He aimed the automatic but an oncoming sight froze him stiff.

Coming north on Washun Road, an armored car stamped with a Rising Sun insignia trundled forward, following by a wall of Japanese Marines. Lighting the way with flares, the bluejackets kept a safe distance behind, but their rifles opened fire. Bullets crashed into the crowd, scattering people in all different directions. A sinister turret atop the armored car wobbled and took aim, sending a staccato volley into the chaos. Bullets screamed and whined, slapping the ground, the Mercedes' windows, and human flesh. Tom, Mei-chen, and the henchman all joined Feng on the ground as they took cover.

Dear God, they must be firing at him! After all, he was armed and it was easy to mistake him as a soldier in this darkness. Up ahead, the congestion was too great to make an escape, so they'd have to beat a retreat back the way they came. In the chaos, the henchman grabbed Feng Lung-wei – who still held his precious Tommy gun – and bundled him into the Mercedes. The thug took the wheel, fired up the engine, and rocketed northward down Washun Road, away from the Mikado's warriors.

A good idea. Before the Japanese could fire another volley, Tom and Mei-chen turned and ran westward on Kungwoo, deeper into Chapei.

CHAPTER THIRTY-FIVE

As Tom and Mei-chen ran, the streets grew more deserted and ghostly. Those brave enough to flee were already gone while the rest just hunkered down and prayed. Understandable. A squadron of fighter biplanes swarmed up above like hornets whose nest had been disturbed. There was just enough illumination from the International Settlement's neon lights to make out the Rising Sun roundels on their wings. Elsewhere in Chapei, the clouds of acrid smoke funneled high into the sky.

Just where the hell were the Chinese planes to intercept them? Maybe there weren't any. Instead, the Japanese pilots soared through the Shanghai sky as if it were a barnstorming performance. Up ahead, Tom could make out four uniformed figures in the gloomy distance. As they neared, aspects of their uniforms stood out – peaked caps, blue tunics, white gaiters. Some of the Mikado's Marines, no doubt.

Tom grabbed Mei-chen and dove behind a parked car, still intact despite the bombing. He raised the Browning automatic up, angling for a clear shot. But as the four figures approached, the uniforms became even clearer. Their peaked caps were ornamented with the White Sun emblem of the Kuomintang. Never in his life did Tom Lai expect to be grateful to see cops from the Public Security Bureau, but today was a strange day. He pocketed the Browning in his overcoat and Mei-chen called out.

"Chinese! Don't shoot!"

The four cops spun around, jerking their guns – three rifles and a Mauser pistol. It was obvious from the weaponry that these police officers were headed to the front lines.

"Who are you?" the senior officer barked, keeping his Mauser leveled.

"We just fled from the Japanese on Kungwoo Road," Tom said.

The officer's eyes widened. "Japanese? How many?"

"At least a full platoon," Tom said, before adding, "and an armored car."

The four policemen looked like they'd just swallowed broken glass. Still, their leader tried to dash any pessimism.

"We'll meet these invaders head on! Right men?"

The other cops gave languid nods.

"Where is the 19th Route Army?" Mei-chen asked.

The senior officer snorted. "The 19th Route Army has taken up defensive positions. As soon as the Japanese devils are in place, we'll spring the trap! We're on our way to give them support."

A harsh droning sound filled the air. Tom looked up and saw a white biplane offset by blood red roundels beginning to dive. Behind the buzzing propeller, a pair of machineguns spat flame and lead down at the street below. Tom and Mei-chen dove behind the nearby automobile, while the four police officers crouched down and fired their guns. The bullets kicked up chunks of pavement but failed to hit anything aside from parked cars and signposts.

The cops continued firing well after the Japanese plane disappeared into the murky night. Tom and Mei-chen emerged from behind the car, now riddled with bullets.

"Stinking dwarf bandits," the senior officer spat out. "We'll make them pay. This won't be like Manchuria, I swear it!"

"All well and good," Tom said, "but where are the Chinese planes? The Japanese have full control of the skies!"

"The Nationalist Government is sending planes down from Nanking, but it will take time," the officer said, examining Tom with a contemptuous sneer. "Who are you to criticize? An able-bodied man like yourself should be in the 19th Route Army!"

"I've already fought in a war," Tom said.

"Oh, have you now?" The senior officer looked Tom up and down. "Let me guess…former warlord soldier turned gangster?"

"I'm an American," Tom snapped back.

The officer sneered again. Mei-chen stepped forward, clasping her gloved hands together.

"Please elder brother, we're just trying to find shelter. Is there anywhere we can take refuge?"

She added an imploring smile, perfecting the image of a demure, helpless Chinese beauty. As if on cue, the cops caved.

"There's a few empty warehouses and cotton mills two blocks north. Hide in there until these planes disperse," the officer said, gesturing with his Mauser.

"Thank you, oh thank you, elder brother," Mei-chen cooed. The senior officer mustered his men and they marched eastward, toward the conflagration. Up above, the planes continued to circle the city like vultures over carrion.

*****

Just like the cop said, there were plenty of empty buildings to take refuge in, for the time being at least. Heavy artillery or bombs could pound them into dust in a moment's notice. Tom thought back to his time in the Argonne Forest. That war had been mostly been fought out in the fields, away from civilians. Sure, Zeppelins had bombed London and the Germans had shelled Paris, but the bulk of the war was between soldiers in the mud and slime of the trenches. This war was taking place in the most congested city on earth, block by block, house by house. The only hope now was that it'd be short.

They approached a dingy-looking cotton mill and yanked the door handle. Locked. Tom whipped out his Browning, fired a shot into the lock, and pushed the door open. Tom went in first, followed closely by Mei-chen. The first floor was comprised of several doors – all locked – so they ascended the stairs to the second story. A musty odor hung in the air, the concoction of years of sweat, tears, and blood. Imposing equipment lined the floors, the spinning machines and pirns that twirled cotton into all types of clothes. Just by the filth on the floor – dust, stains, and an occasional dead cockroach – Tom could tell that this cotton mill produced the cheapest goods for the hoi polloi of Shanghai.

Still, a refuge was a refuge, and they couldn't complain. But the smell was unbearable, so Tom walked over to the elongated window and cracked open a pane. Chilly air flooded in, and Mei-chen rubbed her gloved hands up and down her bare arms. Spy or not, Tom couldn't let a beautiful woman suffer. He rummaged in his coat pocket and removed the Browning pistol, but also grabbed the documents Whitfield had forged – the phony passport and birth certificate.

He slid the documents into his jacket, then removed the overcoat and threw it over Mei-chen's shoulders. On the second story, they had a clearer view of the International Settlement, bathed in a warm neon glow. For a moment, everything was forgotten and an aura of romance engulfed Tom. Without thinking, he leaned forward to kiss her, but stopped when the angry hum of planes buzzed up above.

As Mei-chen huddled close to him and Tom held her tight, they tensed into statues. A well-placed explosive would tear the cotton mill asunder and pulverize them into bloody smears. Would they be lucky enough to survive two bombings in one night? After minutes that felt like hours, the propeller drone faded and they both expelled relieved sighs.

"I'm sorry about Club Twilight," Mei-chen offered, wrapping the overcoat tighter around her.

Tom chuckled. "That's the one thing that isn't your fault."

"Still, I know how much it meant to you. It was a beautiful club."

"Yes…yes it was…"

They stared out the window at the twinkling lights of International Settlement. What a difference a few hours made. He'd gone from handing her over to the Green Gang, to being saved by her, and now they were on the run together like star-crossed lovers who'd just eloped.

Tom cleared his throat and asked, "Why did you save me? Back at the club…"

Mei-chen continued to stare out the window. "For all the trouble I've caused you…it's the least I could do."

Tom couldn't argue with that. He wasn't ready to forgive Ho Mei-chen – or whatever her real name was – but he could try not to hate her.

"What are we going to do?"

Tom shrugged. "What can we do? Try and survive the night. Hopefully, a truce will be declared soon."

"I hope so…"

They stood in a tense silence, punctured by the crack of rifle fire and fading screams in the distance. They'd have to stay here throughout the night and, come morning, try and make it into a neutral zone. Down on the street below, a pair of headlights sliced through the darkness. A bullet-riddled Mercedes ground to a halt and out stepped four sinister figures. Feng Lung-wei, brandishing the Tommy gun like a torch, his gorilla henchman, and two Chinese police officers – Sergeant Frankenstein and Lieutenant Kuo.

CHAPTER THIRTY-SIX

Tom and Mei-chen crouched down but kept close to the open window. They shared an apprehensive look before peering back down to the street below. With a torn suit and overcoat and bloody splotches around his mouth, Feng Lung-wei looked as if he'd returned from the dead. But the others huddled around him like baseball players around their coach.

"You're sure Lai Huang-fu is here?" Feng asked, lisping slightly from a bloody mouthful of broken teeth.

"My men reported that they saw two people matching the description of Lai and his little whore," Lieutenant Kuo said. "They directed them to hide out here and wait for the bombing to end."

Feng snorted. "Fine. We'll search the warehouse," he said, pointing with his Tommy gun across the street. "You and the Sergeant will take the cotton mill." He pointed up toward the window. Tom and Mei-chen crouched lower.

"But Mr. Feng," Kuo whined. "The Sergeant and I need to return to our men. The Police are the first line of defense against the Japanese—"

Feng shoved the barrel of the Tommy gun underneath Kuo's chin, nearly lifting the Lieutenant off his feet.

"What the hell do I pay you for? Lai Huang-fu dies first. I can't have him going off and talking to my uncle. As soon as Lai is dead, then we'll kill those dwarf bandits one by one. Understand?"

"Yes, sir! Whatever you say, sir!" Kuo gurgled out, and Feng tore the Tommy gun away. The gangsters broke off and entered the dim, forbidding warehouse, while Lieutenant Kuo and Sergeant Frankenstein advanced into the cotton mill. Tom whipped out the Browning automatic and gestured for Mei-chen to follow him. Toward the back of the room, they crouched behind a row of spinning machines which provided them ample cover. Peering through the gaps between spindles, they waited.

Heavy footsteps on the first floor announced the hulking Sergeant Frankenstein was searching down there. Softer steps ascended the stairs and soon, Lieutenant Kuo entered the second floor. Brandishing a Mauser pistol, he crept through each row of spinning machines. Tom probed the Browning through the spindles, but the rows and rows of machinery obstructed a clear shot. It was only a matter of time before Kuo made his way around the corner, where he and Mei-chen would be sitting ducks. Better to go on the attack.

"Stay here," Tom whispered to Mei-chen, "and don't move."

She nodded and wrapped herself deeper into his overcoat, like a tortoise retreating into its shell. Still crouching, Tom walked around the corner. Lieutenant Kuo bended another row of spinning machines, coming into range. Tom stood, took aim, and fired. A bullet tore a spindle apart, sending scraps of cotton floating down like snowflakes. Alarmed, Kuo thrust out his Mauser pistol and answered with gunfire. Flame brightened the dank cotton mill and lead smashed into the elongated window.

Tom ducked back down behind the safety of the spinning machines as Lieutenant Kuo continued firing. An incessant hammer of bullets ripped through the spindles, blanketing the filthy floor with twisted hunks of metal and white bits of cotton. Tom braved another shot but Kuo had disappeared. Peering into the darkness, Tom saw the outline of a dark blue uniform and peaked cap slinking closer. Lieutenant Kuo rounded the corner and took aim straight at Mei-chen.

Across the aisle, Tom drew a bead on Kuo and fired. A flash of flame flooded the cotton mill and Tom saw a slug catch Lieutenant Kuo right between the eyes. The force threw him backward, knocking off his peaked cap as a final indignity. Kuo's corpse twitched and jerked, but his fingers held firm onto the Mauser. Out of his periphery, Tom saw another uniformed figure emerge from across the room. Twisting around, he fired the Browning in a renewed attack.

Sergeant Frankenstein's shoulder exploded in a cloud of blood. His thick fingers released his pistol – also a Mauser – and he began charging at Tom like a stampeding rhino. He struggled to draw a bead on the oncoming beast, but the Sergeant was too fast. His enormous hands slammed Tom hard against the spinning machine. The jagged metal dug deep into Tom's back, and he exhaled a pained scream.

Frankenstein's grip was like steel, no matter how hard he struggled. With one hand, he clutched Tom by the throat and squeezed. A terrifying numbness spread throughout Tom's body and began dimming his mind. His muscles strained to bring the Browning automatic up, but the Sergeant swatted it away, then resumed strangling. Tom kicked and flailed but to his horror, he couldn't feel his legs anymore.

His breathing lapsed into gasps, and his vision blurred. He was going under and couldn't fight it any longer. The last thing he'd see was this son of a bitch's smirking face. But thankfully, something covered his ugly mug nice and tight. Frankenstein's beefy hands released Tom's throat, dropping him to the floor. As sensation tingled throughout his arms and legs, Tom took in what was happening.

The Sergeant's face was entirely covered by his overcoat and the brute was being pulled backward. Mei-chen had wrapped it around Frankenstein's ghoulish kisser and pulled him backward over one of the spinning machines. Although a dainty little lotus, she nevertheless heaved and pulled with all her might. Frankenstein lashed out his huge hands for his attacker but was helpless as his neck was caught between the spindle.

Moments passed by as Sergeant Frankenstein flailed and grasped in vain, but Mei-chen kept tugging and pulling on the overcoat, still smothering the bastard's face. Soon, the

Sergeant's massive arms swung impotently beside him, and all movement ceased. Tom shook out the remaining tingles in his hands and feet, then snatched up the Browning. He looked at Mei-chen, still wrapping the overcoat around Frankenstein's face.

"You can let go now," Tom said, "he's dead."

The statement seemed to awake Mei-chen from a trance. She unwound the coat and slid it back over her shoulders without a second thought. Most Chinese women would be appalled to wear such a coat, convinced evil spirits had now attached themselves to it. But Tom reminded himself that this woman was an agent of the Japanese Empire, trained in espionage and – apparently – hand to hand combat. A sudden chill swept over him, realizing that she had always been – and still was – quite capable of killing him.

Angry shouts from below drew them over to the window. Feng Lung-wei and his henchman were exiting the warehouse, now aware of their presence. In the bright, beaming headlights of the Mercedes, Tom saw Feng raise his weapon up and open fire. In an instant, he and Mei-chen hit the floor as the cackling rat tat tat of the Tommy gun shattered the window into glass shrapnel.

Still shielding himself from the onslaught of falling shards, Tom looked up and saw a back exit behind the rows of spinning machines. Motioning to Mei-chen, they crawled on the filthy floor, past the two dead cops and to the exit. The door was locked, but a blast from the Browning automatic burst it open. Behind him, Tom heard slapping footsteps ascend the stairs. The gangsters would be here in moments.

Tom and Mei-chen tore open the back exit and raced down another flight of stairs, leading to a final door. Mercifully, it opened from the inside and deposited them back out into the streets of Chapei. Out in the frigid night air, a hideous chorus of gunshots, screaming, and droning planes turned Tom's insides into jelly. They were back in the war, but anything was better than confronting Feng Lung-wei. Without looking back, they ran into the darkness.

CHAPTER THIRTY-SEVEN

After ducking in and out of alleyways and down narrow side streets that jigsawed throughout Chapei, Tom felt confident enough that they'd lost Feng Lung-wei. Fatigue soon overtook Tom and Mei-chen, slowing their frantic run into weary, plodding steps. Minutes passed by in aimless wandering, until they spotted a movement up ahead at an intersection. It was a grim procession – mothers carried squealing babies on their backs, old men and women hobbled along on canes, and a cross-section of Shanghai's hoi polloi shuffling forward. The luckiest were carried along in rickshaws, although upon closer inspection, it was only because they were missing an appendage or two.

"Where are you headed?" Tom asked no one in particular.

"The Red Swastika Society," an elderly woman said without stopping. "There's a relief station a few blocks west."

That was a relief. The Red Swastika Society was a Chinese equivalent to the Red Cross, running soup kitchens, poorhouses, and relief programs in areas devastated by famine, flood, and war. If anywhere in Chapei was safe, it would be there. Tom and Mei-chen merged into the procession and let themselves be swept along.

*****

The Red Swastika Society had made their relief station out of a warehouse. People rested and slept on and in between stacks of crates and barrels, all full of textiles, toys, and trinkets. Red swastikas were stamped on banners and flags, both inside and outside the warehouse. As a respected symbol in Buddhism and Taoism, the swastika designated the area as a neutral ground, a no man's land in this urban jungle.

Unfortunately, there wasn't much "relief" at this relief station, just a kitchen dispensing *congee* rice gruel and a rest area attended by a few overwhelmed medics. Wounded Chinese soldiers received special attention and large portions of *congee* to compensate for their suffering. Bullet holes were the most common, though some soldiers were missing hands, feet, or legs, while others were mummified in blood-soaked bandages.

Tom thought back to the field hospitals in France, full of Doughboys who'd been chewed up by heavy artillery. At least they had the luxury of morphine, but these poor boys had to make do with an opium pipe being passed around. After a few puffs, their cries and wails died down to a numbed, stupefied gaze. Hopefully, this war would end soon or else there would be a Chinese "Lost Generation."

Tom and Mei-chen each managed to get a single paltry bowl of *congee* and retreated to a less crowded corner of the warehouse. In between a stack of wooden crates labeled "FUR COATS," they crouched down alongside a frazzled-looking mother and her two young daughters. At least the boxes provided some concealment, just in case Feng Lung-wei decided to show up.

Tom slurped down a spoonful of steaming *congee*. It was bland and slimy tasting, nothing like his mother's. *Congee* was usually flavored with pork or chicken, but such luxuries seemed obscene now. After swallowing a few more mouthfuls, Tom looked up and saw the two little girls staring wide-eyed at him. He knew the type – child laborers who toiled away at the cotton mills like the one they'd just escaped. Their mother probably slaved away in a factory by day and pimped herself out as a street walker at night, just to make ends meet. And their father? Probably a coolie rickshaw puller or day laborer who found himself in the wrong street when the bombs started falling.

Tom extended his bowl of *congee* and – after a moment's hesitation – one of the girls took it and began slurping it down. Mei-chen followed and handed her *congee* over to the second girl. The mother nodded and blubbered her gratitude in rapid Shanghainese.

Tom smiled and ignored an irritated rumble in his stomach. He searched around for something to take his mind off food and found a discarded issue of the *Shanghai Evening Post* strewn out on a nearby crate. It was an extra edition, put out immediately after hostilities began. Skimming the main article, his heart sank.

"What's wrong?" Mei-chen asked in English.

"Listen to this," Tom replied. "'Admiral Shiozawa stated that the Japanese Special Naval Landing Forces were being sent into Chapei to restore order and protect Japanese civilians.' Just as I thought!" he scoffed. "Apparently, those protests gave the Mikado's boys just the excuse they needed to start a war."

"Are you blaming the Chinese for being attacked?" Mei-chen snapped.

Tom tossed the *Shanghai Evening Post* aside and glanced over at the two little girls, wolfing down the bowls of *congee*.

"There are enough hotheaded idiots in every country," he said. "They start the wars and everyone else suffers."

Mei-chen said nothing and sank deeper into his overcoat – the same coat she'd just murdered a man with. Still, if not for her, that brute Sergeant would have snapped his neck. That was twice she'd saved his life. But if not for her in the first place, he wouldn't be in this mess. However – regardless of her treachery – Club Twilight would have been destroyed regardless. But maybe Charles Whitfield would still be alive if she hadn't…

Tom sighed. There was no point going down this road of dead ends and self-pity.

"I understand why you want to leave Shanghai," Tom said, clearing his throat. "This city has been heaven for me, but hell for you."

Mei-chen said nothing but gave a grateful nod. Tom fished into his pocket and removed the documents he'd confiscated earlier, then pressed it into her gloved hands.

"Here, Miss Margaret Wong. You'll need that to get back to America."

"Tom...I...thanks…"

"Don't thank me yet. We still need to make it to the International Settlement."

"Think we have a shot?" she asked, already sounding like an American.

Tom shrugged and said, "I think we'll have better odds once the sun comes up."

She nodded and they both fell into a deep silence, surrounded the droning noise of cries, moans, and worried murmurs that echoed all throughout the warehouse. In between a stack of crates, he could see a nurse – wearing a red swastika armband – standing in the center of the warehouse, clasping her hands together. Through moans, wails, and worried murmurs, she began to sing.

"Overthrow the foreign powers, overthrow the foreign powers,

Eliminate the warlords, eliminate the warlords,

The National Revolution is successful, the National Revolution is successful,

Let's all sing together, let's all sing together!"

Tom recognized the tune, and not only because it was sung to the melody of "Frère Jacques." It was the "Song of the National Revolution," the anthem of the Kuomintang during their Northern Expedition to defeat the warlords. Captain Tung had taught him that song shortly after they first met, and Tom always had the Twilight Band play it on Double Ten Day, the founding of the Chinese Republic. It was clumsy, awkward, and somewhat ridiculous, but it spread an infectious patriotism. The wounded Chinese soldiers – those who weren't completely doped with opium – managed to sing along, its strains filling the warehouse like a symphony.

The little girls – now satiated with *congee* – jumped up and down, bellowing out the refrain. Tom looked over at Mei-chen, fast asleep. Fatigue gnawed at his entire body, drooping his eyelids and pulling out a loud yawn. Tom found himself humming "Song of the National Revolution" before exhaustion overtook him completely.

CHAPTER THIRTY-EIGHT

Shrill wailing stirred Tom awake. The woman and her two little girls were gone now, replaced by a young mother and her squalling baby. Tom checked his Rolex – almost seven o'clock. It would be sunrise soon, and that meant they could make their way south to the International Settlement with a little more ease. He reached out and shook Mei-chen awake. She blinked her reddened, bleary eyes and fixed Tom with an inquisitive look.

"I feel like I could sleep forever," she said with a sigh.

"You can sleep all you want once we get down to the International Settlement," Tom groaned, rising to his feet.

Despite the early hour, many people were awake, but most stared straight ahead into dumb nothingness. Tom peered over a line of crate to the pit of wounded soldiers. Most slept or remained dazed by opium, and he wondered how many would be fortunate to wake up again.

Tom and Mei-chen snaked their way through the rows of wooden crates until they came out to the main loading area, now converted into a makeshift kitchen. The gate was wide open for any new stragglers, welcomed by a Red Swastika banner flapping in the early morning breeze. Several members of the Red Swastika Society busied themselves with large pots, preparing a new batch of *congee*.

"Breakfast will be ready soon," an old man rasped, a red swastika armband wrapped around his silk *changshan* long shirt.

"Thank you, uncle," Tom said, "but we won't be staying."

"We appreciate your kindness," Mei-chen added.

"You're going outside?" The old man's eyes goggled. "You can't! All of Chapei is a battlefield! The 19th Route Army and Japanese devils fight for every block."

Tom and Mei-chen exchanged dark glances. "That may be, uncle, but we have to reach the International Settlement. You see," he looked over at Mei-chen, "we're Americans."

Mei-chen flashed him a surprised smile, before they walked out into the street.

*****

Shanghai looked like a ghost town in the misty morning light. There were no people out, but evidence of battle was all too apparent. Broken glass carpeted the streets and glittered like fine jewelry. Bullet holes pockmarked buildings and broken rubble lay strewn about in piles. Up ahead, Tom and Mei-chen saw movement at an intersection. Tom peered into the distance and saw figures moving about in a fortified outpost. It was hard to make out any features aside from their uniforms – blue-gray tunics with field caps. Chinese soldiers of the 19th Route Army!

Tom rifled through his overcoat, still draped around Mei-chen's shoulders, and yanked out a white handkerchief. Dangling it overhead turned it into a makeshift flag of truce, and they began advancing toward the outpost. Their steps were slow and plodding as they avoided the twisted debris and glass.

Coming closer, the Chinese soldiers spotted them and raised their rifles to defensive positions. Tom waved the white handkerchief with more pep, but the soldiers kept their weapons at the ready. Several troops were busy stacking sandbags a few feet high, but other than that, these soldiers – no stronger than a platoon – were without a robust fortification.

Rifle barrels flashed in the morning sun, and Tom counted at least ten were trained on them. As they approached, an unarmed soldier marched out to meet them just a few feet from the outpost.

"Greetings," Tom glanced at the soldier's collar rank insignia, "Corporal. Can we speak to your commanding officer?"

The Corporal snorted. "Our lieutenant and two of our sergeants were killed last night. I'm in charge of this platoon now."

"I'm sorry," Tom said.

The Corporal seemed unmoved. "Why are you out here? Civilians should remain indoors."

"We're heading down to the International Settlement," Tom answered. "We're Americans who lost our way."

Shrewd skepticism wrinkled the Corporal's face. "You're Americans? Then let's see your papers."

Mei-chen handed over her phony passport, and the Corporal scrutinized it. Tom searched for his until remembered that it must have been left behind somewhere in the smoldering ruins of Club Twilight.

"I apologize, Corporal, but in last night's chaos, I lost my passport," Tom said, reaching for his wallet.

Perhaps a small bribe would be enough identification. This was still Shanghai after all. But as Tom's hand drifted to his pocket, the ten or so rifles raised and leveled straight at his heart. Tom lifted and opened his hands in a token of submission.

"No sudden movements!" the Corporal bellowed, snapping Mei-chen's passport shut. He jerked a hand in Tom's direction, and another soldier lowered his rifle, then began fishing through his clothes.

"Watch out, I'm ticklish," Tom said in English, hoping that would vouch for his nationality. Instead, the soldier continued prying into his jacket before plucking out the Browning automatic from his shoulder holster. The soldier presented it to his superior, then raised his rifle back at Tom's chest.

"And what's this?" the Corporal asked, gripping this pistol.

"A gun, apparently."

Scowling, the Corporal said, "Don't try and be funny. Why would a civilian, Chinese or American, have a gun?"

"Shanghai is a dangerous place," Tom answered with a shrug.

The Corporal was unamused. "We've been harassed by those Japanese *ronin* lately. Are you one of them?"

"Do I look Japanese to you?"

"Maybe not," the Corporal scoffed, "but you could be in their pay."

Tom glanced over to Mei-chen. Would the gods be so cruel as to allow him to be executed as a Japanese agent and let her go free? He hadn't escaped an execution by the Green Gang just to let the 19th Route Army shoot him. The hell with that. Tom Lai was a man who made his own destiny.

"Look Corporal, my name is Thomas Lai – Lai Huang-fu – and I'm a Kuomintang member. I've supported the Nationalist Government and Generalissimo Chiang for years now. If you need further verification, you can contact Captain Tung Hsi-shan. But I'm telling you straight, I'm loyal to China."

The Corporal flashed suspicious glances between him and Mei-chen. Not that Tom blamed him – after all, one of them actually was a spy for the Mikado. As he continued his scrutiny, one of his men stacking sandbags gawked at them with an elated expression.

"Ho Mei-chen? Is that you?" the young soldier – still just a teenager – asked, drawing closer. His simple, blocky face possessed an unknown familiarity.

"Private, you know these two?" the Corporal asked.

"Yes sir, this is Ho Mei-chen," the Private said with eager nods, "the famous taxi dancer at Club Twilight. And this man is Mr. Lai, the owner!"

"Oh yes," Mei-chen cooed, shaking the boy soldier's hand. "I remember you, Private. Such a graceful dancer you are!"

Tom shook his head. Boy, could she lay it on thick. Still, he'd fallen for her act as well, so who was he to judge? The

Private blushed and looked positively smitten. Of course! Tom had seen this young soldier dancing with Club Twilight only days ago, right after he'd returned from Feng's opium den horror show. It only figured that nobody, especially a simple soldier, could forget Ho Mei-chen.

"Alright, Private. Return to your work," the Corporal ordered. The Private saluted and flashed a broad smile at Mei-chen, before trotting back over to the sandbags.

"Your club is popular with a lot of the officers and men," the Corporal conceded. "Taxi dances were always half off for soldiers."

"Anything for China's fighting men," Tom said with an ingratiating smile. "I was a soldier too once…"

The tension began to melt and they traded respectful nods, soldier to soldier. Just then, the hammer of gunfire echoed off the buildings. Tom peered into the distance down the street and gasped. A force of Japanese Marines advanced down directly toward them. Tom began counting and quickly realized just how outnumbered the Chinese were.

"You were once a soldier?" the Corporal snapped. "Prove your loyalty to China by helping us right here and now!"

He pressed the Browning back into Tom's palm. Before he could think it over, Tom found himself dumbly nodding. He'd always claimed Shanghai was his new home – now he would fight for it.

CHAPTER THIRTY-NINE

Tom turned back to Mei-chen, her face clouded with concern and confusion. He strode toward her and grasped her by the shoulder.

"Go and hide." Tom pointed to a Buick Coupe, parked nearby. "Don't come out until I come get you."

Mei-chen's concern and confusion gave way to indignation. "You're going to fight? Have you gone insane?"

"The Japs are blocking the way down to the International Settlement," Tom snapped back. "We either stand and fight or hide like rats in Chapei."

Mei-chen opened her mouth to speak, but a cacophony of gunfire shut her up. Instead, she nodded, turned, and dashed toward the Buick. Crouching low, she vanished from sight behind its hood. Tom joined what remained of the Chinese platoon, taking a position next to the Corporal. Kneeling down, he thrust out his pistol and took aim.

The Japanese Marines were closer now, firing potshots at them. Bullets whizzed overhead or slammed against the sandbags. Their Arisaka rifles – fastened with bayonets – were almost as tall as they were, but the Mikado's warriors handled them with finesse.

The Browning automatic now felt like a brick in Tom's hand. Still, the Chinese soldiers held their position, taking aim but not firing. For a moment, Tom Lai left Chapei, left Shanghai, left the Orient, and found himself back inside a damp, muddy trench in the Argonne Forest. A shrieking bullet crashed into a nearby sandbag and brought him back to the present.

The Corporal fired his rifle, echoed by the remainder of the platoon. The Browning automatic jerked in Tom's hand, blasting out a steady stream of lead at the onrushing enemy. Some of the Marines fell, clutching their bellies, arms, or legs, screaming in agony. Tom didn't need to speak Japanese to understand their suffering.

The carnage wasn't one-sided. Japanese bullets found their mark, ripping through two Chinese soldiers, their bodies sagging limply over the sandbags. Both sides kept firing, but despite being outnumbered, the Chinese had the upper hand. Although their fortifications were paltry, the Mikado's men were completely exposed and found themselves inside a shooting gallery. Most were lowly seamen, identified by their Cracker Jack uniforms and white gaiters, but an officer – with silver insignia on his collar and brandishing a sword – urged his men forward.

"*Tenno Heika Banzai!*" the screamed out in unison, rushing forward. Long live the Emperor.

Tom reloaded his pistol then aimed at the officer leading the wave of advancing Marines. The gun spat out quick staccato bursts, hurling the Japanese officer back. The sword dropped from his hand, clattering onto the ground. But the Marines continued their charge, running straight into a wall of lead. Bullets shredded blue uniforms and flesh, dropping almost half of their force to the ground. Those that survived halted in their tracks and crouched low, taking defensive positions.

However, without an officer to lead them, and with half their unit gutted, the Marines began edging back down the street. Both sides continued to exchange gunfire, but with the conflagration was tempering now, and fresh casualties had mercifully subsided. Within minutes, the retreat and withdrawal of the Mikado's Imperial Marines was complete, leaving Tom with the mixed sensation of numb ecstasy.

The Chinese Corporal rose his fist and cheered, "For the Republic! Long live China!"

"Long live China!" the troops chorused. Without thinking, Tom joined in, surprised by his own passion.

*****

Tom holstered his pistol and stood, but the Corporal gripped him by the arm.

"Where are you going?"

Tom let his confusion show. "I'm not one of your men, Corporal."

"Please," the Corporal whined with imploring eyes. "Captain Tung promised us reinforcements, but they won't arrive for another hour or two. We need every man in case the Japanese devils make another assault."

There was such sincerity in the Corporal's voice, Tom couldn't refuse. But his eyes drifted toward the Buick Coupe, where Mei-chen stood behind.

"Very well, but let me speak to my…" Tom trailed off, unsure of how to describe Mei-chen now. The Corporal didn't press and dismissed him. Tom detached from the platoon and joined Mei-chen beside the car.

"Thank God you're okay," she cried. "Let's get out of here."

Tom stared back at her, scrutinizing that pretty face for any vestiges of duplicity. How he yearned to embrace her, kiss her, and love her again. But could a spy even love? Maybe not, but she had saved his life. Or maybe she was just keeping him around long enough to escort her back to the International Settlement. It didn't matter either way. Nothing would be the same anymore. Not for him, not for Ho Mei-chen – whoever she really was – and not for Shanghai, if it still existed after all this. All that mattered right now was surviving. There was something thrilling in fighting back rather than skulking through alleyways like frightened mice. Perhaps Tom Lai was still a soldier after all.

"We can't," Tom said. "The Japanese are everywhere. But if we wait for reinforcements, then we'll have protection. Or maybe they'll be a truce and—"

"Enemy approaching!" someone cried out. Tom turned and found the Chinese soldiers resuming their positions. Glancing back at Mei-chen, he ordered her to hide before running over to the platoon. Crouching next to the Corporal,

Tom slid out his Browning and peered down the street. In the distance, a few Nipponese Marines were visible, clustering around an imposing, steel beast – an armored car.

Rifle fire erupted from the Chinese platoon, pummeling the vehicle with lead. Tom emptied his clip and reloaded, the last of his ammunition. Bullets pinged and whined off its sturdy hood, but the armored car continued to lumber toward them, implacable and unstoppable. The turret swiveled and aimed its machine gun straight ahead, then raked the Chinese fortification with a lethal spray. Sandbags were ripped asunder, their contents spilling out onto the street. The armored car fired again, pumping out waves of bullets which cut the Chinese platoon to ribbons. Soldiers vomited out death rattles, then convulsed over what remained of the sandbag fortifications.

Tom kept his head low and tried to draw a bead on any Japanese who exposed themselves. He fired off the remainder of his clip until there was an empty click. Just then, heavy weight pushed against him, distorting his aim. Tom glanced over and found the Corporal – his face reduced to gory pulp by a well-placed bullet – leaning against him. Sliding the corpse off, Tom saw what remained of the platoon beginning to retreat.

They turned and ran pell-mell, but a renewed volley of machine gun fire cut them down like rabbits in an open field. As the armored car trundled closer and closer, the Marines fanned out to mop up any remaining resistance. No point in staying put. Tom low-crawled out of the fortification and toward the Buick Coupe, now riddled with bullets.

"Mei-chen!" he cried, still crouching low.

Her terrified face appeared behind one of the windows. Glancing around, Tom saw the Mikado's Marines finish off the few remaining Chinese defenders with their bayonets. Before he could think, one of the Japanese bounded toward him. Within seconds the Jap had him covered, his rifle and bayonet aimed point blank at Tom's head.

"*Kosan se yo!*" the Nipponese Marine screamed. Tom didn't know much Japanese, but he understood a command to surrender in any language. There was nowhere to go now, except a prison camp – if he was lucky. The Browning pistol slid from his fingers and clattered onto the ground. Holding his arms up, Tom stood and lowered his head in submission.

To his left, he saw Mei-chen step around the Buick, her hands also raised. To his right, he saw the body of that young private – who'd shared a dance with her – writhing out on the ground. Blood frothed at the soldier's lips as he cast a lingering stare at Mei-chen. Satiated, he released a gruesome death gurgle, before his eyes slid shut forever.

CHAPTER FORTY

The Marine began to unload a torrent of angry Japanese at Tom, drawing his bayonet closer and closer with each word. Wearing civvies in a battlefield was an invitation to a firing squad. There was only one thing that could possibly save him now.

"*Amerika-jin*," Tom said, pointing at himself and at Mei-chen. The Jap blinked, dividing his attention between them both. Maybe this Nipponese would think twice before executing two Americans. Mei-chen began talking in fluent Japanese, jarring Tom slightly. Even after all this, it was still strange to hear her speak that language, as if she was pulling off yet another mask.

Mei-chen pulled out her phony passport and presented it to the Marine. After a few moments, he scrutinized Tom again, then called over one of his comrades. An older man – a petty officer judging by his peaked cap – marched over and began conversing with the Marine.

"What did you tell them?" Tom muttered in English, under his breath.

"That we work for the American Consulate," Mei-chen answered. "They can kill coolies, but diplomats might cause an international incident."

The Petty Officer inspected them both with cold, suspicious eyes. No doubt he was trying to answer the age-old question – how could someone be both Chinese *and* American? He stopped his scrutiny and scooped up the Browning pistol, then handed it to the Marine. After barking out an order, the Petty Officer returned to his men.

The Marine rattled off a few words to Mei-chen, who translated.

"He's going to escort us to the rear, where their commanding officer will interrogate us."

Tom's breath blew out slowly. There was one thing true about any military – nobody wanted to be stuck making the hard decisions. At least that bought them some time.

"*Susume!*" the Marine ordered, before prodding them with his bayonet. Tom guessed that meant, 'forward march.'

With their hands up in the air, Tom and Mei-chen crossed back over the ruined fortification, strewn with Chinese casualties. Tom tried not to look at their grisly remains and instead focused up ahead at the armored car, now parked and surrounded by Imperial Marines. Raising their rifles, they chanted, "Banzai! Banzai! Banzai!" over and over again until the victory cry echoed in Tom's ears. Pretty soon, he figured, all of Shanghai would hear it too.

*****

The Japanese rear position was situated in an alley, between buildings that had been half-scooped out by bombs. Several Nipponese Marines stood guard while a hoisted Rising Sun flag with jutting rays fluttered in the chilly morning breeze. On the other side, an enormous painting loomed over them. A smiling Chinese beauty in a silky *cheongsam* held a bottle of Coke up to her luscious lips. In English and Chinese characters it proclaimed, "Coca-Cola means 'delicious' in any language!" Tom suddenly felt a passing homesickness.

Underneath the wall advertisement, a scraggly-looking man in a silk shirt stood across from a Japanese firing squad. A Navy officer held up his sword for a moment, then brought it down. The rifles cracked and the man dropped face-first to the ground. Two Marines hoisted the corpse up and dragged it to a nearby pile of bullet-ridden bodies.

"Well, this just went from bad to worse," Tom whispered to Mei-chen.

"They might think we're snipers or spies," Mei-chen replied.

"A good guess," Tom said. "We're going to have to convince them to call the US Consulate. That's our only hope of—"

"*Damare!*" their Marine escort barked.

The officer strode toward them before exchanging salutes with his subordinate. Like all officers of the Mikado's Navy, he wore a high collar, cherry blossom insignia – denoting his rank as an ensign – peaked cap, and leather gaiters, which suggested he was attached to the Imperial Marines rather than the Imperial Fleet. His uniform was smarter than the enlisted rank and file, with their Cracker Jack outfits, sailor caps, and white gaiters. Still, wearing any uniform would be a welcome relief right now. At least then he'd be treated like a prisoner of war with all its rights and privileges.

The Ensign conversed with the Marine briefly, then cast his attention toward Mei-chen.

"Pasupōto," he said, extending his open palm.

Mei-chen presented her passport, casting a nervous glance over to Tom. The Ensign flipped through it, then handed it back. He thrust out his hand, demanding Tom's. Mei-chen intervened, explaining in Japanese. For a brief moment, a dark thought crept into Tom's mind. All Mei-chen had to do was sell him out, admit she was a Nipponese spy and cut him loose. That would be fitting for a rube like him. He swallowed hard and prayed he was wrong.

The Ensign examined him up and down, then rubbed his chin.

"What did you tell him?" Tom asked Mei-chen.

"I said you lost your passport last night, but that we're both Chinese-Americans attached to the US Consulate."

"Let's hope he buys it."

The Marine presented his superior with the Browning automatic. He pointed to Tom's direction, chattering in accusatory Japanese. The Ensign nodded and gestured to the pistol, then began asking questions.

"He wants to know if that's your gun," Mei-chen said.

Involuntarily, Tom nodded. The Ensign started up again.

"Why does an American own a Belgian pistol?" Mei-chen asked for him.

"Tell him that Americans love all guns, regardless of where they're from."

Mei-chen rattled off his reply in Japanese, but the Ensign kept a dour expression as he barked another question.

"He asks why an American was fighting alongside the Chinese 19th Route Army?"

Tom searched his mind for a placating excuse. "Tell him that the Chinese forced me at gunpoint to fight for them."

Mei-chen translated with such sincerity, Tom almost believed it himself. Unfortunately, the Ensign shook his head dismissively.

"He says he doesn't believe you," Mei-chen said.

"I can tell. Look, just ask him to call the American Consulate. That ought to by us a little more time."

Mei-chen conversed with the Ensign for several more rounds, but each plea was met with a stern, pitiless stare and laconic answers.

"He says since you can't prove you're American, you're either a spy or a sniper," Mei-chen said, her bottom lip trembling. "And that he has every legal right to shoot you along with the other snipers."

Tom cast a glance over to the pile of Chinese corpses, all in civilian clothes. Well, he couldn't be sore at the Ensign. After all, you didn't survive on the battlefield by taking unnecessary chances. Still, a deep anger welled inside Tom. Here he was again, trapped like a rat and at someone else's mercy. Whether it was the Japanese or the Green Gang, Tom Lai was tired of running. If only he'd taken Captain Tung up on his offer. At least then he could die fighting.

"*Amerika-jin!*" Tom snapped, thumping his chest. He summoned what little Japanese he knew and shouted, "*Watashi wa Amerika-jin desu!*"

"*Damare!*" the Ensign snarled, then ordered the Marine forward.

Prodded by the bayonet, Tom was led down the alleyway, right underneath the wall painting. The squad of Nipponese Marines resumed their position and raised their rifles. Tom looked up at the giant woman, smiling with her soda. Dying in front of a Coca-Cola advertisement. What could possibly be more American? And here he was – after everything he'd been through – about to be executed as a spy. Or maybe they thought he was a sniper? It didn't really matter anymore. Tom sucked in a deep breath and braced himself for the end.

CHAPTER FORTY-ONE

Ignoring Mei-chen's frantic pleas, the Ensign drew his saber. The blade gleamed in the morning sun, but it possessed a strange beauty. At least he'd be given the martial dignity of a firing squad. Tom wondered if his parents would ever find out how he died. Maybe Mei-chen could let Mama and Papa Lai know how their son bit the dust. Tom wracked his brain for some escape but came up empty. The only shot would be if this Ensign's commanding officer intervened on his behalf.

That's it! Tom didn't have much influence in the Nipponese Navy, but he did know one officer.

"Mei-chen!" he called out. She and the Ensign turned with perplexed stares. "A man deserves a final smoke before he dies."

Mei-chen nodded her understanding, then translated his words to the Ensign. A few moments ticked by before he finally relented. Perhaps this Nipponese was an officer *and* gentleman after all. The Marines lowered their rifles, but kept them raised just enough to cut Tom down if he ran.

Tom dug into his jacket, pulled out his cigarette case and lighter, then lit himself up a Lucky Strike. Drawing the tobacco smoke deep into his lungs calmed his rattled nerves and allowed him to sort out his plan further. It was a long shot, but he had nothing to lose at this point. Taking another drag, he called over Mei-chen. The Ensign allowed her to proceed with a nod.

"I have an idea but you're not going to like," he said to her.

"What is it?"

Tom paused and blew out a trail of smoke. "Commander Fukuzaki."

Mei-chen's eyes bulged, then narrowed. "What do you mean?"

"He's the only Jap with enough clout to save my skin."

Brow furrowing, Mei-chen rubbed her bare arms. No doubt she was weighing the options in her mind. After all, she – as Margaret Wong – had an American passport.

"He can confirm my identity and nationality. The Japs might be more hesitant to shoot an American citizen."

Mei-chen glanced over to the Ensign. "And what if *he* refuses?"

Tom took another drag. "How could any Japanese officer say no to one of the Mikado's spies?"

She'd have to blow her cover, but it was his only chance. The dark thought from before crept back into his brain – could he really trust a Japanese spy? All she needed to do now was keep her mouth shut and she had a free ticket to the States. But after a moment of grueling hesitation, Mei-chen nodded, her eyes like brown pools of sympathy.

"Okay…I'll do it…"

Mei-chen went back to the Ensign and began speaking in animated Japanese. Most words were indecipherable, but the Ensign did straighten up whenever '*Fukuzaki Chusa*' was mentioned. Tom finished his Lucky and ground it underneath his heel. Tense moments went by, before the Japanese officer called over one of the Marines. After a brief exchange, the enlisted man saluted and trotted off. The Ensign beckoned Tom closer, drew himself up, and spoke a few terse lines.

"He says he will confirm your identity, and mine, once Commander Fukuzaki arrives. Otherwise, you will be executed accordingly," Mei-chen said, unable to hide her worry.

Tom couldn't suppress a relieved smile and lit up another cigarette. "Tell him I said, '*arigato*.'"

*****

The minutes dragged by in agonizing slowness. Between staring up at the Coca-Cola advertisement and exchanging worried looks with Mei-chen, Tom kept quiet, smoking away the remainder of Lucky Strikes in his cigarette case. The Marines remained aloof and silent, not that he could blame them. You always wanted to be alone with your thoughts before battle, just in case it was the last time to have them. Gunshots and explosions wailed in the distance, confirming that the war was still on. At this point, Tom hoped he'd survive long enough to see who won.

After almost an hour, a motorcycle sidecar rumbled up to the Japanese outpost. Tires squealing, it ground to a halt right next to the flapping Rising Sun flag. An enlisted Marine – goggled and helmeted – was the driver, but in the passenger car sat Commander Jiro Fukuzaki. Like the Ensign, he wore a high-collared blue uniform and peaked cap, but his polished shoes were more appropriate for a ballroom dance floor than the battlefield.

Regardless, as he stepped out of the sidecar, Fukuzaki exuded such authority that it was almost palpable. The Ensign and Marines snapped crisp salutes as he strode toward Tom and Mei-chen. His reputation as chief of Naval Intelligence in Shanghai must have been well-known, even to these grunts.

"Ah, Mr. Lai," Commander Fukuzaki purred in English, "we meet again."

"Howdy Commander," Tom said, taking a drag on his last cigarette. "Wish it were under better circumstances."

A furtive glance from Mei-chen made Tom wonder if Fukuzaki knew he'd unmasked his Beautiful Pearl as a Nipponese spy. Best to play dumb and keep mum.

"This is Ho Mei-chen," Tom said with his best poker face. She extended a gloved hand and Fukuzaki took it. "I'd invite you to have a drink at Club Twilight, Commander, but it was blown to bits last night."

"Not to worry, the Golden Unicorn is still standing," Fukuzaki said with a wry grin. "Mr. Lai, I'm sorry for this regrettable situation, but you were found on the battlefield with enemy soldiers. In civilian clothes, no less. I'm sure you're aware that without a uniform, you are not entitled to be treated as a prisoner of war."

"Maybe so, but I'm still an American citizen. My country is neutral in your little war."

"But you didn't remain neutral, did you Mr. Lai? Wearing a suit, you aided our enemy. Japanese Marines are plagued by dishonorable Chinese snipers in civilian clothes, shooting from rooftops and behind rubble." Fukuzaki shook his head. "Is it fair that our men's uniforms make for easy targets while the Chinese hide behind silk shirts?"

"No it's not, but neither is bombing Chapei. Besides, it's not like the 19th Route Army attacked Little Tokyo, did they?" Tom countered, his temper inflamed.

"Indeed they didn't Mr. Lai, but Chinese mobs did molest Japanese civilians. Since the Shanghai Police were unable to deal with this crisis, the Imperial Navy took control."

"And started the war you and your *ronin* wanted," Tom snapped. "But that's neither here nor there, Commander. As an American citizen – and one who has friends all over Shanghai – I demand to speak to the US Consulate."

Fukuzaki gave a mischievous smile as he eyed Tom, then Mei-chen, up and down. "And who would you speak to, Mr. Lai? Charles Whitfield?"

Whitfield's bloodied body, writhing in agony in a bed of broken glass, resurfaced in Tom's mind. He'd forgotten about that horror for the past few hours, superseded with countless other horrors, but now it bubbled back up with full fury. Unable to disguise his sorrow, Tom blanched.

"Too bad he's dead," Fukuzaki continued. "His body was discovered last night. Shot in the chest. How sad. Apparently, a Russian doorman saw two Orientals – a man and a woman – exiting his apartment building. You wouldn't happen to know who they were, would you Mr. Lai?"

Tom balled his fist and cast a sideways glance to Mei-chen. Her face remained rigid, but her eyes shone with mute fear. The son of a bitch was just toying with them now.

"Commander, I have no idea what you're insinuating, but—"

Fukuzaki waved a dismissive hand. "There is no point denying it, Mr. Lai, I can see the truth in Miss Ho's face. To kill our best source of information! I expected better from her. Truly an amateurish mistake."

Mei-chen cast her gaze downward, like a schoolgirl about to be punished in front of the class.

"Last time we met, you were searching for my spy and you found her," Fukuzaki said with a sigh, shaking his head bitterly. "And if you figured out her true identity, then perhaps someone else did? Or perhaps you told others? I ask you, Mr. Lai, what good is a spy who no longer enjoys anonymity?"

"I didn't tell anyone," Tom said through gritted teeth.

"Perhaps you did, perhaps you didn't. Better safe than sorry, as you Americans say."

Snapping his fingers, Fukuzaki ordered the Ensign forward and rattled off a few commands. The Ensign nodded, and gripped Mei-chen's bare arm. Shoving her to her knees, he circled around and drew a pistol from his side holster. She stared back at Tom with pleading eyes.

"What are you doing?" Tom demanded. "You'd kill your own spy?"

Fukuzaki shook his head again, sorrow and regret etched into his gray face. "A pity. I had a fondness for the girl. But she has failed in her duty."

"She doesn't even deserve a firing squad?"

"This is more fitting for a spy. But don't worry, Mr. Lai. Your actions merit a military execution."

"My actions?"

"You cannot expect us to treat our enemies with impunity, especially if they are in civilian clothes," Fukuzaki said, his mood lightening a little.

"But the American Consulate—"

"Will never know what happened to you. With your skin, you'll be reported as just another executed Chinese sniper. After all, besides Mr. Whitfield, you don't have many friends in the American Consulate, do you Mr. Lai?"

No, he didn't, Tom conceded. Most of Tom's acquaintances in Shanghai were gangsters, riff-raff, and crooked politicians. Charles Whitfield was one of the few real friends he had in Shanghai. Yan Ping was another, and he'd gotten them both killed.

Only Captain Tung remained. If only he was here to save them now. Tom swallowed hard and cast a regretful look at Mei-chen, now with a pistol to the back of her head. He'd be joining her soon enough.

CHAPTER FORTY-TWO

His mind blank and numb, Tom stared at Mei-chen, kneeling on the ground. He'd played his last card and came up short. He mouthed the words "I'm sorry" to her. Meager compensation but it was all he could offer. Mei-chen nodded, then squeezed her eyes shut. Even Commander Fukuzaki appeared remorseful with a dour frown. After all, he was about to lose one of his best spies. Then again, good spies didn't get caught.

Fukuzaki raised his hand and held it there. Was he having second thoughts or just flaunting his power? It didn't matter any longer. Tom turned away and bit his lip.

The crack of a gunshot ripped through the air. Tom looked up and gasped. The Ensign wobbled, and fell to the side, blood spurting out from his temple. Mei-chen opened her eyes and stared at the dead Ensign in stunned silence. Angry cries erupted from the Marines as they raised their weapons, searching for the hidden threat. Across the street, the glint of a rifle barrel snaked out of an open window. Apparently, the Japanese fears about snipers were very real.

Another gunshot tore straight through a Marine's forehead, hurling him backward. Disregarding the danger, Commander Fukuzaki strode past Mei-chen – still cowering on her knees – and pointed at the sniper's nest.

"*Utee! Utee! Utee!*" Fukuzaki shouted for the Marines to open fire, his guttural voice descending into an animalistic roar.

Having found their footing, the Marines began firing enough ammunition into the sniper's nest to make the fireworks at Chinese New Year look tame. The window cracked and shattered, but more bullets rained down at the Japanese and found their deadly mark. Another Marine was struck and slammed to the ground, blood and gore spilling out all over his Cracker Jack uniform.

Through the incessant hammer of gunfire, Tom saw an opening. Rushing forward, he helped Mei-chen to her feet, clutched her hand and raced in the opposite direction down the alleyway between buildings. Passing under the enormous Coca-Cola wall painting, Tom dared a brief glance behind him. The Mikado's Marines kept shooting, including Commander Fukuzaki, taking pot shots with a pistol. Somehow still alive, the sniper continued showering bullets at them.

Running alongside Mei-chen, Tom felt a mixture of both gratitude and envy toward him.

*****

Only when the gunshots faded did Tom and Mei-chen stop to catch their breath. They were in southern Chapei now, just blocks away from the International Settlement and safety. The damage was just as bad here, and few storefronts survived without cracked windows or bullet holes. All of Shanghai would look like this before long. And Tom Lai was running away from it all. What kind of man was he? The Japanese had invaded his city, destroyed his nightclub, and almost executed him.

A coward – that's what he was – if he fled into the International Settlement. Besides, Feng Lung-wei was still out there. Even if he survived the Japanese, he couldn't escape that gangster brat. The Green Gang would still be watching every port, so he couldn't run away to San Francisco with his tail tucked between his legs. No, better to stand and fight here, like a man. Besides, the 19th Route Army would need all the help it could get.

"Look Tom! Look!" Mei-chen squealed, pointing up ahead. "We're almost there!"

Tom peered down the street and – through the wispy fog of the early morning – stood the Stone Bridge. Thronged by a mass of seething, desperate humanity, it offered the only chance of survival. As Tom and Mei-chen approached, a squad of red-turbaned Sikh police officers became visible, struggling to control the onrushing crowd.

You had a better chance of beating back a tidal wave, Tom thought. There was a magnetic pull emanating from the panicked swarm, but Tom's feet remained planted to the ground. His future spread out before him in vivid clarity. Whether he lived or died, it would be in Shanghai.

"Mei-chen, I'm…I'm not going." Tom's throat felt strained as the words were forced out.

"What do you mean?" she asked, her face swirled with a mixture of worry, bewilderment, and irritation.

"My city needs me," Tom said, standing firm.

"Why? Don't be a fool, Tom. You're not a soldier! You don't even have a gun anymore! Leave the fighting to the 19th Route Army!"

"I can't keep running. Wherever I go, Feng Lung-wei will find me."

"Not if you go back to America and—"

"The Green Gang has every exit out of Shanghai covered. They'll be watching me, but not you."

Mei-chen shook her head. "Then wear a disguise! Anything! Tom, this city is going to burn to the ground. Do you really want Shanghai to be your grave?"

Without hesitation, he gave a firm nod. "I can't think of a better city to be buried in."

The joke pulled a little laugh out of her. "My God Tom, what are you saying?"

Tom rested a hand on her shoulder. "Go to America and live the life you've always wanted."

Mei-chen bit her lip and nodded. "You're too good for this wicked city, Tom. It doesn't deserve you."

Tom shook his head. "I thought you were my true love, Mei-chen. But now I realize it's this city. Shanghai and I were made for each other. And a man doesn't run when the love of his life is in trouble."

"Tom, my real name is—"

He raised his hand and slid it over Mei-chen's mouth. "It doesn't matter anymore. You'll always be my Beautiful Pearl."

Tom let his hand drop and Mei-chen's lips curled into a bittersweet smile. Although her mascara ran, her lipstick was smeared, and her black hair was mussed, she was still look painfully beautiful. Without thinking, Tom leaned over and kissed her, holding her tight. The cacophonous shouts from the nearby throng died away and "Sing-Song Girl of Old Shanghai" played in his mind.

He let her go, and the hideous sounds and sights of the present came rushing back. She nodded, turned, and ran toward the Stone Bridge, gateway to her new future. Tom watched her go, wondering who she was and who she would become. Ho Mei-chen was an enigma, one he could never truly know. But at least for a little while, she was his.

Within moments, the seething crowd swallowed Mei-chen up and carried her out of his life forever.

CHAPTER FORTY-THREE

Tom doubled back and headed deeper into Chapei and the war. Hopefully, that enlistment offer from Captain Tung was still valid. He'd be at the North Railway Station, provided he wasn't dead already. The crisp air carried the sounds of gunfire from blocks away. And here he was – walking through a war zone without a weapon. He'd need some form of protection if he was going to make it to the North Railway Station. The best he could hope for now was pilfering a firearm from the corpse of a soldier. Or a gangster. Suddenly, the gruesome image of that flattened Green Gang thug from last night entered Tom's mind.

He pressed northward, toward the remains of Club Twilight. The deeper into Chapei, the more severe the damage became. Skeletal frames of burnt out automobiles lined up against buildings gutted by bombs and artillery, while bloodied bodies of soldiers and civilians lay strewn about like trash heaps on the empty streets. It fueled him, propelled him forward, and stoked a burning resolve to fight back.

The sound of gravel popping beneath tires halted him in his tracks. Someone – either friend or foe – was near. Tom dashed into the safety of a nearby alleyway and pressed his body up against the wall. The rumbling grew louder like the growl of some angry tiger approaching. A truck loaded with Japanese Marines – wearing steel helmets and with fixed bayonets – sped by, followed by another, then another. They were pouring men and materiel into Chapei for a final push.

Soft crying inside the alley caught Tom's attention. A few feet away, partially hidden in the darkness, a mother and her baby had taken refuge there. Peering into the shadows, Tom could make out her face, smudged with dirt, and her eyes were wide and fearful. The woman grasped her infant tighter and curled into a defensive position. Although they'd never met, this woman could have been a photographic print of the same woman he'd seen at the Red Swastika Society.

Tom fished into his pocket and pulled out what remained of his money. He grabbed her trembling hand and pressed it into her palm. He wouldn't need it anymore. Not where he was going.

"Get down to the International Settlement," he said. "This should be enough to give you a new start."

The woman stared blank-faced for a while, then closed her fingers and pocketed the money. She nodded and bowed her thanks, causing the baby to give another soft cry. Tom put a finger to his lips, then stuck his head out of the alleyway. The coast was clear and the harsh rumbling of Japanese trucks faded into the distance. Without looking back, Tom slipped out to the street and pressed on.

*****

Tom approached the ruins of Club Twilight with a mix of apprehension, disgust, and homesickness. Here was his past life, smashed into hunks of brick, splintered glass, and pulverized wood. There was no time to ruminate about what happened or stew in self-pitying bitterness. All Shanghai was in peril now, and just like in 1918, Tom Lai was going to do his bit.

Stepping through the rubble, he scanned the remnants for any signs of a weapon. Most of the bar still stood, a defiant, mocking gesture. Tom suppressed the urge for a drink and kept fumbling through the wreckage. Half of Club Twilight's structure remained upright, but an occasional groan from its beams suggested it was ready to topple over any minute.

Tom soon came across the mutilated body of Chow, staring back at him through shattered spectacles. All of his scheming and double-dealing had led him here. A fitting end to such a crooked snake. Funny, this nightclub had been

Tom's entire life, yet it was also the reason he'd been marked for certain death. If there had been no war, Tom would be in Chow's place and Club Twilight would have become Feng Lung-wei's Pleasure Palace. Maybe the club's destruction was actually a mercy killing.

Tom continued onward, before stumbling upon the grisly remains of the Green Gang thug, smashed between thick piles of debris. Dried blood crusted around his lips, nose, and eyes, turning his bloated, swollen face into an enormous scab. Tom planted one shoe – now caked with dust – on solid footing, gripped some loose rubble, and heaved. The rest of the gangster's body became visible, along with his firearm – a Smith & Wesson revolver. Tom snatched it up and slid it into his pocket.

He turned to leave, but sentimentality kept him put. Instead, he wandered around what had been the dance floor where the Twilight Band had played "Chinatown, My Chinatown," "Limehouse Blues," and every other jazz song this side of Harlem. Now, every melody rang out in Tom's head like a dirge, a funeral march for Club Twilight. The table where Charles Whitfield regularly sat was now reduced to a pile of splinters. Through a gaping hole in the wall, the back storage room was visible where poor Yan Ping had met his gruesome fate.

The upstairs had been blown away, leaving only the twisted husk of the stairs that had led up to where his private apartment had been. He saw ghosts of the past, Mei-chen, Whitfield, Yan Ping, the band, the bartenders, the taxi dancers, and clientele streaming in and out of Club Twilight, an endless parade of light. Within moments, it was all gone, replaced by a battered shell.

At least it had existed – at least they had all existed – even if it had been fleeting. Tom lowered his head and said a prayer – for Yan Ping who was with his ancestors now, for Whitfield who he forgave and hoped forgave him, for Mei-chen longing to escape the demons of her past, and for Club Twilight, his kingdom, his home, now just a memory.

Squealing tires jerked Tom's head upward. A black Mercedes screeched to a stop across the street. Tom ducked behind the back wall into what remained of the back storage room and peered out through the gaping hole. Feng Lung-wei and his surviving henchman hopped out of the Mercedes and strode toward the ruined main dance hall.

Clutching his Thompson submachine gun like a one-man army, Feng Lung-wei bellowed, "Oh Tommy! Come out, come out, wherever you are!"

CHAPTER FORTY-FOUR

With the Tommy gun firm in his hands, Feng Lung-wei looked like a Hollywood gangster – flashy, yet dangerous. However menacing Feng was, he had seen better days. He'd cleaned the blood off his face, but his fancy pinstripe suit and overcoat were wrinkled and torn. That brutish, hulking henchman of his lurked nearby, brandishing a revolver of his own. How the hell did these two idiots survive the war so far? This vicious whelp must have been even more determined to kill Tom than he'd thought.

"No use hiding, Tommy," Feng called out. "We saw you scurry in here like the rat you are. I knew you'd come back here, so we parked the Mercedes just a block away and waited. What have you got stashed away here? Money? Guns? Or maybe you just want to drown yourself in Scotch and memories?" He croaked out a rattle of cruel laughter. "If you come out now I won't make you suffer *too* much."

Tom peered through the hole in the wall and called out, "Who's calling who a rat? I'm surprised you didn't piss your pants, run back to Frenchtown, and beg Uncle, or should I say 'Papa Tu,' for protection!"

Feng swiveled the Tommy gun around and blasted away. Tom dove down as the bullets flew through the hole and pinged off what remained of the half-ruined wall. Cracks grew and groaned under the added pressure and injury. It would keel over if this kept up.

"Pretty clever, aren't you Tommy? Well, you'll never live to tell anyone you figured out who I really am," Feng went on. "Besides, I can't have you spilling the milk about my plans for Club Twilight."

"That's 'spilling the beans,' you idiot," Tom called back at him.

"Beans, milk, who cares? All that matters is that if Tu Yueh-sheng knew I tried to make a little money behind his back, then even I – his own son – wouldn't survive the night. Not only that, he'd probably cut every tendon in my body for trying to kill you, his precious 'American nephew.'"

Still crouching low, Tom yelled out, "I'm touched that your pop still has a soft spot for me."

Feng barked another laugh. "He'd be relieved to hear that your twist was the spy and not you. Say, whatever happened to sweet little Mei-chen?"

Tom whipped the revolver out of his pocket, slid in front of the hole, and fired back. Feng and his henchman took cover behind heaps of debris. Tom ducked back down and avoided a steady blast of bullets from Feng's Tommy gun that poured through the open hole and smashed against the wall. More cracks emerged, wooden beams began to splinter and snap. A few more of these exchanges and what remained of Club Twilight would all come crashing down.

With that much firepower in Feng Lung-wei's hands, there was no way Tom could outshoot him. But maybe with a little extra effort, that gangster brat and henchman would be crushed like cockroaches. Edging closer to the hole, Tom cupped his mouth.

"Mei-chen was sick and tired of Shanghai. Said there was too many two-bit punks who fancy themselves real public enemies here!"

"Tommy you...son of a bitch!"

"Your English is improving! Did you learn that one from *Black Mask*?" Tom taunted, then hit the dirt.

Feng Lung-wei responded in Chinese, screaming, "*Sha! Sha! Sha!*" Die! Die! Die!

Another wave of lead crashed against the wall, ripping out huge chunks. The submachine gun's hideous scream of rat tat tat continued uninterrupted for long, excruciating moments. Explosions continued to tear the wall asunder, showering Tom with splinters and debris. Finally, the Tommy gun ceased and the violent bursts were replaced by a high-pitched wail. The cracks in the wall were widening, ready to give way. Tom leaped to his feet and – concentrating all his strength into his shoulder – rammed the wall like a juggernaut. The structure cracked and bent, pulled down by the sheer weight of itself.

Through the massive hole, Feng Lung-wei was visible, grasping his Tommy gun. Fear ignited in his youthful face. The gangster brat spun around and ran, along with his brutish henchman. The wall came crashing down, sending up a thick cloud of dust, rubble, and pulverized debris. Tom struggled to see, but the acrid cloud obscured his vision and left him gasping for air.

Instead, he turned and ran the opposite direction, away from the smoldering rubble. He stumbled into the back alleyway, where his Bentley – still squashed like a pancake – remained parked. Steadying himself against the crushed hood, Tom sucked up as much clean air as he could, soothing his burning lungs. Looking back, the dust cloud was dispersing and revealed the two gangsters to be very much alive and retreating to their Mercedes parked across the street.

Raising his revolver, Tom aimed and squeezed off a few shots, but Feng and his thug were too far away. Within moments, they were back in the safety of the Mercedes, which roared to life and rocketed forward. Squealing tires announced its new direction – they were doubling back for a renewed assault. The Mercedes swerved around and rumbled over the ruins remains of Club Twilight like a tank treading across no man's land.

Tom fired a few more shots of his revolver, which pinged against the Mercedes' hood. Fighting off an overwhelming horror, Tom ran and ducked back into an alleyway, too narrow for the gangsters to follow. There was no way to outrun or outgun Feng Lung-wei now. Not unless he had help. The North Railway Station offered the only chance of protection now. If he could reach it, that is.

CHAPTER FORTY-FIVE

Tom ducked out of the alleyway and onto the Woochen Road. A caravan of refugees passed him on the other side, a pathetic mass of wounded civilians hobbling south. Only he was crazy enough to head north, deeper into the war zone. But only the 19th Route Army could match Feng's Tommy gun in firepower.

Tom kept running and glimpsed behind him. The Mercedes hooked onto Woochen Road and sped forward. There was no slowdown, not even for the throng of refugees that clogged the street. Tom kept running, but he couldn't take his eyes off the hideous sight behind. The Mercedes slammed headfirst into the crowd, tossing bodies aside, flipping them up onto the hood, or mercilessly crushing them beneath its tires.

There was nothing Tom could do, not yet anyway. He kept stealing glances behind him and realized that this tragedy had bought him some time. The Mercedes had slowed down as if bogged down in a swamp. Behind the steering wheel, the Green Gang thug tried to maneuver around the caravan to no avail. Feng Lung-wei leaned out of the passenger window, aimed his Tommy gun, and fired wildly. The bullets ripped through the crowd and cut down the remaining survivors.

That bloodthirsty madman. He'd get his, so long as Tom managed to reach the 19th Route Army in time. Tom ran, fear and anger propelling him faster. Up ahead, the North Railway Station came into view, looming above the rest of Chapei's squat buildings. It was now a magnificent fortification, surrounded by barbed wire, sandbags and mounted machine guns, supplemented with dozens of armed Chinese soldiers. Most majestic of all was the red and blue flag fluttering in the chilly morning breeze, stamped with the

White Sun of the Kuomintang – the standard of the Chinese Republic.

Tom tore into his jacket pocket and whipped out a white handkerchief. He waved it to and fro as a token of peace. The Chinese soldiers remained at their defensive positions, but beckoned Tom forward. Just a few hundred feet and he'd be home free. Screeching tires from behind jerked him around. The Mercedes had broken through the massacred heap and was roaring toward him. Feng Lung-wei, his face contorting with hate, leaned out of the passenger window, and leveled the Tommy gun.

"*Sha!*" he screamed again as the Tommy gun cackled, blasting an endless stream of fire and bullets. Tom dove onto the ground and covered his head with both hands. The Mercedes kept coming, closer and closer, and the Tommy gun blazed away in an endless, earsplitting rat tat tat.

Suddenly, a new symphony of gunfire burst out and slammed into the oncoming Mercedes with such tremendous force, the automobile erupted in hundreds of small explosions. The Chinese soldiers fired a wall of lead that tore through the Mercedes, shattering windows, tearing out chunks of metal, and shredding the tires to tatters.

The conflagration devoured the car, like a ravenous monster, before spitting it back out. The heavy hammering of gunfire ceased, leaving Tom dazed, numb, and almost deaf. He watched as the Mercedes – now a twisted hunk of scrap metal – skidded off the street before smashing into a nearby building. Other than smoke billowing from its engine, the car was rendered inert.

Still clutching the white handkerchief, Tom rose and made his way toward the wreckage. Through the shattered glass window, he could see Feng's henchman – or what was left of him – slumped over what remained of the steering wheel. Bullets had torn golf-ball sized holes out of his beefy face, reducing him to a pile of red jelly.

Tom walked around to the other side and found Feng Lung-wei hanging prostrate out the side of the passenger door. Or rather, he thought it was Feng. He'd suffered some nasty wounds in the past few hours, but now the gangster brat no longer looked human. His pin striped suit was ripped to shreds, and his torso clung together by only a thin strip of flesh since the volley had almost sawed him straight in half. His face had been pulverized into a thick, bloody pulp, robbing Feng Lung-wei of any defining features. Even his big ears had been blown clean off, reduced to specks of gory flesh that trailed behind the Mercedes.

Funny enough, he still clutched that Tommy gun in what remained of his fingers. Tom inspected the weapon, but realized it too had been fatally wounded. In his peripheral, he became aware of Captain Tung approaching.

"Lai Huang-fu, what are you doing here?" he cried in disbelief. Tung Hsi-shan looked magnificent in his blue-gray tunic, jackboots, and field cap – the modern Chinese warrior.

Tom sucked in a deep breath and answered, "Taking you up on your offer. I'm here to join your company, Captain." To show his sincerity, Tom stood at attention. A warm glow shone on Tung's face, before souring.

"Who were these two?"

Tom glanced back at the two mutilated corpses. If he survived this war, his life would become even more complicated if Tu Yueh-sheng discovered he was responsible for Feng's death. Whether or not the Grandmaster of crime hated his despicable bastard son, familial ties were strong in China and would demand retribution. Tom searched for a placating answer.

"One of those Japanese *ronin*," Tom said, pointing at what was left of Feng Lung-wei, before jerking at thumb at the remains of his henchman. "And some Chinese riff-raff he hired."

Captain Tung sneered. "We've heard reports of *ronin* attacking our forces. At least these two won't cause us anymore trouble."

Tom smiled. "Happy to help the cause, Captain."

They retreated back inside the fortifications and into the main courtyard of the North Railway Station.

"Have the Japanese attacked yet?"

Captain Tung nodded. "Twice, but we beat them back. Didn't we, men?"

A cheer arose from the entire company. With defenses like this, maybe they'd win the war after all. Captain Tung went into the main railway terminal, then returned carrying a field cap and rifle.

"Sorry, we don't have any spare tunics and pants. But this will identify you as one of us," Tung said, handing the field cap over.

Tom examined it – a simple, blue-gray design, decorated with a blue and white Kuomintang sun badge. Nothing flashy, but he couldn't suppress a deep inner pride as he removed his fedora and tucked it on his head. Tom accepted the rifle and gripped it with both hands.

"Still remember how to use one of those?" Tung asked.

"I never forgot, *dai go*."

They shared a smile, a brief respite of friendship before the approaching inferno.

"What changed your mind, Lai Huang-fu?"

Tom gave the question some thought. Charles Whitfield was dead and so was Yan Ping. Mei-chen was gone and Club Twilight was a smoldering ruin. All that was left was Shanghai. Tom Lai didn't run from a fight. Not from the Green Gang, not from the Japanese Empire. This was his home, and he'd stop anyone from burning it to the ground. However he reinvented himself after this, it would be in Shanghai.

"This city has been awful good to me," Tom answered. "I'm going to pay her back."

Captain Tung nodded and smiled warmly at his surrogate little brother. Before he could respond, a soldier cried out, "Incoming enemy! Incoming enemy!"

The soldiers in the courtyard grabbed their weapons and took up positions around the perimeter. Tom and Captain

Tung ran over to the section overlooking Woochen Road. Past the shattered Mercedes, past the mangled pile of corpses, a horde of Japanese Marines approached, led by not one, but three armored cars. In their white gaiters and steel helmets, and clutching bayoneted rifles, the Mikado's warriors never looked more fearsome. Tom had a newfound respect for how hard the Nipponese fought, but he and Captain Tung would show just how tough Chinese soldiers were.

Tom looked around at the steely-faced troops of the 19th Route Army, waiting in silence for the enemy. The machine gunners took aim but held their fire. Others kept the rifles trained, still as statues. Captain Tung drew a Mauser pistol from his holster and crouched down over a sandbag. Tom knelt beside him, angling his rifle into position. The Japanese had moved past the pile of bodies, the rumbling armored cars leading the advance. They would be upon them any minute now, but Tom knew there would be no more running.

Here in Shanghai, Tom Lai would stand and fight, no matter what. He took aim and opened fire.

Afterword

Shanghai Twilight is set during the run up to the 1932 Shanghai War, known in China as the January 28th Incident and in Japan as the Shanghai Incident. Tom Lai, Ho Mei-chen, Yan Ping, and Feng Lung-wei are all fictional, but Tu Yueh-sheng was a real historical figure. As the Grandmaster of the Green Gang, Tu ruled Shanghai's underworld until the Communist takeover in 1949. Tu had many children, some legitimate and some not, so I created Feng Lung-wei as his nephew/illegitimate son in order to have some dramatic license.

Charles Whitfield, Chow Chun-wah, and Captain Tung Hsi-shan are also fictional, but Chiang Kai-shek, Wang Ching-wei, Mayor Wu Tieh-cheng, and General Tsai Ting-kai were all historical figures who played large roles in the 1932 Shanghai War.

Jiro Fukuzaki is also fictional, but there were real cases of intrigue which led to the outbreak of war in 1932. Most famous is the case of Major Ryukichi Tanaka and his mistress, the Manchu Princess Aisin Gioro Xianyu aka Yoshiko Kawashima. They exploited the very real anti-Japanese boycott and sentiment in Shanghai in order to precipitate a conflict within the city. The reasoning for this was threefold.

1) The Japanese Army wanted to distract international attention away from Manchuria, where they were launching the final offensive against Harbin.

2) To punish the Chinese for allowing the anti-Japanese boycott to hurt Japan's economy.

3) The Japanese Navy were eager to show off their fighting prowess after sitting on the sidelines during the Manchurian Incident.

Tanaka and Kawashima paid a gang of Chinese thugs to assault a group of five Japanese Buddhist monks to exacerbate tensions. One of the monks died, which gave the Japanese Navy more incentive for military intervention. In the end, Mayor Wu accepted all the Japanese demands, but citing violence against Japanese citizens, the commander of Imperial Naval Forces in Shanghai – Admiral Shiozawa – launched an assault into the district of Chapei on January 28th, 1932.

The Chinese Nationalist Army unit in Shanghai – the 19th Route Army – fought hard and eventually almost annihilated the Japanese Marines. They were forced to request the Imperial Army for help, which arrived in late February 1932. With their increased strength, the Japanese launched a counterattack, forcing the 19th Route Army to evacuate Shanghai on March 3rd, 1932. The League of Nations soon mediated a ceasefire. The international community was shocked, but did little to aid China.

Although the war was brief, it nevertheless had a lasting impact. It was the first conflict that had bombers attack large civilian areas, urban warfare, and set the stage for further tension within Shanghai.

Thank You

Thank you for reading *Shanghai Twilight*. If you enjoyed this novel, please leave a review on Amazon and Goodreads! Honest reviews from readers like you are absolutely essential for authors to survive in today's marketplace.

Also, if you would like to see more of Tom Lai's adventures in Old Shanghai, please let me know! I have several other ideas for a full series, but would like your feedback.

Thanks!

About the Author

Matthew Legare has always loved reading, writing, and history. He's combined his passions to tell stories set during little-known, but fascinating, events of the past. His style is a smooth blend of old pulp magazines and contemporary thrillers, which makes for a pulsating read.

Matthew would love to hear from his readers! Please contact him at:

Website: https://matthewlegare.com

Twitter: @mlegareauthor

13275521R10136

Made in the
USA
Monee, IL